THE HESITANT HERO

BOOKS BY GILBERT MORRIS

THE HOUSE OF WINSLOW SERIES

The Honorable Imposter
The Captive Bride
The Indentured Heart
The Gentle Rebel
The Saintly Buccaneer
The Holy Warrior
The Reluctant Bridegroom
The Last Confederate
The Dixie Widow
The Wounded Yankee
The Union Belle
The Final Adversary
The Crossed Sabres
The Valiant Gunman
The Gallant Outlaw
The Jeweled Spur
The Yukon Queen
The Rough Rider
The Iron Lady

The Silver Star
The Shadow Portrait
The White Hunter
The Flying Cavalier
The Glorious Prodigal
The Amazon Quest
The Golden Angel
The Heavenly Fugitive
The Fiery Ring
The Pilgrim Song
The Beloved Enemy
The Shining Badge
The Royal Handmaid
The Silent Harp
The Virtuous Woman
The Gypsy Moon
The Unlikely Allies
The High Calling
The Hesitant Hero

CHENEY DUVALL, M.D.[1]

1. *The Stars for a Light*
2. *Shadow of the Mountains*
3. *A City Not Forsaken*
4. *Toward the Sunrising*
5. *Secret Place of Thunder*
6. *In the Twilight, in the Evening*
7. *Island of the Innocent*
8. *Driven With the Wind*

CHENEY AND SHILOH: THE INHERITANCE[1]

1. *Where Two Seas Met*
2. *The Moon by Night*
3. *There Is a Season*

THE SPIRIT OF APPALACHIA[2]

1. *Over the Misty Mountains*
2. *Beyond the Quiet Hills*
3. *Among the King's Soldiers*
4. *Beneath the Mockingbird's Wings*
5. *Around the River's Bend*

LIONS OF JUDAH

1. *Heart of a Lion*
2. *No Woman So Fair*
3. *The Gate of Heaven*
4. *Till Shiloh Comes*
5. *By Way of the Wilderness*
6. *Daughter of Deliverance*

[1]with Lynn Morris   [2]with Aaron McCarver

GILBERT MORRIS

the HESITANT HERO

William W. Harvill
APR. 2012

◆ BETHANYHOUSE
Minneapolis, Minnesota

The Hesitant Hero
Copyright © 2006
Gilbert Morris

Cover illustration by William Graf
Cover design by Josh Madison

Published by Bethany House Publishers
11400 Hampshire Avenue South
Bloomington, Minnesota 55438

Bethany House Publishers is a division of
Baker Publishing Group, Grand Rapids, Michigan.

Printed in the United States of America

ISBN-13: 978-0-7642-2945-9
ISBN-10: 0-7642-2945-1

Library of Congress Cataloging-in-Publication Data

Morris, Gilbert.
   The hesitant hero / Gilbert Morris.
     p. cm.
   ISBN 0-7642-2945-1 (pbk.)
    1. Americans—France—Fiction. 2. France—History—German
occupation, 1940-1945—Fiction. 3. Jewish orphans—Fiction. I. Title.
II. Series: Morris, Gilbert. House of Winslow.
   PS3563.08742H47   2006
   813'.54—dc22   2006013582

To Rev. James Golden and his companion Murlene—
my Golden Missionaries—

Your faith witness to the glorious gospel of Jesus
has been a wonderful testimony to me for many years.
I keep my memories of you among my most
prized possessions—so thanks for the memories!

GILBERT MORRIS spent ten years as a pastor before becoming Professor of English at Ouachita Baptist University in Arkansas and earning a Ph.D. at the University of Arkansas. A prolific writer, he has had over 25 scholarly articles and 200 poems published in various periodicals and over the past years has had more than 180 novels published. His family includes three grown children, and he and his wife live in Gulf Shores, Alabama.

CONTENTS

PART FOUR
July 1940

THE HOUSE OF WINSLOW

★ ★ ★ ★

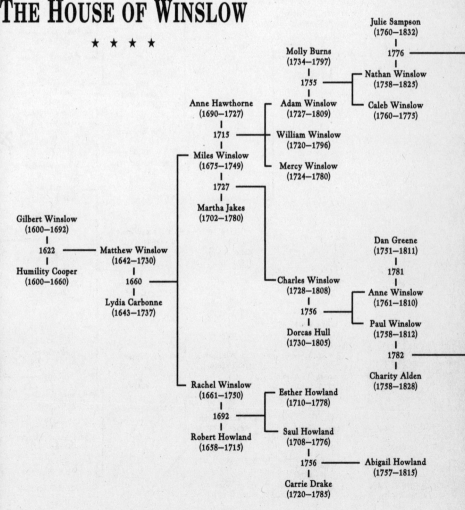

Julie Sampson
(1760—1832)
|
1776 —————

Molly Burns
(1734—1797)
|
1755 —————
Nathan Winslow
(1758—1825)

Caleb Winslow
(1760—1775)

Anne Hawthorne
(1690—1727)
|
1715
|
Miles Winslow
(1675—1749)
|
1727 —————
Martha Jakes
(1702—1780)

Adam Winslow
(1727—1809)

William Winslow
(1720—1796)

Mercy Winslow
(1724—1780)

Gilbert Winslow
(1600—1692)
|
1622 ————— Matthew Winslow
(1642—1730)
|
1660 —————
Humility Cooper
(1600—1660)

Lydia Carbonne
(1643—1737)

Dan Greene
(1751—1811)
|
1781
|
Anne Winslow
(1761—1810)

Charles Winslow
(1728—1808)
|
1756 —————
Dorcas Hull
(1730—1805)

Paul Winslow
(1758—1812)
|
1782 —————
Charity Alden
(1758—1828)

Rachel Winslow
(1661—1750)
|
1692 —————
Robert Howland
(1658—1715)

Esther Howland
(1710—1778)

Saul Howland
(1708—1776)
|
1756 ————— Abigail Howland
(1757—1815)

Carrie Drake
(1720—1785)

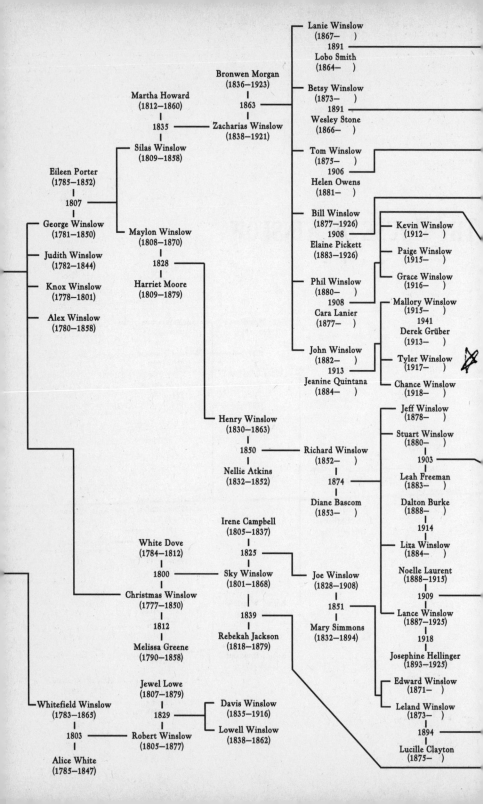

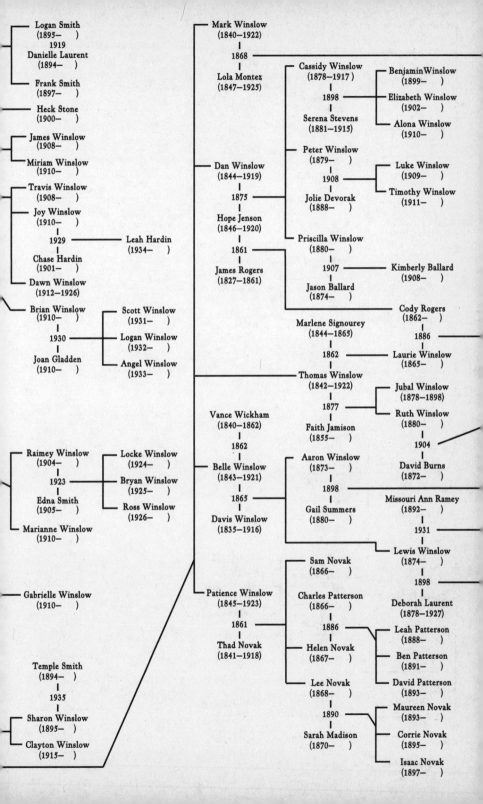

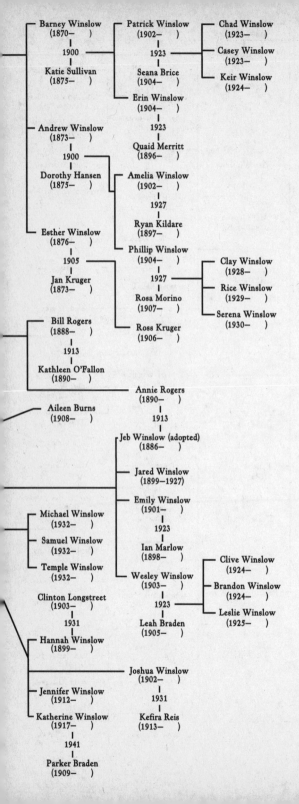

Barney Winslow
(1870—   )
1900
Katie Sullivan
(1875—   )

Patrick Winslow
(1902—   )
1923
Seana Brice
(1904—   )

Chad Winslow
(1923—   )
Casey Winslow
(1923—   )
Keir Winslow
(1924—   )

Erin Winslow
(1904—   )
1923
Quaid Merritt
(1896—   )

Andrew Winslow
(1873—   )
1900
Dorothy Hansen
(1875—   )

Amelia Winslow
(1902—   )
1927
Ryan Kildare
(1897—   )

Esther Winslow
(1876—   )
1905
Jan Kruger
(1873—   )

Phillip Winslow
(1904—   )
1927
Rosa Morino
(1907—   )

Clay Winslow
(1928—   )
Rice Winslow
(1929—   )
Serena Winslow
(1930—   )

Ross Kruger
(1906—   )

Bill Rogers
(1888—   )
1913
Kathleen O'Fallon
(1890—   )

Annie Rogers
(1890—   )
1913

Aileen Burns
(1908—   )

Jeb Winslow (adopted)
(1886—   )

Jared Winslow
(1899—1927)

Emily Winslow
(1901—   )
1923
Ian Marlow
(1898—   )

Michael Winslow
(1932—   )
Samuel Winslow
(1932—   )
Temple Winslow
(1932—   )

Wesley Winslow
(1903—   )
1923
Leah Braden
(1905—   )

Clive Winslow
(1924—   )
Brandon Winslow
(1924—   )
Leslie Winslow
(1925—   )

Clinton Longstreet
(1903—   )
1931
Hannah Winslow
(1899—   )

Joshua Winslow
(1902—   )
1931
Kefira Reis
(1913—   )

Jennifer Winslow
(1912—   )
Katherine Winslow
(1917—   )
1941
Parker Braden
(1909—   )

PART ONE

October 1939–May 1940

★ ★ ★

CHAPTER ONE

THE COLONY CLUB

★ ★ ★

"Come on, Tyler, have some dinner with me. I'm starving!"

Tyler Winslow lolled back in the seat of the yellow cab and grinned faintly at the woman who was pulling at his arm and urging him to get out.

"I should go home. I've had a little much to drink."

Caroline Autry was not in the habit of begging for favors. As the daughter of Denton Autry, one of the richest men in New York City, she was more accustomed to having her smallest whims fulfilled. "None of that!" she urged. "Come on. I'm famished."

With a groan, Tyler allowed himself to be pulled out of the cab. He stood there for a moment swaying, then closed his eyes, muttering, "Is the whole world turning around, or is it just me?"

"You're all right. Here, driver, keep the change."

"Thank you, miss."

Tyler opened his eyes and looked at the building in front of them. "This is the Colony Club. You know I can't afford it, Caroline."

"Well, *I* can."

Indeed, the jewelry that adorned Caroline Autry could probably have made a good start toward buying the famous restaurant. Diamonds glittered at her ears and an enormous ruby necklace decorated her throat, and when she moved her hands, more diamonds caught the reflections of the lights of the club and flashed like stars. The October night was chilly, and she wore a chinchilla coat over her shoulders. Looking up at Tyler, she said, "The night's young and so are we, so let's live it up."

"All right, honey, if you say so."

A tall, handsome doorman greeted them with a smile. "Hello, Miss Autry. And how are you, sir?"

"Hello, George," Caroline said. "Is it a full house tonight?"

"Pretty crowded, but they'll find you a good seat, I know."

They went in and were greeted again by a small, dapper man in a tuxedo who smiled slightly. "Ah, Miss Autry, so good to have you."

"We want good seats, Henry."

"The very best that we have available. If you'll walk this way, please."

As the two followed the maître d', Tyler was only vaguely aware of the ornate decorations. The Colony Club was located on Sixty-Second Street and was one of the most famous and fairly notorious restaurants in America. *Vogue* magazine had stated, "It's harder to get a good table at the Colony than it is to hit a hole in one."

Indeed, nothing was too good for the clientele who willingly paid the enormous prices. The famous guests were treated like visiting royalty. Every time Bernard Baruch dined at the Colony in the heat of a New York summer, the management had the air-conditioning turned off because Baruch hated it.

Something about the atmosphere of the Colony Club was displeasing to Tyler Winslow. Having been brought up in the more primitive parts of Africa, he had spent most of his life in a simpler way. Now as he glanced around the crowd, noting that the waiter was taking them to one of the better tables, he thought of how snobbish some people in New York were. He was well aware that there was a section of the Colony Club known as Siberia. It had gotten its name when socialite Peggy Hopkins Joyce had been shown to one of the less-than-desirable tables and had demanded, "Where are you taking me to? Siberia?"

But there was no way that Caroline Autry would be taken to what had been dubbed the penal section in the Colony Club—where the common people ate as opposed to the stars.

They reached a table and the waiter bowed. "I trust this will be satisfactory."

"Yes, of course," Caroline said as she nodded carelessly. She sat down in the chair, which the waiter held for her, and then glanced around. "Look, Tyler, there's John Barrymore," she said. "I think he's the handsomest man I've ever seen." Then she turned and smiled. "Present company excepted, of course."

Tyler grinned. He had been told he was a roughly handsome man, although he had none of the smoothness of Barrymore. He was exactly six feet tall and carried a trim, hard one hundred seventy pounds of muscle, put on over years of an active life in Africa. His thick brown hair had a very slight curl, and women always told him they liked his intense blue eyes.

Caroline leaned forward and playfully tousled Tyler's hair but then stopped, lightly pulling his hair straight up. "I never noticed that before. Where'd you get that scar, Tyler?"

He touched the scar on his forehead that was usually covered with hair. "A leopard."

Her eyes widened. "Are you serious!" she exclaimed. "You mean a real leopard?"

"It wasn't imitation."

Caroline stared at the scar. "I can't imagine such a thing."

"I didn't have to imagine it."

"Were you out in the jungle?"

"No, sleeping in my bed."

"He came into your house? Didn't you keep the doors locked?"

"I don't think we had any locks on the doors. And we had to keep the windows open for air."

"And he just came right in?"

"Sure he did. I was just a kid, and we were out in a village, my folks and I. Leopards often come into villages at night. Lots of children have been stolen away. I was lucky, though," he said. "Dad always kept his gun by his side. We were all sleeping in the same room. When the leopard made a grab at my head, I hollered, and Dad shot out of bed, grabbed his gun, and killed it. I was a bloody mess. There was no doctor, so Dad had to sew my head up himself."

Caroline was fascinated by Tyler Winslow. Ordinarily she would never have given the son of poor missionary parents a second look, but she had encountered Tyler at an art show and had been struck by his rugged good looks. She had flirted with him, and he had asked her out. Since then she had found it a pleasure to show him the more expensive sides of New York, which he would never have been able to afford. He was an artist studying painting, but it was too soon to tell if he had enough talent to make it.

Aware that she was studying him, Tyler said, "I can read your mind, Caroline."

"I doubt it."

"You're wondering why in the world you put up with a poor, struggling artist when you could be running around with rich bankers."

"Bankers are boring."

"Painters can be boring too. I've met enough of them who are." He toyed with his glass of water, turning it in his hand and studying the fine crystal. "Some of them can't talk about anything but art."

"You're not like that. You can talk about all kinds of things." She winked suggestively and laughed. Looking around the room, she motioned to the waiter, who came scurrying forward. "What's good tonight?" she asked.

"Almost anything you desire, Miss Autry."

The food at the Colony Club was legendary. Waiters were pushing carts of hors d'oeuvres, roasts, soups, and even ice sculptures through the dining room. One waiter was flamboyantly displaying food skewered on flaming swords.

"I think I'll have a hot dog on one of those swords," Tyler said. "Set it on fire, will you, please?"

The waiter stared with astonishment. "Sir, we don't serve hot dogs."

"I thought you served everything."

"Nearly everything, sir, but not hot dogs."

"He's only ribbing you," Carolyn told the waiter.

"May I suggest the pheasant Souvaroff." The waiter reeled off a list of other choices, and finally Caroline ordered eel ragout, and Tyler ordered roast lamb.

"And bring us a bottle of your best wine," Caroline instructed. "I'll let you choose."

"I will do my best to please you, Miss Autry." The waiter bowed and left.

Tyler leaned back in his chair and shook his head. "All this rich eating's going to make me fat."

"You'll never be fat. What did you eat in Africa?"

Tyler grinned. "When we were visiting the Masai, the host would milk a cow, then he would open a blood vessel in the cow's neck and fill the rest of the cup up with blood. Mighty tasty."

"Not really!" Caroline shuddered. "How awful!"

"Well, the Masai men were some of the finest I've ever

seen. All of them over six feet, strong, and more guts than you can imagine. Who knows? Maybe it was from drinking all that blood."

"You've come a long way, Tyler. All the way from drinking blood and milk to being a promising art student in New York."

"I don't know how promising I am. My teachers don't seem to think so."

"They are teachers because they can't paint themselves. You know what they say. Those who can, do. Those who can't, teach." She laughed aloud. The waiter soon came back with the wine, allowed Tyler to taste it first, then poured them each a glass.

"My brother's been after me to stop drinking," Tyler said as he picked up his glass. "You met him once, but you may have been a bit too drunk to remember him."

"Of course I remember him. His name was Chance. A very proper, upright man. Not like you at all."

The remark struck something in Tyler, and he drank half of his glass in one gulp. "You're right. He's not like me. He's the good one. I'm the bad apple."

"Don't put yourself down."

"I don't need to put myself down. I've got plenty of other people doing that."

"You mean your brother?"

"For one. He's trying to convert me."

"Your family are missionaries, all of them? Your parents and your brother too?"

"Pretty much. I'll be glad when Chance goes back to Africa. I'm nothing but a disappointment to him." He drank more of the wine and shook his head. "Our folks won't be happy when he tells them what I've been up to, although he'll think of something good to say about me to make the folks feel better."

"Come on. Let's dance while we're waiting for our food."

As they walked to the dance floor, Tyler said, "It's

hard for two drunks to dance well together."

"We're not drunks!"

"We get drunk all the time. What do you think makes a drunk?"

"That's your family talking. There's nothing wrong with drinking and having a good time."

"Sometimes they're not the same thing."

"What do you mean by that?"

"Most of the time when you drink you don't have a good time. You just think you are. And then you wake up the next day with your mouth tasting like a birdcage and someone trying to drive an ice pick through your skull. You call that having a good time?"

Caroline laughed at him. "Talk all you want to, but we *are* having a good time. I am, anyway."

As they moved around the floor, she seemed to be studying him in a strange way. Finally she said, "You know, we could get married."

Tyler's mind was not clear, and he blinked his eyes with surprise. "We can't do that."

"Why not?"

"In the first place, I couldn't support a wife."

"But I can support a husband."

Tyler flashed a sour grin. "That's all I need, Caroline, to be a kept man."

"You're too old-fashioned. This is 1939, not the Middle Ages."

"I know what year it is. I know what month is it too."

"Why, it's October."

"Does that mean anything to you—October 1939?"

"No."

"Ten years of the Depression. It was ten years ago in 1929 that the Depression hit. The whole country's gone downhill. I wasn't here for most of it, but there are still hard times in this country."

The music ended and they went back to their table just as the food arrived. Tyler only picked at his food. He was troubled, and finally Caroline shoved her own food away. "You're not much fun tonight."

"I know it. I'm feeling guilty."

"What are you feeling guilty about?"

Tyler looked up, a disturbed look on his face. "My folks sacrificed a lot to send me over here to college to learn how to paint. They had to do without. Chance had to make some sacrifices too." He suddenly shoved the plate back, poured another glass of wine, and gulped it down. When he put the glass down, he said with determination, "But when I make it big as a painter, I'll make it up to them."

"You're funny about some things," Caroline said. "Maybe that's why I like you."

"Funny about what?"

"Well, most struggling young artists wouldn't mind marrying a rich woman. You wouldn't have to worry about money. Daddy's got oodles of it."

"It's not the same thing. I wouldn't want to have to depend on your dad."

"You've got some archaic ideas." She stood up. "I'm going to the ladies' room."

Tyler watched as she got up and made her way through the crowd. He sat there and stared at the wine bottle. He started to pour himself another drink but stopped. "What's the matter with you, Tyler Winslow?" he muttered. "You didn't used to be a drunk." Indeed, he didn't especially like to drink. When he had first come to America, he had drunk very little, but in Caroline Autry's circles, alcohol was just part of the atmosphere. The years of prohibition had somehow changed America, and now it seemed that people were trying to make up for the lost years by drinking more.

He pulled his billfold out of his pocket and opened it. A grimace touched his wide mouth and he shoved it back. *I'll have to ask the folks for more money.* The very thought of it was abominable, and with grim determination, he thought, *I won't be any more of a burden on them. I can't.*

He sat there unhappy and heavy in thought until finally he looked up to see Caroline coming across the floor. As she moved through the crowd, a big man suddenly stepped in front of her. She tried to get by, but the man laughed and took her by the arm.

Despite his alcoholic haze, Tyler hastened toward the two, anger running through him like a jolt of electricity. Even above the loud music he heard Caroline crying, "Let go of me!"

"Ah, come on, pretty lady—don't be so stuck up."

Tyler clamped his hand on the man's wrist and squeezed hard. The man winced and turned around.

"What are you doing?" the man growled.

"Let the lady alone or I'll send you to the dentist."

The big man released his grip, and his face was flushed. "Get out of here, sonny. I'm talkin' to the lady."

"Come on, Caroline." Tyler reached for her hand, but the big man knocked his arm away. Without thought, Tyler swung and caught the man right on the mouth with a devastating blow. He watched with satisfaction as the man went reeling backward, the back of his legs striking a table.

The blow would have put most men down, but Tyler saw that despite the blood on the man's lips there was a light in his eyes. He came forward with a shuffle, and his stance warned Tyler that this man had done his share of fighting.

Tyler managed to get his arms up and turned, but the fist caught him on the shoulder with frightening power, driving him backward into another table, which collapsed beneath him. The two women at the table screamed as they tried to get out of the way. Tyler scrambled to his feet and threw himself at the big man in a frightening fury. Only vaguely aware of what was happening, he threw blow after blow and received many in return. Both men were bleeding now, but Tyler was getting the worst of it. He saw the big man pick up a chair and he tried to dodge it, but the edge of it caught him on the head. He sank down, his surroundings growing darker. He could hear Caroline's voice but could not make out her words.

Finally he felt hands pulling him to his feet. He winced and reached up to touch his head, discovering that it was damp. He looked at the blood on his hands and then at Caroline, who was being held back by a burly policeman. Another officer was holding him by the arm. "You'll have to come along with me."

"He started it," Caroline cried.

"The judge will decide who started what. Let's go." Tyler was pulled along, and he glanced back to see the big man glaring at him. "What about him?"

"You don't know him?"

"No."

"That's Oliver Blalock. He's a district attorney. He's got lots of pull with the judges. You picked the wrong man to hit, young fella."

"But he started it!"

The policeman had a red face and a battered countenance. He grinned as he pulled Tyler out of the crowded room. "Don't matter who started it. He's the man with the weight. Next time be more careful who you bust."

"It's not fair!"

" 'Course it ain't fair," the officer answered. "Most things in this here world ain't fair. If things were fair, we'd all be born to rich people. But I didn't make the rules and looks like neither did you. That's why you're going to the slammer and Oliver Blalock ain't."

Tyler glared at the policeman but knew it was hopeless. His head was splitting, and all he could think of was what his parents would say when they heard about this little escapade.

CHAPTER TWO

FLUNKING OUT

★ ★ ★

By the time the squad car had reached the hospital and Tyler had been led to the emergency room by the policeman, Tyler had sobered up considerably. He had a splitting headache, and the blood that trickled from the cut in his scalp had stained his white shirt. He had put a handkerchief on it to staunch the flow, but it had become sodden.

"Go ahead and find some lunch or something, Dan," the officer told his partner. "This could take a while."

"All right. I'll be back in an hour."

The officer got out of the squad car and helped Tyler get out of the back seat. "That's a bad cut you got there, Winslow," he said as he led Tyler into the emergency room. "I reckon you'll have to have some stitchin' done."

Tyler's head hurt too much for him to reply, and, in truth, he was ashamed of himself for the whole incident. His temper was a fearful thing, and he had struggled most of his life to control it. Now he knew there would be no way to keep this from Chance, and inevitably his parents would hear of it.

The officer went to the desk and said, "We need to get this guy fixed up right away. He's bleedin' to death."

The woman behind the desk gave him a wry smile. "This is an emergency room, Officer Murphy. Everybody's bleeding to death in one form or another."

"Ah, come on, sweetheart," Murphy said. "Give us a break. We ain't got time to wait."

"All right. Sign him in, and I'll see what I can do."

The paper work took little time, and before long an attractive woman was leading Tyler and Murphy through a door that led down a corridor and then through a door in which there were six beds, two of them occupied.

"Now, what can I do for you?" the woman asked Tyler.

"I guess I've got a pretty good cut on my head," he said as he pulled the handkerchief away from his forehead.

"All right. Take this bed here."

"How long is this gonna take?" Murphy asked.

"It shouldn't take too long, Officer."

"Okay, I'm going to go get something to eat, but I'll have to lock him to the bed. Come on, Winslow, put yourself down here."

Tyler gloomily lay down on the bed and watched as Murphy took out a pair of handcuffs, clamping one side to his wrist and the other to the bed rail. "You stay here and let the doc patch you up, then we'll be goin' downtown."

"What did he do, Officer, rob a store?"

"No, he just got into a fight and busted the wrong guy."

Officer Murphy left as the woman bent over Tyler. Her brown hair was pulled back off her forehead and gathered in a bun. "Does it look bad, Nurse?"

"It's going to have to be stitched, and incidentally, I'm not a nurse."

"So you're a doctor?"

"Not yet." She stood up. "I'll need to shave part of your scalp before I can put the stitches in."

Tyler lay on the bed feeling worse by the moment. He shut his eyes and wished fervently he had not gotten himself into such a situation. He was certain he would not go to jail, at least not for any significant time. Caroline would see to that. One word from her father would be all it would take. Tyler was disgusted as he realized he was depending on a man who despised him. Denton Autry, Caroline's father, had little use for artists of any kind—especially for those who ran around getting drunk with his only daughter.

"Well, what happened to you?"

Tyler opened his eyes and saw a man standing in front of him wearing a white coat with a stethoscope over his shoulder. "I got hit in the head with a chair by another drunk."

"I'm Dr. Lawrence. Let me see that head." Lawrence looked more like a defensive tackle than a physician. He wasn't as gentle as the medical student was as he inspected Tyler's cut. "That's a pretty good cut you've got there, but you'll live," he said cheerfully. He turned and said, "I think I'll let you do this one while I go check on another patient, Jolie. Can you take care of it?"

"Yes, Doctor."

"I'll be back to check after the stitches are in." He grinned down cheerfully at Tyler. "I hope you had a good time. How much have you had to drink?"

"Too much."

"Good thing you came here. Dr. Vernay's got great hands. She'll take good care of you."

Tyler glared at the doctor, and as he left, he turned his head to the young woman, wincing with pain. "He's pretty cheerful about how much I hurt, isn't he?"

"Oh, that's just his way. He's really a fine doctor."

"What kind of an accent do you have?" he asked, more to take his mind off his problems than anything.

"French. Now, this will be a little painful while I numb your scalp."

Tyler tried to lie motionless as he watched the young woman work quietly and efficiently. "I thought you weren't a doctor yet."

"I'm in my last year of medical school."

"Then you'll be a doctor."

"Then I'll be a doctor, but I'll still have to do my internship." She stood up straight for a moment to stretch her back. "How did this happen?"

Tyler caught his breath as she hit a spot that wasn't completely numb, but he was determined to show that he had a little manhood left.

"My girlfriend and I were in a nightclub. A fellow there got fresh with her, and we got into it."

"Was he arrested too?"

"I don't think so. He's a big shot here in New York."

"You shouldn't hit big shots."

Tyler glanced up and saw that she was frowning at him. "Or anybody else, I imagine," he said.

When the woman was nearly finished, Officer Murphy returned, a cup of coffee in his hand. He watched with interest and said, "Say, Doc, you're real good at that."

"Thank you, Officer."

"The next time I get shot I'll be sure to come by and have you take care of me." He flirted with the young woman as she tied the final knot and bandaged the wound. "There, Officer, all done." Turning to Tyler, she said calmly, "You need to get those stitches out on Thursday. Come by and I'll take care of it."

Murphy shook his head. "You make house calls?"

"No, I don't."

"Well, you won't be takin' these stitches out. Winslow here is headed for the slammer." He grinned and said, "I called the station. Lawyer Blalock is mad as hops. He's pullin' strings to get you at least six months in jail. Come on." Unlocking the handcuffs, he said, "Thanks a lot, Doc. Send the bill to the City of New York."

Tyler felt miserable, weak, and shaken as Murphy led him outside and put him into the squad car, where Murphy's partner was waiting behind the wheel.

When Murphy got in he said to Dan, "Good-lookin' broad in there. If I get shot, take me to her."

"Yeah, I'll do my best to remember that."

Tyler put his head back and reached up to feel the bandage. Although it was numb at the moment, he knew when the feeling came back it would be sore.

Won't I ever learn? he moaned inwardly. *You think a man would get a little sense as he got older, but I never do!*

★   ★   ★

Tyler stood beside the bars of the jail as his fellow prisoner, a tall, lanky man named Simms, talked constantly. He paid little attention, but Simms was apparently used to that. "What'd he give you, Winslow?" Simms asked. "The judge, I mean."

"A fine and a year's suspended sentence. If I so much as spit on the sidewalk in the next twelve months, that's it."

Simms laughed. "Don't spit, then, would be my advice. That ain't bad, you know."

"I know. It could have been a lot worse."

His attention was caught by the guard who was walking toward his cell. "Come along, Winslow, you're sprung."

"Take it easy and don't spit," Simms said with a laugh.

As the steel door closed behind Tyler, he vowed, *I'm not coming back to this place.* He hated to be closed in, and as he accompanied the guard down the line of cells, that resolution was the strongest thing on his mind. When he stepped outside, he almost stopped, for he saw Chance standing there—and beside him was Caroline Autry.

Caroline came toward him and hugged him. "Tyler, how awful for you!"

Tyler took her hug, then turned to his brother. "Sorry you got involved in all this, Chance."

"I didn't do much. Miss Autry here paid your fine."

Something in Chance's face gave his feelings away, and Tyler knew exactly what it was. Chance was a good man but somewhat puritanical—at least for Tyler's tastes. He was embarrassed that he'd had to be bailed out of his trouble by a woman and said, "I guess you'll have to tell the folks about this."

"No I won't. You tell them if you want to." Suddenly Chance said, "I've got to leave."

"Your ship leaves when?"

"Tomorrow. This is good-bye." He turned to Caroline. "Thank you very much for your help, Miss Autry."

"Well, the whole thing was really my fault, Mr. Winslow."

Chance shook his head almost imperceptibly and then put out his hand. "Good-bye, Tyler. I'll be in touch."

"Good-bye. Tell the folks I'll . . ." Tyler could not complete the sentence, but added weakly, "Tell them I'll write soon."

"I'll tell them that." Chance Winslow turned and walked away, his back straight.

"He's not very pleasant, is he?" Caroline remarked.

"He can be, but he's right to be sore at me."

"Wasn't your fault," Caroline said. "Come on. I've got my car here. I'll take you home."

She took his arm possessively and led him out to the car. "How's your head feel?" she asked as she pulled out into traffic.

"Not bad. Could have been worse."

"When do the stitches come out?"

"Thursday."

Tyler sat quietly until she pulled up in front of his apartment. "I'm sorry you had to pay the fine," he said.

"Why, that was nothing." Caroline leaned over and pulled at him until he turned toward her. "Don't let this get you down. It'll all be forgotten. It could have happened to anyone." She pulled his head toward her and kissed him. "Call me tomorrow."

Tyler nodded. "I will." He got out of the car, waved good-bye, and watched her pull away. He turned heavily and made his way into the building. It was a small building with only four units—one of them occupied by the landlady, who kept close tabs on all her tenants.

On the way up the stairs he met his landlady and her eyes flew open. "What happened to you? What's wrong with your head?"

"Just a little accident, Mrs. Brown. Nothing to worry about."

Unlocking his door, Tyler stepped inside and closed the door. His eyes fell on the canvas that he had been working on before he had gone out with Caroline. He had thought it was good at the time, but now nothing he did seemed to please him. He stood in front of the canvas and studied the images of children playing in front of a tenement. He turned away in disgust, muttering, "Whatever makes me think I can make it as a painter? I don't even have enough sense to stay out of brawls with fancy lawyers."

★ ★ ★

The week following his release from jail was not a pleasant one for Tyler. He had to face up to the fact that he was failing most of his classes at college, and he also had to face the anger of his art teacher. Professor Tibbs was waiting for him when he went into the studio and without preamble began bawling him out.

"So I see you've decided to grace us with your presence," he said sarcastically.

"Sorry, Professor Tibbs. I had a little personal problem."

The man's eyes went to the bandage on Tyler's head. "Did you fall off of a building and split your head?"

"Something like that, sir."

Tibbs stared at Tyler and then shook his head. "I think you need to change your major."

"Change my major? Why would I do that?"

"Because whatever it takes to make an artist, you don't have it," he said bluntly. "You don't even try. It takes time and practice, two things you go out of your way to avoid."

"I'll try harder, Professor. You'll see. I can do it."

"No you can't. You don't have any discipline. You always take the easy way out. I've seen it in your art, time and time again. Look at this one." He strode across the studio. He shuffled through some paintings on a table and stopped when he found the one he was looking for. "Look. There's your last effort. You know what grade I'm going to put on it?"

"Not very good, I would suppose."

"An F—total failure. The frustrating thing is you had a good idea here, but you couldn't finish it."

Tibbs was referring to a painting of the Brooklyn Bridge. Probably ten thousand paintings had been made of that particular bridge, but Tyler had determined he would find a new perspective, something that hadn't been done before. He had decided to get down beneath the bridge, looking at the underside of it as it soared into the sky. He had spent the better part of a week trying to make it come alive. He had thought he had something, but then Caroline had come along, and the two had gone out every night and had spent every hour together that he wasn't actually in class, and he had even cut some of those. The deadline for the painting had come, and he had finished it in a slapdash manner. Now he looked at it and just felt sad. "I thought I had a good idea there," he said lamely. "It just didn't work out."

"*It* didn't work out! What do you mean *it*? What's *it*?" Tibbs demanded. "I'll tell you what didn't work out," he said grimly. "*You* didn't work out, or you just quit. I don't know what you do in your spare time, but I can tell you you're wasting your time here."

The scene with Tibbs was only the beginning of bad news. The dean of academics had left a note in his mailbox instructing Tyler to come to his office, and Tyler wearily made his way across the campus.

Dean Smith started by showing Tyler his grade point average, which was depressing enough. "You've just scraped by every year since you've been here." Dean Smith was a tall, spare man with a set of hard eyes and a mouth like a trap. "You've been on probation almost constantly. Your departmental chairman tells me that you're loafing and doing nothing. You're wasting your money—or I should say your parents' money."

"I know I haven't done well—"

"Done well? You've done *nothing*! Mr. Winslow, I suggest you find yourself a job. Evidently the academic world doesn't suit you."

"But, Dean Smith—"

"Listen, Tyler. I'm going to give you one more chance. But if you don't show some real discipline and vast improvement real soon, the next time you're in my office will be the last. Do you understand?"

"Yes, sir."

Tyler left the office, sobered by the reality of his situation. He had done a good deal of thinking lately about his financial problems. His parents had always paid his bills, and although he had worked summers to help, he knew it had been a hardship for them. They had never complained, and he had more or less taken their support for granted. Now as he mentally added up his bills and compared the sum to his available funds, he saw that there was little hope he could get by unless a miracle occurred.

★ ★ ★

Tyler began to work harder at his studies, trying to play catch-up, which was difficult. He even admitted to some of his instructors that he had been remiss and would do better. They had all given him a rather doubtful look, which he knew he had earned.

On Thursday afternoon, Tyler was glad it was time to go back to the emergency room to get his stitches out. He had endured the humor of his fellow students about the fight and felt like a fool with the top of his head shaved and crisscrossed with catgut.

The hospital was on the edge of the campus, so it took no time to walk there. He remembered that the medical student's name who had sewed him up was Jolie. When he asked at the desk, the woman said, "Yes, she's on duty. Have a seat until you're called."

He took a seat in the waiting room and paged through a six-month-old issue of *Collier's* magazine but found nothing in it that interested him. Finally his name was called, and he followed a nurse down the hall.

He sat on the edge of the bed and the medical student he remembered entered the room. "Do you remember me?" he asked her. "You told me to come back and you'd take these stitches out."

"Yes. We'll see how you're doing."

She picked up the chart the nurse had hooked to the end of the bed. "Your name is Winslow, is that right?"

"Yes. Tyler Winslow."

"Tyler? Is that a nickname?"

"No. My mother's brother was named that. She wanted to keep the name going."

"Unusual name."

Tyler studied the young woman as she took some instruments out of a cabinet. He had forgotten how attractive she was. Once again her hair was pulled back into a bun, emphasizing her beautiful blue eyes and incredibly even complexion. When she came closer, he noticed her full name on her name tag: Jolie Vernay. He sat still as she examined his head.

"It looks like it's healing very well. We can take the stitches out."

As she began to remove the stitches, Tyler felt her firm grasp and noticed also a faint perfume. "I never went to a woman doctor before." When she did not answer, he said, "Where I come from we don't have too many doctors of any kind."

"And where is that, Mr. Winslow?"

"Africa."

Jolie leaned back. "Africa?"

"Yes. My parents are missionaries there. I only came here a few years ago to go to school."

"I've often wanted to go to Africa. I don't know if I'll ever get the chance."

"It's quite a place," he said. Then he asked curiously, "You said you're from France?"

"Yes."

"Did you come to this country to study medicine?"

"No."

Tyler waited for her to explain, but she did not. He tried to make conversation as she went back to work on his stitches, but she only supplied brief answers.

Finally she stepped back and said, "There, all done. I'd try not to get hit in that spot again if I were you."

Tyler grinned crookedly. "I'll try. Listen, when you get off, do you suppose we could get something to eat?"

"No, I don't think so."

"I might have a relapse. I'd need a doctor there."

The woman smiled, and he saw an appealing dimple

36

on her right cheek. "You have a dimple," he remarked.

Instantly the smile went away. "I hate it."

"I think it's cute."

"Well, I don't. Now, you'll have to excuse me."

"I really would like it if you would come out and have dinner or at least coffee with me." She appeared to be examining him, and he said quickly, "I may have a lot of faults, but I'm rather persistent."

Somehow his remark amused Jolie, and she said, "I won't be off for two hours."

"It's a date. I'll meet you in the waiting room in two hours."

★　★　★

As Jolie stepped out into the waiting room, she saw Tyler Winslow relaxing in a chair. He got up at once and came over.

"Are you finished?" he asked.

"Yes."

"I'm starved. How about you?"

"I'm always hungry when I get off."

"Do you have a favorite place close to the hospital?"

"I have a favorite Italian place. Do you like Italian food?"

"I love it."

The two walked to the small restaurant called Gregorio's. "They have very good Italian food," Jolie told him as he opened the door for her.

When they entered, a short, rather rotund man greeted Jolie with a big smile. "Ah, Doctor, good to see you again."

"Good to see you too, Gregorio. We're awfully hungry. Just bring us something good. You pick it."

"The very best for you, Doctor, and for your friend."

As the two sat down, Tyler said, "You've been here before."

"The food is cheap and good, and it's handy to the hospital."

Tyler was studying a painting of an Italian landscape on the wall near the table.

"Do you get involved in fights very often?" Jolie asked abruptly.

"Well, not as a rule," Tyler said. "This one was sort of forced on me."

"I'd like to hear about it."

"It's not a very pleasant story."

"Are you ashamed of it?"

He felt like squirming. "I'm not proud of it." He tried to change the subject, but the conversation was stilted, and Tyler was feeling more and more awkward. Finally Gregorio strutted from the kitchen with two plates held high and set them on the table.

"Escarole with fresh lemon juice, chicken parmigiana, and green beans with olive oil and lemon," he explained. "This you will like!"

"Thank you, Gregorio," Jolie said. "It looks delicious, as always."

Gregorio made a little bow, and Jolie clasped her hands in her lap and bowed her head.

"That's what my folks always do," Tyler said when she opened her eyes.

"You don't say grace over your food?"

"I've kind of gotten into bad habits since I've come to this country."

"Tell me about yourself," Jolie said as she took a bite of escarole.

"Well, not much to tell. I'm studying art. I want to be a painter."

"I love paintings."

"Really? What kind do you like?" he asked.

"I like the Flemish school. That's one reason why I like

New York. There are so many good museums. I've been to all of them, I think."

"Maybe we could go to one together someday."

Jolie took a bite of her chicken and chewed slowly.

"What about you?"

"I'm studying to be a doctor."

"Well, I know that, but you're from France? Why didn't you study there?"

Jolie toyed with the food on her plate, shoving it around with her fork. Finally she looked up and said, "I had to come to America to help my father."

"Your father? What's wrong with him?"

"It's not a very happy story."

"I'd like to hear it."

Jolie shrugged, and he saw again the strength that was in her. Her cool eyes seemed to mirror some sort of ancient wisdom. He was intensely aware of the perfect curve of her mouth, and her abundant brown hair lay smoothly pulled into the bun on her head. He was also aware, even as she sat there, of the lovely turnings of her throat and the clean-running lines of her body. "Do you have a large family in France?"

"Just my mother."

She saw the question in his eyes and shrugged, a typical French gesture. "My father is an American. He fought in France in the Great War. He and my mother fell in love, but he did not like it in France, and she did not want to come to America, so they separated."

"That's a hard one. Have you seen him often?"

"No. Never until I came here. I was studying medicine at home, but when we found out he was ill and had no one to care for him, I came over to help take care of him."

"Is he very ill?"

"He cannot live long."

Tyler shook his head. "I'm sorry to hear that."

"Tell me more about yourself, Mr. Winslow," she said, obviously wanting to change the subject.

"Like I said, I'm studying to be a painter." He took another bite of his chicken, savoring the flavor. Jolie turned her full attention to Tyler and began to ask him questions about his art. Tyler soon found that she knew as much about art history as he did. He found himself in awe of the combination of beauty and intelligence that she possessed.

As the two continued to talk, Tyler started telling Jolie about some of his problems with his parents and some of his bad behavior. "Hey, that's enough about me," he said. He wiped his mouth and put his napkin on his empty plate.

"Yes, it's time to go. I have to see to my father." She paid for her own dinner and thanked Gregorio for the fabulous meal.

When they were outside, Tyler said, "I'd like to see you again."

"No, I don't think so."

"Maybe we could go to an art gallery or something."

"I don't think I'd like to do that."

He was puzzled. "What's the matter?"

"I'd rather not say."

"It's not hard to see. You don't like me."

"Mr. Winslow, we're not going in the same direction. It would be pointless for us to try to see each other."

"Why?"

"I will not date a man I wouldn't consider marrying," she said quietly, "and the man I marry must be strong. You are not a strong man. Good night." She turned and walked toward the hospital.

Tyler stared at her, feeling his anger build, but as he started in the opposite direction, he thought, "Actually, I guess she's right about that." It was a discouraging thought, and he kept his eyes down in shame.

CHAPTER THREE

AN UNWANTED GOOD-BYE

★ ★ ★

As October slowly passed, Tyler threw himself into his work at school almost in a frenzy. He had not heard from his parents, so he knew Chance had not informed them of his actions, which pleased him but at the same time made him feel guilty for keeping things from them. He felt like he had when as a boy he had hidden a misdeed from his parents.

For two weeks he steadfastly kept at his work, staying up late and rising early. Only three times did he go out with Caroline, which upset her. She did not understand his new work ethic any more than Tyler himself understood it, but she put his reluctance to spend more time with her down as a mark against her own charms. As a matter of fact, she had found herself falling in love with Tyler, which even surprised Caroline. Her father and mother were not happy about the situation, for they saw nothing in Tyler that could appeal to them as a son-in-law, but they knew they had spoiled their daughter to the point that she was difficult to reason with.

As hard as he tried, Tyler could not forget what Jolie

Vernay had told him after they had dined at Gregorio's. *"The man I marry must be strong. You are not a strong man."*

More than once, after Tyler went to bed, that scene came rolling before him almost like a motion picture. He remembered the tone of her voice and the look of disdain in her eyes, and for hours he would toss in bed vacillating between dislike and desire.

There was something inexplicable in Jolie Vernay that drew him. Perhaps it was her clean beauty, but more likely it was the old story of the moth being drawn to the candle. She had hurt him and humiliated him with her words and with her attitude, but that did not seem to matter. More and more he began to grow introspective, and even when he worked for long hours on a painting, trying to blot out the memory of her words, they would come floating back to him.

In truth, Tyler Winslow had always been somewhat successful with women. He had never been seriously attached to any of his girlfriends, although he had fancied himself so a few times. His rugged good looks, quick intelligence, and cheerful wit appealed to women, and now for the first time, he was discovering what it was like to be rejected. It was humiliating. As time went on, he spent more and more time thinking of how he might change Jolie's opinion of him.

★　★　★

Every time Tyler was anywhere near the hospital, he came close to going inside and asking Jolie out, but he always refused the impulse. "She's nothing but a snob," he muttered once. "I hope she winds up a sour old maid." He knew this was not very likely, and finally the unpleasant truth pressed upon him that she was stronger than he was. She had left her home and come to a foreign country to complete an obligation that must be very difficult. He himself had never stuck to any course of action that had caused him any discomfort, and the thought that Jolie Vernay could do what he could not was a reproach to him.

Finally one Wednesday afternoon he found himself standing in front of the hospital gazing at the cheerless gray building almost as if it were a human antagonist. It was a cold day and already the sun was hidden in a bleak iron heaven in the west. The air had the taste of cold in it, and even as he stood there, a few flakes of snow fell on his face, burning slightly like tiny bits of fire. He turned his head up and studied the sky and blinked as the snow touched him; then with a burst of resolution he entered the building.

When he discovered that she was on duty, he told the receptionist, "I've got an important message for Dr. Vernay."

"I'm sorry. She's busy with patients," the woman answered.

"It's pretty important."

"I'll have to know more than that. We can't have people interrupting the doctors."

"It about a personal matter." He leaned over and said, "Come on, be a sport."

"Oh, go right on back," the receptionist finally assented with a grin. "Let me know how it all works out."

Tyler quickly turned and went down the hall. He found Jolie in one of the large rooms with several beds, standing over a female patient. He watched her for a moment, realizing he was probably setting himself up for another embarrassment. *She'll probably give me the bum's rush, but she'll have to be persistent, because I won't quit.*

When Jolie started around the bed, she saw him in the doorway and her eyes widened. She recovered from her surprise quickly and came over to him.

"Hello, Tyler."

"Hi. I don't mean to bother you, but I have something to ask you."

"What is it?" Her eyes were cool as always, and she seemed on guard as she waited.

"Do you mind not standing there like you're a soldier ready for an assault?" Tyler asked with some asperity. "I just wanted to ask you out again."

"I thought I made myself clear about that."

"Well, *I* didn't make myself clear." Having nothing to lose, Tyler went ahead with his plan. "I need to talk to you."

"About what?"

"I can't talk here."

"Neither can I."

Tyler smiled and winked at her. He'd had considerable success with his smiles and winks in the past. "What time do you get off?"

"Six o'clock, but I don't—"

"I'll be in the waiting room, and I won't take no for an answer." He was a bundle of nerves, and all the pressure that had been mounting in him was evident. "I'm not going to bite you," he said. "I just want to have something to eat and talk."

Jolie looked as though she wanted to turn and walk away, but finally she shrugged and said, "All right. We can have dinner—but that's all."

"Good. I'll be waiting for you. I'll be the one looking anxious out there."

Jolie smiled, and the expression lightened her whole attitude. "I'll be able to pick you out, then."

★ ★ ★

Tyler took Jolie to a small restaurant he liked because it was usually quiet and a good place to talk. She only ordered a cup of soup and a salad, and he contented himself with a small sirloin steak and a baked potato. As they ate, Jolie was willing enough to talk.

She had had dinner the previous evening with some close friends of hers, Jack and Irene Henderson. Jack was one of the other medical students who worked at the same hospital, and the family went to the same church as Jolie did.

"You should have seen little Barbara in her high chair," Jolie told him. "Irene put some peas on a plate in front of her, and she picked them up one at a time and dropped them on the floor. And then when she got tired of that game, she poked her finger into the ones that were still on her plate and squished them." She laughed. "I love children. You never know what they're going to do next!"

She went on to tell him about a mother who had brought her child into the emergency room that day, very upset that he had swallowed a penny. "I told the mother that the coin wouldn't hurt the child, and she said, 'But it's a very valuable penny. It's part of my collection.' Here I was working myself up thinking she was worried about the child, and she only wanted the penny."

"Do you get many like that? People who don't really need a doctor?"

"Not too many. Although we sometimes get some pretty grim cases there."

"Some people die, I suppose."

"Yes, that does happen. People hesitate to seek medical care until it's too late, and they die before we can help them."

"I don't think I'd like to be a doctor. It sounds like a pretty depressing business."

"Oh, not always." She took a sip of her soup. "It feels pretty good when you help someone."

"How long have you wanted to be a doctor?"

"Since I was a little girl, I think. Of course I never had any idea I could. We were very poor. There was no money for school, but my mother and I both worked hard and got me through college. My grades were good so I got into medical school. It's been a struggle, though."

As he listened to her, he felt a twinge of guilt. He had no hard luck stories to tell her, for his life had been much easier. He had two good parents, a fine brother, and a sister he was very proud of. Even though his parents didn't approve of his choice of profession and wondered if he would be able to make a living with his art, they made it possible for him to study in New York. He felt a twinge of guilt at how lightly he had taken their sacrifices.

He poured some more steak sauce onto his meat. "Did you say your father is sick? That's why you came to New York?"

"Yes. He's in the last stages of lung cancer." There was a slight tremor in her voice. She picked up her coffee cup and took a quick sip. When she put the cup down, she shook her head. "He was exposed to gas in the war, and his lungs were never strong after that. To top it off, he persisted in smoking, which I'm sure didn't help anything."

"What's your dad's name?"

"Dennis Franklin."

"His last name's not the same as yours?"

"No." She sipped her coffee again. "He never married my mother."

"Oh, I see."

"He's not a very strong man, Tyler. He always took the easy way out, from what Mother said. I think he loved her, but he couldn't face up to taking a foreign bride home and making a living for her."

Tyler digested that slowly and then he met her eyes. "Was it hard for you to come to the U.S. and take care of a man who . . ."

He wasn't sure how to finish his sentence, but Jolie managed a smile. "Who's done me a disservice? It was at first, but my mother is a wonderful woman. She married before I was born, so I was given her husband's last name—Vernay. Of course, I grew up believing he was my father. My mother didn't have any contact with my real father for years, and then two years ago we got a letter from him, telling us about his illness. She decided it was time to tell me who my real father was. It was a hard decision to come here, but I don't regret it now."

"I don't think I could have done that."

Jolie did not answer, and her silence seemed like a rebuke to Tyler. He thought, *That's exactly what she meant when she said I didn't have any strength.* He picked up his fork and cut at a corner of his steak, but he had lost his appetite. Putting the fork down, he said, "I've been thinking about what you said after we ate at Gregorio's—that I'm not strong."

"I'm sorry. I've always been too blunt." Jolie laughed, and the dimple appeared in her cheek. "I like to think I'm just straightforward, but *Maman* always says I have no tact. It's none of my business what you are, Tyler."

"Well, it made me angry when you said it, but the more I've thought about it, the more I think you're right. Things have been pretty easy for me compared to the problems you've had."

"Oh, I've had a good life. It was hard coming here, of course. It's hard to see my father so sick, even though I never knew him before."

She put her fork down and leaned forward. "I've been thinking about your passion for art since the last time I saw you. You're the first artist I've ever met. It seems that artists who are most successful have an unusual drive." She leaned back in her chair. "I remember reading about Paul Gauguin, the artist who was a friend of Van Gogh. He was so driven he forsook his family and went to the islands of the South Seas and painted constantly. And Van Gogh himself, if I remember correctly, only sold one or two of his paintings. Now each one is worth millions."

"Yes, he was a miserable, unhappy man—Van Gogh, I

mean. But look what he left the world. What a legacy."

"Is that what you want to do?"

The simple question stopped Tyler almost as if he had run into a wall. "I guess I haven't thought that far ahead. I just like to paint."

"That's not enough, though, is it? Most of the great artists had to work hard and overcome all sorts of obstacles."

The question was like a sharp knife being driven into Tyler. He knew that he was lazy and that he didn't have the kind of energy that drives a man to such an extent that it consumes his life. "I guess so," he finally said, knowing she had touched on a raw spot.

"Tyler, let me tell you something that you might not want to hear. You seem to have forgotten that God gives people talents, and anyone who wastes them is a fool."

He could not meet Jolie's eyes. He dropped his focus to the tablecloth and was silent for so long that she finally said, "Well, I've hurt your feelings again. I don't think it's a good idea for us to be together. I'm too blunt and at times I get self-righteous." She started to get up.

"Don't go," he said. "It's early yet."

"Tyler, don't you see that we're not alike?"

He did see that, and somehow their differences were what made him interested in her. He saw in her a strength and an intensity that he admired but knew he did not possess—or if he possessed it, it was dormant. After he paid for their meals, they went outside. "Let me see you again," he said. "We'll talk about something else."

"About the weather? About the war in Europe? The world's going to pieces, Tyler. The Germans could attack my country any day and kill half the population. They almost killed off half the men in the last war. This man Hitler is a maniac, and he's not going to stop until the world's on fire."

Tyler was astonished at her intensity. "Hitler's pretty bad all right, but he's promised that he won't do anything else toward expanding German territory."

Jolie's eyes flashed. "He's a liar and a maniac, and he will not stop until the whole world is destroyed!" She pulled her collar tight around her neck. "Good-bye, Tyler. It would be best if you didn't come to see me anymore."

Tyler watched her leave and felt tremendously deflated. He wasn't angry, for he recognized the truth in what she had said. Slowly he turned and made his way back toward his apartment. When he arrived home, he tried to work for a while but found he could not, for the things she had said kept running through his mind.

★ ★ ★

Looking back afterward, Tyler realized that the supper he'd had with Jolie Vernay had acted as a catalyst. For two or three days, he took her words to heart and threw himself into his art and his schoolwork with a vigor he had never shown before. But then Caroline appeared on the scene again, demanding that they go out, and he gave in with little protest.

That night they went to a nightclub, and Caroline shoved a bunch of bills into his hands, saying, "Spend it all. Let's just have a good time."

They enjoyed their evening together, drinking too much, and the next night they repeated the pattern.

The cycle then began, and through most of November Tyler slipped back into the same bad habits that had marked his career. Caroline was now, she declared, completely in love with him, and more than once she had suggested that they get married. "We'll have a place together," she continued the last time they had talked about it, "and you can study art and we won't have to be separated."

"What will you do while I'm studying art?"

She had thrown her arms around him and pulled his

head down to kiss him thoroughly. Her eyes were gleaming, and she had laughed. "You be the artist, and I'll see that we both have a good time."

The temptation was real enough, for Tyler's finances were in shambles. He had to take a job as a grocery cashier just to make his way without asking for more money from his parents. The time spent on the job was time spent away from his studies, and he gave up on art almost altogether except for the projects that he had to do in order to pass his art classes.

November passed quickly, and each time he thought of Jolie Vernay he quickly pushed her out of his mind. Her words still burned in him when he allowed himself to dwell on them, so he solved that problem by drinking enough that he was able to put her out of his mind.

★　★　★

It was on the first day of December that Tyler encountered Jolie again. He had just come out of his last class for the day and had started walking home. He sometimes took another route so that he would not have to pass by the hospital where Jolie worked, but he was tired this evening and took the quickest route. As he approached the hospital, he was startled to see Jolie coming out of the front doors. She was wearing a black cloth coat and a hat that covered most of her hair. She was moving rather slowly, he saw, as if she were weary, and an impulse took him. He hastened his pace.

"Hello, Jolie." She turned, looking startled, but she didn't acknowledge him.

"What's the matter?" he asked. "Is something wrong?"

She stood looking down at the ground and finally said, "Hello, Tyler. No, I'm all right."

"You don't look well." He thought she looked like she

had lost weight, and he stepped closer, studying her face. "Is your father worse?"

"He died two weeks ago."

Tyler knew she was alone in a foreign country and wished he could have been there for her. "I'm sorry," he said awkwardly. "If I had known, maybe I could have—"

"No. There was nothing you could do."

Tyler tried to think of something to say. "I really am sorry," he murmured. "It must be hard for you."

"I'll be going home soon," she said, "so this is good-bye."

Although he knew the thought was ridiculous, Tyler suddenly felt that he was losing an important part of his life. "Let me have your address in France."

"I'd rather not."

The abrupt refusal surprised Tyler. "It wouldn't hurt you to let me write."

"Tyler, I've told you in every way I know how. We have nothing in common. What would we write about?"

"I don't know, but I don't have so many friends that I couldn't use another one. I think you could too."

She shrugged, looking fatigued, but she took a piece of paper and a pencil out of her purse. Using the purse as a brace, she wrote her address down and handed the paper to him. "Please don't get your hopes up," she said. "This won't come to anything."

"When are you leaving?"

"Very soon. Good-bye, Tyler. I wish you well."

He stood there watching until Jolie was completely out of sight, unable to take his eyes from her. He wanted to run after her to argue, but he knew it would be futile. When she had disappeared from his sight, he remained standing where he was. *I should have helped her,* he thought. *If I had had any sense at all, I would have realized that she needed a friend. She told me her father wouldn't live long, and I did what I always do—just ignored it.*

He turned away, his head down, walking aimlessly.

He did not want to go to his apartment, and for a long time that afternoon he walked the streets. His feet grew numb with the cold, and he kept his hands shoved in the pockets of his overcoat, but his face quickly became immobile. Finally in disgust he made himself go home. Somehow he did not want to be alone, and he called Caroline. As usual, she was ready for a night out. As he hung up the phone, he felt the emptiness grow inside him. He had come to America with high hopes and expecting success, and instead of that it seemed that everything he had touched was turning sour.

That night he and Caroline outdid themselves, throwing themselves into the night life with wild exuberance. At one point, Caroline gasped, "Well, you've come alive at last. It's about time!"

But later, when Tyler staggered home and threw himself on his bed fully clothed, so drunk he could not undress, he thought about her words. "No," he muttered, "I'm not alive. Just the opposite."

★　★　★

Tyler went through the next two weeks almost in a daze. He had failed three of the courses he was taking, including the art course in which he had the most interest. He opened his mailbox and stared at the notice that had come from the dean's office instructing him to see the dean immediately. He made his way to the campus, his heart heavy.

The dean wasted no time. "Your grade point average will not permit you to continue your studies here. I'm sorry, Mr. Winslow. You are dismissed from this college."

Tyler left the man's office and for four days he tried to come up with a plan for his future. He drank too much but found it offered no comfort.

On Saturday night, he went out with Caroline as

usual, but he was unable to forget his troubles. By nine o'clock, he was ready to go home.

"What's wrong with you, Tyler?" she asked as they sat in her car outside of his apartment. "You act like you're sick."

"I've got something to tell you," he said. "I've made a mess out of school, Caroline."

"So did I. So do a lot of people. It's no disgrace. Are your grades bad?"

"They're terrible. I've got to go back to Africa."

"Africa! Why, you can't go back there. There's nothing there for you."

"I know it, but I don't have any choice." A bitterness twisted his mouth, and he shook his head. "I guess I could get a job driving a bus or something like that."

"I don't know anything about art," Caroline said, "but you must have thought you could be successful."

"I thought so once. I'm not so sure anymore."

Caroline took his hand and held it against her cheek. "I'll help you," she said softly.

Her words took Tyler by surprise. He often thought of her as being an empty-headed pleasure seeker, but now he saw that there was more to her than that. "I don't think you can."

"I can if you'll let me," Caroline said eagerly. She took his hand in both of hers. "What you need is to forget about all those other classes and do nothing but paint. You need to throw yourself into it. You don't need to be worried about money all the time."

Tyler suddenly grinned. "By George, why didn't I think of that! That's what I need to do—get rich and do nothing but paint. That's a great idea!"

"Don't make fun of me, Tyler," Caroline said. "Listen, you've always talked about going to Europe to look at the great paintings there and maybe find a good teacher. If you'd do that, I think you could make it, and I've got the money."

Tyler stared at Caroline. "Why, I couldn't do that."

"Why not? Don't you care for me at all, Tyler?" She put her hand on his cheek. "I care for you, and I thought you loved me, a little bit at least."

Caroline was showing a vulnerable side of herself that Tyler had never seen, although at times he had sensed that she was covering up a sensitive heart with the wild, extravagant life she led. But he was not in love with her, much as he sometimes enjoyed being with her.

"Oh, we have a good time together, Caroline, but that's different."

"I know I'm silly and foolish and I drink too much, but I do care for you. I want to help you. Listen," she said. "I've got some money put aside that my parents don't even know about. It's enough to buy you passage on a ship to Spain or France or somewhere. You could study hard and become a great painter, and then you could come back here and my parents would be proud to have you as a son-in-law. We could be happy together, Tyler. I know we could! I know your pride's hurt because my family has money, but if you could do this and become successful, why, there'd be nothing to keep us apart."

Tyler was stunned. He could not even speak for a moment, and finally he said, "That's sweet of you to offer, but—"

"But what? What's wrong with it? You know I'll just throw the money away on partying or something stupid. This way I'd be investing in you. I'd be part of you. I'm not smart like you are, but I could help in this way. Please don't go back to Africa. Go to Europe for six months until you find yourself, and I know you will."

★ ★ ★

Tyler, of course, refused Caroline's offer, but the idea

seemed to have taken hold in her, and from that day forward it was all she talked about. As the new year approached and Tyler didn't come up with any better plan, he began to think seriously about what she had said. Actually he had no choice at all. It was either go back to Africa, keep his job at the grocery store, or do as Caroline wished. Of the three choices, the longer he thought about it, the more Caroline's idea seemed to make sense.

Finally, in the last week of December, he was alone with Caroline. They had gone out for a brisk walk in the park, and she had, as usual, begged him to take her offer. Finally the decision that had been coming more and more into focus in his mind solidified. "Caroline, do you really think I should go to Europe?"

"Yes, I do. It's the only thing to do, Tyler."

"I believe you're right. It galls me to have to take your money, but I will under one condition."

"What's that?"

"That you let me pay you back when I begin to sell my work."

"You won't need to pay me back, because when you come back we'll get married. You'll be successful. I'll be the wife of a famous painter. Then it won't be my money or your money, it'll be *our* money. Oh, Tyler, I'm so excited!" She put her arms around him and kissed him. "I'll miss you so much, but we'll write all the time, won't we? And when you come back, we'll get married. I'll be so proud to have a famous husband."

Tyler held her tightly and at that moment all of his doubts fled away. *Why, of course I can do it. It's what I've been needing all the time, and Caroline's right. She would have thrown the money away on booze or a fur coat or jewelry. And I'll pay her back.*

★ ★ ★

On the night of January the third, Tyler stood at the dock saying good-bye to Caroline. The two clung together, and as the whistle blasted in the morning air, she held to him tightly. "I'll miss you so much! You write me as soon as you get to France."

"I will, and if I ever amount to anything, Caroline, it'll be your doing."

"No it won't," she whispered. "I don't have the talent for much of anything, but you do. This way I'll be a part of your life. I want it this way so much!"

The two hugged again, and then the last call sounded. Tyler kissed her once more, made his way up the gangplank, and stood at the rail. She was waiting, a small figure in the crowd, her eyes fixed on him. When the ship began to move out, Tyler waved at her, smiling.

Before long, he could see her no more. The passengers began to disperse, but he went to the stern of the ship and watched America recede. Suddenly it all seemed wrong, but it was too late now. He had a crazy impulse to jump off the ship and swim to shore, to tell her that it wasn't going to work—but he pushed that idea away with some effort.

"I'll make it up to her," he murmured. "I'll work hard and be a success, and she'll be proud of me. And so will my folks." With that thought in mind, he left America and headed for the Old World.

CHAPTER FOUR

MORE DISAPPOINTMENT

★ ★ ★

Although the ship that carried Tyler Winslow from America to France bore the rather magnificent name *The Flying Eagle,* in reality, it had none of the speed of an eagle. It seemed to crawl over the gray surface of the Atlantic so slowly that if it weren't for the vibrations of the engines, Tyler oftentimes would have felt that the ship was standing absolutely still. For the first day or two he prowled the ship out of curiosity, but after he had thoroughly explored the vessel, he spent as much time as possible on deck. He had not always been a deep thinker, but he had a lot on his mind these days.

While the meals were adequate, each day they became less satisfying. The cook had apparently never heard of seasoning, and Tyler had to add salt and pepper to whatever was set before him for it to have any flavor at all. There were activities of various kinds at night, with the passengers gathering to play games or dance. One woman in her late thirties apparently took a fancy to Tyler and flirted with him, but there was something predatory about her. Tyler found himself remaining in his cabin or walking around the deck rather than be thrown into her company.

When word finally came that land was in sight, the passengers crowded around the railings to watch *The Flying Eagle* approach Le Havre. Tyler was one of the first passengers to disembark, and as he passed through customs, he enjoyed hearing the musical sounds of people speaking French. He had studied French in college and quickly discovered that he could speak the language better than he could understand it. He wanted to ask everybody to slow down, but he knew that he was the one who would have to change. He determined to avoid speaking English as much as he could and to try to speak French at all times.

Anxious to get to Paris, Tyler went at once to the railroad station and bought a ticket to Paris. He found that the train was leaving in three hours, and since he was not at all sleepy, he bought a good meal at a restaurant and sat at the table listening to the babble of voices.

The train pulled out of Le Havre exactly on time, and Tyler found himself in a car with only four other people. The young couple who looked to be in their early twenties were totally involved with each other and ignored the rest of the passengers. A tall older man with white hair and something of a military bearing sat beside the window staring out and saying nothing, and a talkative Frenchman who spoke very good English and looked every inch a businessman sat beside Tyler.

He had a sallow face and a pair of eyes that seemed to pop out of his head, and he spoke almost explosively. He also had the irritating habit of knowing more about any subject than anyone. The man had first tried to engage the silent man sitting across from him but got limited responses. He then turned his artillery of words on Tyler. He inquired into Tyler's reason for coming to France and determined the part of the United States he came from, and when he learned that Tyler had been raised in Africa, he proceeded to give a lecture on Africa's role in the world economy.

When the businessman finally fell silent, perhaps to gasp for air, Tyler asked, "What do you think of this war?"

"Ah, the war. It will come to nothing."

Tyler stared at him. "Come to nothing? How can you say that, sir? It's already come to something. Hitler's already taken big chunks out of Europe, like Czechoslovakia and Poland."

"He's a bad man, but he's not a stupid man. He has taken territory, but he knows that if he tries to take any more, France will stop him."

"They haven't done much in that line so far," Tyler remarked.

Tyler's words seemed to irritate the businessman. "You do not understand, sir. You are not European. Hitler is an astute man. He knows that if the British joined with France, they would stop him in a minute. Believe me, he will take no more territory."

"You are a fool!" exploded the older man by the window in heavily accented English.

Both Tyler and the businessman and even the young couple turned swiftly to look at the man.

"Do you speak to me?" the businessman asked. "You call me a fool?"

"Yes. You *are* a fool. So is anyone a fool who believes Hitler will stop. The Boche will never stop. He will take all of Europe before he's stopped, and even then he will attack Russia."

"But France and England—"

"France has no army. All it has is a dream."

"A dream, sir! What do you mean?" the businessman demanded.

"The generals put their trust in the Maginot Line. They are trying to prepare as if this war will be like the last one, but it will not be."

"You were in the Great War, I take it, sir?" Tyler asked quietly.

"Yes, I was." He was silent for a minute and then said, "I saw men die until it became sickening. Then it was trench warfare. I remember battle after battle where we would lose hundreds or even thousands of men to gain a hundred yards of ground—and then lose it the next day." He seemed to sag. "But this war. It will not be fought in trenches. If you read the papers, you know how mobile the Germans are."

"The Maginot Line is impregnable, sir, I assure you," the businessman said. He seemed irritated and his voice took on a high-pitched angry tone. "It cannot be pierced, I tell you."

"Apparently you cannot read. The Germans have no attention of attacking the Line. They will simply go around it or over it. Something that could not be done in the Great War, but now the Germans are using the blitzkrieg, the lightning war. They will overleap our defenses as they have already done with smaller nations. They will pay no attention to the line but will crush all opposition with their air power and their tanks and artillery."

"Do you really think there's no hope, sir?" Tyler asked.

"There's hope only in a miracle, and miracles have become rather uncommon in our world." The man turned to look out the window again, and the businessman began to speak loudly, as if by volume he could overcome the old soldier's arguments.

As the train approached Paris, Tyler wondered how much of what the old man had said was true. It sounded ominous, and he filed his thoughts away, determined to ask more about the military dangers in which France seemed to be engulfed.

★ ★ ★

After Tyler got a room in Paris, finding it was somewhat more expensive than he had expected, he wrote at once to Caroline and to his parents. His letter was full of enthusiasm and excitement, for he felt that his luck had to change. He was determined to make it as an artist and said so in the letters. He wasn't sure how to close his letter to Caroline. He knew that her feelings for him were much deeper than his for her, but it was her money and advice and help that had brought him this far and given him a second chance. So he ended the letter warmly and promised to write regularly.

For the next week Tyler roamed the streets of Paris. There was so much to see, and he was determined to see it all. By the end of the week he had found that he could make himself understood to most people, though with some difficulty. *Give me six months, and I'll speak like a native.* He did not make this boast aloud, but he did constantly try to improve his French.

He spent several days going to the art museums and was stunned by the magnificence of the Louvre. Day after day he would stand before the masterpieces of the ages in awed silence. One day he studied a single painting by Rembrandt for almost two hours, unable to take his eyes off it.

A guard had watched him for a long time and finally said, "I trust you're not planning to steal it, *monsieur*?"

Tyler grinned. "No, though I'd like to."

"Many people would. Are you an artist yourself?"

"Well, to tell the truth, I thought I was. But now looking at these masterpieces, I think I'm just a dabbler."

"You must take heart," the guard said, smiling with encouragement. "All these artists, they had to begin somewhere."

"But all of them had genius in them. I'm not sure I have that."

The guard offered a few more encouraging words, and when Tyler finally moved on, he thought, *Not every-*

body will be as encouraging as he was.

★ ★ ★

The weather was not much different than it had been in New York. It snowed several nights in a row, but by midmorning the snow had been churned into a slush by the thousands of automobiles and trucks that plowed through the city. More than once, despite the cold weather, Tyler saw artists out braving the frigid air to paint on the street. He would inevitably stop and watch, and sometimes he would strike up a conversation. He found that some artists were almost sullen and would not return more than a monosyllable, but others were quite open with their views.

One Thursday afternoon, he stopped near a young woman who was painting a picture of the *Arc de Triomphe*. He stood off to one side and did not bother her, and finally she turned and caught his eye.

"L'aimez-vous?" she asked with a smile. She was a pretty girl who looked to be in her midtwenties with cheeks whitened by the cold.

"Yes, I do like it," he answered in French. "Have you been painting long?"

"I can't remember when I wasn't painting. You are what, English?"

"No, I'm an American. I was raised in Kenya but went to college in New York."

"Oh, I've always wanted to go to America."

"Well, I always wanted to come to France," he said, "and I made it. So maybe you'll make it to America someday too." He was starting to tell her about New York when a man wearing a uniform approached them and she introduced him as her husband.

"Your wife paints better than most of the painters who are actually making a living at their work in America."

"That is good to hear," the man replied.

"You're in the army, I see. What's the situation?"

A cloud crossed the soldier's face. "It is not good. You have come to France at the wrong time, sir."

As always, Tyler got what information he could, which was not a great deal. The soldier and his wife were happy, but there was a cloud over them, he saw.

★ ★ ★

The art institute that Tyler ended up enrolling in was not particularly well known. With so many art schools in Paris, he simply chose the one closest to his room in the heart of the city. It was housed in an ancient brick building with tall windows to allow as much light as possible. Tyler went there on the twentieth of January to enroll. He found himself speaking to a small man wearing a gray suit and a gleaming white shirt. His name was Dever, and he seemed preoccupied and irritable. He had Tyler fill out several papers, which he glanced over with a frown on his face.

"You have samples of your work?"

"As a matter of fact I don't, Monsieur Dever. I didn't have room to bring them with my luggage."

"We do not take people without talent."

"I hope I have a little of that."

"It takes more than talent. It takes devotion, dedication."

"Well, I trust I have a little of that too, monsieur."

"I will allow you to enter on probation, Monsieur Winslow."

Tyler gave the man a check for the tuition, and then Monsieur Dever said, "I will assign you to one of our instructors. You will be here Monday morning at eight o'clock."

"Certainly, sir. I trust I will be able to meet your standards."

Dever's look said, *I doubt it*, but he refrained from saying anything.

As Tyler left, he thought, *They need a better recruiter here. Quite a cold welcome.*

On Monday morning he was at the school on time and found his instructor was quite different from Dever. His last name was Genis, and he was a huge bear of a man with fingers like bananas, and already, although it was early, he had spots of paint on his hands. He had a loud roar of a voice and seemed to shout everything. The teacher showed Tyler where the supplies were and got him set up by the window.

"Come let me know when you have something for me to look at."

Somewhat intimidated by Genis, Tyler began work at once. He decided that painting a still life might be the safest thing to do, so he gathered a few props that were sitting on the counter. He arranged a teapot, teacup, and saucer on a white tablecloth that he folded in waves. A number of other students were coming in, but no one stopped to talk with him.

He worked as quickly as he could, but it took him two days before he finally got the effect he wanted. He was nervous, but he went to Genis and said, "Monsieur Genis, would you look at my work?"

The man grunted and walked over to the easel without speaking. He examined the still life but still did not speak, which made Tyler's nervousness increase.

Finally the instructor said loudly, "If this is the best you can do, you need to go someplace else. This school is for those who have achieved a certain level, which you have not."

Genis's voice was loud enough so that everyone in the large room heard it. There were at least ten other artists at work, and Tyler felt that every one of them was looking at him, hiding smiles. He stood there as Genis pointed out the flaws of his painting, and finally the man said, "I will have Monsieur Dever refund your tuition."

"You won't let me try?"

"You are not ready to try here. Go learn some fundamentals. Come back in a year and we'll see." He lowered his voice then and stepped closer. In a hoarse whisper he said, "You would be wasting your time if you stayed here, Winslow. There are numerous other schools that will teach you the basics. Monsieur Dever can give you the addresses of some of these."

"Thank you," Tyler said quietly. He waited until Genis left to begin putting his supplies away. He knew his face was flushed, and when he left the room, every student was taking pains not to look at him. In humiliation, he stopped by Monsieur Dever's office to collect his refund, but he was too discouraged to ask the man for the names of other art schools he might recommend.

★　★　★

The shame of being dismissed from the art institute ate at Tyler, and after depositing his still-wet painting in his room, he went out and walked the streets. He did not feel the cold air; all he could feel was the deep embarrassment of being rejected. It had never occurred to him that he would be turned away like this, and after a time he stopped at a bar. Several women approached him while he drank, but he gave them no encouragement. Finally he went back to his room, undressed, and got under the covers. Even in his numbed state, he couldn't forget that he had failed in France just as certainly as he had failed in New York. Finally he fell into a restless sleep, but he woke up several times during the night hearing the voice of Genis, saying, *"Go learn some fundamentals. Come back in a year and we'll see."*

He rose early and spent another day roaming the city. This time he went to art shops and studied the paintings that were for sale. There seemed to be hundreds of small shops selling art of all kinds. He recognized that most of the paintings were far better than anything he had ever done. Totally depressed, he did not eat again until late that night, and again he drank more than he should.

"I've got to do something," he muttered, "but what?"

★ ★ ★

On Thursday morning Tyler got up, his head throbbing, and when he looked at himself in the mirror, he saw a bum. He had not shaved for three days, his hair sprang in every direction, and his eyes were bloodshot.

"I've got to do something," he told himself loudly for the umpteenth time that week. He knew he should enroll at one of the schools whose standards were not as high as the one that had refused him, but somehow he could not force himself to do it.

"Clean yourself up and do something—anything," he told himself sternly. "You cannot continue to wander the streets of Paris without a plan." He wet his hair down and combed it into place and then got out his razor. As he pulled the blade across his chin, he thought of Jolie Vernay. She had no idea that he was in France, for he had not written to her for several months. Why not go visit her now? *I'll go there and get a place, and I'll learn to paint better. Then I'll come back and enroll in a different school here.*

It might not have made complete sense, but at least it was a plan, and he threw himself into it. He spent the morning buying art supplies, for he wasn't sure if he would be able to find any in Ambert, the village where Jolie lived, and then bought a train ticket.

He found one of the last vacant seats in the car and settled in. He said not a word to anyone but was occupied with his own doubts. It began snowing shortly after the train left, and he sat there looking out at the signs beside the small villages. The names of the towns meant nothing to him, but once when the train stopped for some time at a small village called Moulins, it required all of his strength not to get off the train. *What am I going to see Jolie for? What can she do?* The question penetrated his dark thoughts, and he almost got off and headed back to Le Havre and a ship to take him back to America.

But there was nothing to go back to, so he remained in his seat. Finally he put his head back and dozed off and then later, when he woke up, he saw that they were pulling into a small village. When he saw that the sign said Ambert, he got up at once and grabbed his luggage.

He was the only person who had disembarked there. He went over to an elderly man who was sitting on a bench. "Can you tell me, sir, where a family named Vernay lives? *Mademoiselle* Jolie Vernay?"

"But of course, the doctor. You take this road until you come to a big white house with turrets. Turn left and go until you see a small house set off to the right. It is green. That is where Mademoiselle Vernay lives with her mother. You are English?"

"No. American."

"You come to France at a bad time." He shrugged before continuing. "Madame Vernay, the doctor's mother, works at a watchmaker's shop. It is right down that street, you see. She might still be there if you care to see her before going to the house, although it may be a little late," he said as he looked at his pocket watch. "You have business with the Vernays?"

"Yes." Tyler did not feel like divulging his business with this man or with anyone else, so he picked up his luggage and trudged away. He felt the man's eyes on him as he left, and with great misgiving started down the street, wishing desperately he had never come to France in the first place.

CHAPTER FIVE

A Birthday Party

★ ★ ★

The shrill wind howled as Jolie Vernay made her way toward the green house set back off the road. She had to lean against the strong wind while sleet bit at her cheeks. It was about a kilometer from the orphanage to the house, and she normally enjoyed the walk, but today her feet and cheeks, and even her hands, despite the wool gloves, were growing numb.

The sleet swept over the street, and as Jolie turned off the main road and walked quickly toward the house, she looked forward to the evening ahead—good food, warmth, and rest. She had returned from the United States too late to start an internship immediately, but she would begin the following fall at the hospital in Clermont-Ferrand, a city not far from the village where she had lived most of her life.

In the meantime, she had accepted a post as a half-time staff physician and half-time secretary at the large orphanage in town. She found the work very satisfying as well as a welcome relief from the stress of working in the emergency room in New York. She still carried some of that stress with her.

Opening the door, she stepped inside, took off her boots, and slipped her feet into warm house slippers. She took off her hat and coat, wet and heavy with sleet, hung them on the coat-tree, and took a deep breath. *Good to be home.* She went down the hall and into the kitchen. The good smell of food cooking was in the air, and her mother was standing by the stove.

"Hello, *Maman.*"

"Ah, you are back. Go stand in front of the fire and thaw yourself out. It's cold enough to freeze an Eskimo."

"Yes, it is very cold."

Marvel Vernay did not look her forty-six years. Her hair was the same brown as that of her daughter, and her eyes were the same blue. She was small, but her posture was so erect she appeared taller. Her cheeks were flushed by the heat of the stove, and as she smiled at Jolie, she exposed perfect white teeth. "Did you have a good day?"

"Very good. We've got the chicken pox epidemic brought to a standstill, I think."

"Chicken pox is difficult, but it's not as bad as some other things that children can get."

"You're right. Thank God."

As the two women shared the details of their days, and as Jolie thawed out, she began to set the table with the fine china. "We never use plain dishes," she commented, "always this expensive china even for just the two of us. Why is that, Maman?"

Marvel smiled. "There are so many things in this world that we can't have, so the things we can have, I intend to use. They are only dishes. If we break one, it doesn't matter. Now, you make the tea while I take the roast out of the oven." A knock at the door interrupted her words.

"Are you expecting someone, Maman?"

"No. Not that I know of. It's probably *Madame* Dalon

from next door. She probably needs to borrow something for supper."

Walking to the door with quick steps, Madame Vernay opened it, but instead of finding her neighbor, she saw a tall man holding a large suitcase.

"Madame Vernay?"

"*Oui*, I am Madame Vernay."

"My name is Tyler Winslow." He spoke French with a heavy accent and seemed to be searching for the words he needed. "I am a friend of your daughter. We met in New York. I wonder if she's at home."

"Why, yes, indeed. Come in, Monsieur Winslow. Bring your things with you. They'll freeze solid out here." Marvel stepped back as the man entered. "I remember my daughter wrote me about you," she said with a smile. "But she didn't tell me you were coming."

"I didn't really know myself, Madame Vernay."

"Well, put your things down, take off your coat, and we'll surprise her." Marvel waited until he had hung up his coat and stomped his feet on the mat before leading him down the hall. Turning into the kitchen, she said, "Jolie, a surprise for you. A visitor."

Jolie turned, and Marvel saw her eyes open wide and her lips part with astonishment. "Why—it's you!"

"It's me," Tyler said with a broad smile. He was shocked at how glad he was to see her again. "I have bad manners like all Americans. Just come rushing in without an invitation."

"Not at all." Jolie came close to him and put her hand on his arm. "It's good to see you, Tyler, but it is a surprise."

"I came to Paris to study painting. I didn't expect I would get to see you, but things happened and here I am."

"Well, you came at an opportune moment," Marvel said quickly, seeing that her daughter was apparently at a loss for words. "It's very fortunate that I cooked enough for three. By all means you must have dinner with us."

"Oh no, I couldn't—"

"I insist. Come. I will show you where you can wash up and refresh yourself."

Marvel led the way out of the room and showed the American to the guest room. "I will bring you some hot water."

"Oh, please, Madame Vernay, don't bother."

"It is no bother. I'm glad to have company, especially from America. And you even speak French."

"Not very well, but I'm learning."

"Wait here and I will get the water."

Marvel went back to the kitchen and took the kettle off the stove. "You did not expect him?" she asked her daughter.

"No, I didn't."

"I remember what you said about him. But let me take the water." She left the room while Jolie continued setting the table.

When her mother returned, Jolie said, "I can't imagine why he's here."

"He said he came to study painting. You told me he was an artist."

"He didn't mention a thing about coming to France when I knew him."

Marvel studied her daughter's face. "You're upset by his arrival?"

"No, not exactly. I'm just shocked."

Marvel said no more, but she knew her daughter well enough to know that she was perturbed. After a moment Tyler appeared at the door, and she said, "Come and sit down. It's all ready."

"I feel terrible barging in like this. I should have written."

"It's no bother," Marvel said. "I'll ask the blessing." She bowed her head and immediately Tyler glanced at Jolie and bowed his own.

"Lord, we thank you for this food and for this visitor. We ask you to help us love you more. In Jesus' name. Amen."

The meal consisted of beef roast flavored with Burgundy, new potatoes in a white cream sauce, tiny peas with pearl onions, and chunks of thick, hard bread slathered with sweet-tasting butter.

"This is very good indeed, Madame Vernay," Tyler said. "I've always heard about delicious French cooking, and if this is a sample, then what I've heard is correct."

After Jolie had told her mother about how the two of them had met, she started to question Tyler about why he had come to France and what his plans were.

"I came into enough money to come to France and study painting," Tyler told them, toying with his fragile teacup. It looked very small in his hands as he turned it around and around. "I might as well have stayed in America."

"Why do you say that, monsieur?" Marvel asked. She was interested in the young American and saw that he was embarrassed by her question. "But I do not mean to pry."

"I might as well tell you. My professor at the art school in Paris said that I don't have any talent."

"And what do *you* think?" Marvel asked.

The question seemed to trouble Tyler. "Well," he said, "he's the expert. He should know."

"The experts do not know everything, and they are often wrong. Isn't that true, Jolie?"

"I think Maman is right. You should not let someone else's opinion decide your future."

"That is exactly right," Marvel said with great determination. "I advise you to throw yourself into painting. Forget about that art instructor."

Tyler laughed. "I see where Jolie gets her direct ways."

"It's always best to be direct." Marvel smiled and

added, "I don't have a great deal of tact, and I'm afraid my daughter is the same way."

"I believe you're right—I mean about letting someone else's opinion determine my future—but on the other hand, some people who think they have talent are mistaken." He herded some peas onto his fork. "What I had on my mind in coming here, aside from seeing you again, Jolie, was to rent a little place and try to see if I have any talent at all—and the determination to make it as an artist."

"Why, that's a fine idea," Jolie said, leaning forward, her eyes fixed on Tyler. "I had the impression your life was . . . shall I say *cluttered* in New York?"

"You're right about that. *Cluttered* about describes it. I thought it might help me to come here and do nothing but paint. Perhaps you could advise me about a place to live. It doesn't have to be much. Just a place to sleep."

"I'm sure we can find something. But tonight you must stay here in the guest room."

Tyler shook his head. "I won't argue with you, but tomorrow I'll make a new start."

"I think it would be good for you," Marvel said. "I know little about painting, but Jolie here, she loves it. She can tell you when your work is good or bad."

"Oh, I couldn't do that, Maman," Jolie protested.

"Why, of course you could."

Jolie laughed. "I think Tyler knows enough about my *directness* to believe that I'd be willing to do that. But this is a bad time of the year for painters. Many come here, but most come in the springtime."

"Well, I expected to be painting inside at the art institute, but now maybe I'll learn to paint winter things."

"It's very beautiful here, as I'm sure you've noticed. The mountains are beautiful in every season, and the river sometimes freezes over," Jolie told him. "You should have plenty of subjects for your paintings."

The conversation flowed easily as they finished their

meal, and afterward Jolie took Tyler into the parlor. Marvel joined them after the dishes were done and they talked for some time.

Naturally the discussion turned to the war, and Tyler repeated the words of the old soldier he had encountered on the train. "He seemed very positive that the Germans would come, but I'm not sure," Tyler said.

"The journalists are calling it the Phony War," Marvel said, "but they are wrong. The Germans are just waiting until spring. Then they will come."

"And what will you do then, Madame Vernay?"

"I will survive."

"Yes, I believe you will."

"Long ago I put my life in God's hands. Now whatever happens, it will be the will of God."

"You sound like my parents. They believe the same thing—and I wish I'd listened to them more while I was at home."

"You're not too old," Marvel said with a smile. "God is always faithful, and you need to learn that lesson well."

Tyler admired the woman's determination. He saw the same beauty in Jolie's mother that he found in her and the same strength and determination. "I don't know much about politics," he said finally.

"I expect all of us will learn about life whether we know politics or not. I remember how hard it was in the Great War." Marvel was silent for a moment and then said, "Well, it's in God's hands. You must be tired. I will prepare your room."

As soon as Marvel left the room, Jolie's eyes sparkled. "You're being told to go to bed, Tyler. Maman's like that. Very firm."

"I see she is," he said. "I like her. She's very much like you—very attractive and very strong."

"Thank you, Tyler. That's a nice thing to say."

Marvel came back and announced that his room was

ready, and Tyler left at once. As soon as he was gone, Marvel looked at her daughter with a question in her eye. "Well, what are you thinking?"

"About what?"

"About what! About your guest."

"He's *our* guest, Maman."

"Don't be foolish! He didn't come to see me. You know he is a good-looking man."

"Yes, but he's weak."

"How can you know that?"

"You'll find it out soon enough. He has a charm about him that most Americans don't have. He's witty, and physically he's strong and attractive, I'll admit. But he doesn't have whatever it is that makes people survive."

"It sounds like he's never known a hard time."

"I think you're right. He's always had someone to take care of him."

"Well, sooner or later, times will be hard for him, as they eventually are for all of us." Marvel nodded, as if agreeing with herself. "Then will be the time to say whether he's weak or strong."

★ ★ ★

To Tyler's surprise, his life became vastly different. Jolie's mother found him an upstairs room to rent in the home of one of her friends. It had a skylight, which made it much easier for him to paint indoors. Jolie set aside one day and took him on a tour along the Allier River and up to the Puy de Sancy, the highest mountain in the area, both of which were close enough to Ambert to make the trip in one day. While they were on the mountain, a flock of geese flew overhead. He looked up in wonder until they were out of sight and then set up his easel and tried to capture the moment with paints.

In this environment, he found himself able to paint

freely, with none of the strain or fear he had sometimes experienced. Puzzling over this, he decided it was because no one would be judging his work. After his day at the Puy de Sancy, Tyler worked for hours at a time on the painting he had started there. There was a simplicity and a cleanness to it that his earlier paintings had lacked, and he found inordinate pleasure in looking at it. Usually when he finished a painting, he found himself wanting to alter it in endless ways. But he was satisfied with this one, which he called *Geese Against the Sky*. He liked it just as it was.

★ ★ ★

One day about a week after he and Jolie had taken their day trip, they crossed paths in the village. She invited him to come to a birthday party the following day at the orphanage where she worked, and he readily agreed.

"You don't need to bring any presents," she told him. "The children are always glad to have visitors. Anybody, really, who will give them a little attention. Some of them get very lonely."

"Is it just one birthday or several?"

"It's a party for everyone who will have a birthday in February. We'll have a cake and play games. It means so much to them. They have so little."

Tyler thought it sounded like fun, as it had been a very long time since he'd been around any children at all.

The next day Jolie met Tyler at the door of the orphanage. "I saw you coming," she said. "You're a bit early, but that doesn't matter."

"Who are these children, Jolie?" he asked. He noted that the hall they were going through was whitewashed and clean, and the floors were polished. Children were passing and greeting Jolie. "How many do you have?"

"We have only fifty-two now. The orphanage is sponsored by a church. A wealthy man left an endowment, and the church administers it. As for the children, it's difficult to say. Some of them come from other countries. We have four from Poland. Their parents were all killed in the German invasion. They're new, of course, and having a rather hard time of it."

"Does anyone here speak Polish?"

"Not really." Jolie shook her head. "And that's a problem. They're quickly learning French, though, and we try to make them feel loved."

They turned down a hall and then entered a large room. Three children were already chatting around a table. They all came running toward Jolie, greeting her with hugs.

"Madame Lambert said we could come down here early," the older girl said. "Is that okay?"

"Of course it is, Rochelle," Jolie said. "I brought a special guest today. This is Monsieur Tyler Winslow. He comes from America, and he very much wanted to come and help us celebrate the birthdays. You must speak slowly so he can understand you."

The smallest of the children, a darling girl with blond hair, stood in front of him. "Hello, my name is Yolande Marcil," she said slowly and correctly. "I'll be six years old in two days. How old are you?"

Tyler grinned. "I'm twenty-two."

"That's old! Do you like little girls?"

Tyler winked at Jolie, who was smiling at him. "I like them very much," he said, pronouncing his words carefully.

"This is Damien Rivard," Jolie said, putting her hand on the boy's shoulder. "Damien is nine years old."

"How do you do?" The boy bowed slightly from the waist. He had bright red hair and brown eyes. "We are happy to have you at our party."

"Thank you, Damien. Perhaps when I have a party, you'll come to mine."

"And this is Rochelle Cohen. Rochelle, Monsieur Winslow."

Rochelle seemed to be somewhere between twelve and fourteen. She was a beautiful girl with curly black hair and dark eyes. She smiled shyly and asked very softly, "How do you do, sir?"

"I am fine, Rochelle. It's very nice to meet you."

"Did you bring any presents, monsieur?" Yolande asked, looking up at him seriously.

"Yolande, that's not polite," Rochelle said.

"I don't see why," Yolande retorted.

"I don't see either," Tyler said quickly. "But you see, I didn't know how many would be at the party and who would be celebrating a birthday. So I'll make a list right now, and if Mademoiselle Vernay will allow me to come back, I will come loaded down with presents."

Damien grinned broadly. "Good," he said. "I would like to have a toy airplane."

"You shall have it."

The other children started to arrive as Tyler made his list, and before long the room was filled with children of every age.

"And what would you like, Rochelle?" Tyler asked over the increasing chatter.

"Just anything," she said shyly.

Tyler went over to the table and picked up a piece of paper and a pencil. "'Just anything,'" he said as he wrote it down. "That will be easy."

"And you, Mademoiselle Marcil. What can I bring you?"

"Lots of chocolates."

"Lots of chocolates. You know, I eat lots of chocolates myself. That's why I'm so pretty."

"You're not pretty," the girl exclaimed.

"Well, my mother thinks I am. And I'm sure that

Rochelle does. Don't you, Rochelle?"

She giggled. "Men aren't pretty. They're handsome."

"Well, I suppose that's true," Tyler said, winking at Damien. "Maybe if you eat enough chocolates, you'll be handsome like me."

Jolie had been observing from a distance, surprised at how easily Tyler made friends with the children. When everyone had arrived, she got the group started on a simple game and was pleased at Tyler's willingness to join right in.

After the games the children ate cake and drank lemonade, and then each of the three children who had birthdays that month received presents from the orphanage staff.

After all the sticky fingers were washed, Jolie had the children sit with her on the floor and they all sang "Frère Jacques." When it was time to sing it in rounds, Yolande crawled into Tyler's lap and they sang together.

"You don't sing very well," Yolande said seriously.

"No, I don't, but you sing beautifully."

"Well, if you don't sing so loud, maybe no one will hear how bad you are."

"That's a good idea, Yolande," Tyler said. "I think I'd better do that."

The party lasted about an hour, and after the children left the room, Tyler said, "Let me help you clean up."

"There's really not much cleaning up to do," she said as she started wiping the tables down with a sponge.

Tyler found another sponge and started on another table. "Is something wrong?" he asked when he noticed that she was looking sober.

"Oh, I'm just worried."

Quickly Tyler thought, then said, "Because of the Germans?"

"Yes."

"They probably won't come. Hitler's being very quiet right now."

"He's always quiet just before he strikes. Most Americans don't know a great deal about the history of this conflict."

"That's me, I guess."

"If you go back in history even ten years, you can see what's happening."

"Ten years. What happened then?"

"In 1931 Japan attacked Manchuria. It would have been easy for the League of Nations to stop them, but they did nothing. Then in 1934 Italy attacked Ethiopia. The same thing. The League did absolutely nothing."

Tyler listened as she went over history and was ashamed of his own lack of knowledge. She spoke about how Hitler took the Saar in 1935 and Franco took Spain with German help that same year. And the next year Japan attacked China, and the year after that Hitler seized Austria. "Since then he's taken the Sudetenland and Czechoslovakia, and he's made a nonaggression treaty with Russia so he doesn't have to worry about them."

"And now he's taken Poland."

"Yes, and divided it up with Russia. You know, Tyler, millions of people have been killed in these wars, but I'm afraid Hitler and Japan are just beginning."

"Russia too, I suppose," he said. "I was angry when they invaded Finland." Indeed, when Russia invaded Finland in 1939, it angered the world. But again, no one moved to stop the aggressor.

Jolie took Tyler's sponge and put the two away. "It was kind of you to come, and the children loved it." She hesitated, then said, "The three children you met before the party started . . . it's children like these I worry about—when the Germans come."

"Why do you worry about them in particular?"

"Because they're Jews."

"Oh, I guess I didn't realize . . ."

"Hitler despises Jews. In every conquest he's picked

out what he calls the 'undesirables.' I shudder to think what he's done to them."

Suddenly she shook her shoulders and pasted on a smile. "Let's talk about something else. How's your painting going?"

"You know, Jolie, it's strange, but I think I just painted the best picture of my life."

As he went on to tell her about the formation of the geese against the mountain, she had a hard time concentrating on what he was saying. As good as he had been with the children, she couldn't help but think he wasn't the man for her. *He will fold when the pressure comes. I'm sure of it.*

★ ★ ★

The time passed so quickly that when March came, bringing the first breath of spring, Tyler was taken off guard. He went outside early one Thursday morning. The air was fresh, the grass was turning bright green, and the mountain was clearly outlined against the blue sky. He stood there for a moment thinking how quickly the time had gone. He had returned to the orphanage several times, meeting many of the children, but spending extra time with the three Jewish children. The three were so fond of each other, and he had already grown attached to them.

He painted outside for much of that day, just moving inside when his hands got too cold, and that night he went to the Vernay house for dinner. It was a delicious meal, and there was a great deal of laughter around the table. Afterward they went into the parlor and tried to find some music on the radio, but it was interrupted many times by news bulletins about the war.

After Marvel went to bed, Jolie and Tyler lingered in the parlor and she updated Tyler on the children's activities at the orphanage. Jolie walked him to the door and he pulled her into an embrace. He lifted her chin and gave her a brief kiss. When he released her, she looked down.

"I'm sorry, Tyler," she said. "I shouldn't have let you do that. That was a mistake."

"I don't think so."

Tyler had always been attracted to her, and the time they had spent together in France had only served to increase that attraction. "Why do you draw back, Jolie? You need people. Everybody does."

"Yes," she said quietly. "Every woman needs a man to make her complete—but it must be the right man." She opened the door. "Good night, Tyler. We enjoyed your visit."

"Good night." Tyler left the house, but he was confused and argued with himself all the way home. "My work is going better than ever, but I'm still not happy." It bothered him that he was committed to Caroline, who was waiting for him back in the States. In her eyes, they were engaged. He knew he shouldn't have accepted her money to finance the trip abroad. He couldn't dismiss his attraction to Jolie. "Why can't I let this woman alone? I'm not the kind of man she wants."

★ ★ ★

He slept poorly that night, and the next morning he got up and went to his favorite local café, where he had found good food at inexpensive prices. As soon as he walked in, the proprietor, a man named Poupon, said, "Have you heard the news, Monsieur Winslow?" The man clearly looked agitated.

"What news?"

"The Germans have attacked Denmark and Norway. They are overrunning them." Monsieur Poupon gave him the few details he knew, and then the two stood close to the radio, which was providing more information.

"Next will be Belgium, and then there's nothing to stop them from coming into France," Poupon said.

"I can't believe they can take all of France!"

"Who's to stop them?"

"The English have troops here."

"Not enough!"

"But the French army . . ."

"They are running for their lives."

Tyler sat down and ordered eggs and toast, but the same thought kept repeating in his mind. *The Germans are coming, and the gates are closing. I've got to get out of here!*

CHAPTER SIX

ROUND TRIP TO PARIS

★ ★ ★

The German attack on Norway on April 9, 1940, was completely successful. Tyler listened every day to the radio reports, hoping that somehow the tables would be turned and the Germans' blitzkrieg would be denied.

Almost every day Tyler thought about leaving. He could think of very little worse than being trapped in France by the German army.

During this time he painted steadily, using his art as more of a hiding place than anything else. Despite this he was pleasantly surprised to see that he was improving steadily. Something about his environment in France had enabled him to put paint on canvas in a more meaningful way.

He saw Jolie and her mother several times during April, although as time went on, he knew he had to admit that Jolie's feelings for him hadn't changed. She had made no secret of the fact, from the very beginning of their relationship, that she had no romantic interest in him.

Each week he made it a point to go to the orphanage.

He had become close to several of the children but was especially fond of Damien, Rochelle, and Yolande. Their joy in seeing him pleased him a great deal, and he found their company invigorating.

All of this changed with a series of events that began on May the tenth. The Germans invaded the Low Countries with all the force at their command. As soon as Tyler heard this, he knew he could delay no longer. He had listened to enough talk about strategy and looked at enough maps to know that Hitler could have but one purpose for taking the Low Countries. He would use Belgium as a route to get to France.

On the same day that the Germans invaded the Low Countries, Chamberlain, the Great Appeaser, resigned and was replaced by Winston Churchill. Churchill had been an anti-Hitler statesman for years, while Chamberlain had done little but cave in before the führer. Churchill immediately began leading his country into mobilization for war, and even by listening to the radio and knowing as little as he did about the conditions in Europe, Tyler was certain that within a matter of days Hitler would send his troops into France. In fact, that's exactly what happened within a couple of short days.

Tyler worried and wondered about what to do throughout much of the month, and as May drew to an end, he finally made his decision. "I've got to get out of here," he muttered. "I can't be trapped in the middle of a war that's none of my business."

That very day he went to the Vernays' home and found Jolie and her mother listening to the radio. "We've been listening to the news broadcast," Jolie told him as he took a seat in the living room. "Have you heard about the Netherlands and Belgium?"

"I know they've been under attack for the last couple weeks. Is there something new?"

"They both surrendered."

"Belgium too?"

"Yes," Jolie said, her lips tight. "They were just reporting it on the radio."

"What about the French army and the British forces?"

"They're being pushed back," Marvel said. She looked tired, but she seemed calm. "We must prepare ourselves for what's coming."

For a moment Tyler could not speak, and then he said, "I came to tell you that I'll be leaving France."

"When?" Jolie asked.

"Probably tomorrow."

"I'm actually surprised you stayed here this long, considering the military activity that's been closing in." Jolie pressed her palms together and took a deep breath. "I want to ask you an enormous favor."

For a moment Tyler hoped she would ask him to take her with him, but she said, "I want you to take Rochelle, Damien, and Yolande with you."

His mind was a jumble of thoughts as he considered the enormity of what she was asking. Finally he cleared his throat and said, "I'm sorry, but I can't do that."

"Why can't you?"

"Because it would be too dangerous for them. I would need to get them all the way to the coast, and unless I'm mistaken, the Germans will be right in the way."

"Do you know what will happen to them if this town is taken by the Germans? Do you know what Hitler does to Jews?"

Tyler knew, of course, exactly what Hitler planned for the Jews. But still the thought of trying to protect three children from harm while threading his way to the coast was more than he could take on.

"I'm sorry. I just can't do it. It would be too dangerous."

Something changed in Jolie's face. She held his gaze, and her voice was even as she said, "You're a weak man, Tyler Winslow. You think only of yourself. Please leave the house."

Tyler couldn't believe that she would speak to him
that way. He cast a glance at Marvel Vernay, who had
dropped her head.

"I'm sorry," he said hoarsely, "but it would—"

"Please leave the house."

Tyler did as she asked, but he knew her words would
haunt him. He tried to put the children out of his mind
and went home to finish packing.

He slept little that night, and Jolie's words kept echo-
ing in his mind.

★   ★   ★

The next morning Tyler boarded a northbound train,
not bothering to try for a friendly good-bye from Jolie. He
kept watching out the window, noting whenever the train
paralleled a road that cars and buses crowded the south-
bound lane. There was very little traffic going north,
toward Paris. He asked one of the men in the compartment with him, a small man with black hair greased
down on his head, "Why's the traffic so heavy going
south?"

The man gave him a strange look. "The Germans are
coming. Don't you know that?"

"Yes, but it may not be so bad."

The man gave him a withering look. "You are English?"

"American."

"Then you know nothing!"

"I know—"

"You know *nothing*!" The man shook his head and
closed his eyes, as if he could shut out danger by refusing
to look at it.

★   ★   ★

When Tyler got to Paris, he got off the train and made his way to the other platform to catch his next train. As he was waiting, he watched a family that was sitting on the bench across from his—a father and mother and three small children—one a baby in the mother's arms. The father came over, cigarette in hand, and asked Tyler if he had a match.

"No, I'm sorry, I don't smoke," Tyler said.

"You're catching the train to Le Havre?" The man spoke French with an unusual accent.

"Yes, I am."

"That's good. You are not French?"

"No. American."

"You'll be all right, but I must get my family away."

"You think it will be bad?"

The man gave him a strange look. "We're Jewish."

Tyler could not think of a thing to say, and finally he asked, "You think it would be too dangerous to stay here?"

"We lived in Poland. I was a banker there. When the Germans came, they put all Jews in ghettos and then sent them off to concentration camps. You Americans need to wake up. One day Hitler will be on your shores." He turned and walked away bitterly.

As Tyler sat there, the words of the man seemed to grow in his mind. And without willing it, he saw Yolande with her golden hair and blue eyes. He saw a German soldier gruffly taking her from her friends at the orphanage.

"Are you all right, sir?"

Tyler turned to see the wife of the man who had asked him for a match. In some ways, she reminded him of Rochelle Cohen. She had the same curly black hair and dark eyes. She was looking as concerned as her husband was.

"Yes, I just had a bad thought."

"There are many of us with bad thoughts," she said.

She looked down at the baby in her arms and said, "We pray that we will make it to the coast before the Germans cut us off." She looked back suddenly, as if she could see through the walls and over the countryside of France. "But there are so many of our people who cannot escape. What will happen to them?" The woman began to cry, and she quickly returned to her family.

Tyler could not help but be moved by the woman's pain. The faces of Rochelle and Damien and Yolande seemed to glow in his mind, and then he heard Jolie's words as clearly as if she stood in front of him. *"You're a weak man, Tyler. You think only of yourself."*

As the train appeared a good distance away, Tyler's thoughts were scrambling. He could go back to America and marry Caroline, as she assumed he would. He could go back to Africa and take refuge with his parents. He could return to Ambert and see if Jolie would consider returning to America with him. Or . . .

He made up his mind. He stood and gathered his luggage and then without hesitation walked straight to the ticket window. He presented his ticket to Le Havre and said, "I want to cancel this and buy a ticket to Ambert instead."

The clerk looked at him with astonishment. "But you just came from there. Did you forget something? Your luggage perhaps?"

Suddenly Tyler smiled. "No," he said, "my soul."

The clerk stared at him, shrugged his shoulders, and issued a new ticket. As Tyler walked away, he heard the man mutter, "Crazy Americans!"

★   ★   ★

Jolie had come home at midday and sat at the kitchen table staring at her hands. The news was worse than usual. The Germans were taking France as if they were no opposition at all. The British and the French were in full retreat now. They were bottled up in a little town on the French coast called Dunkirk, and the German army was preparing to destroy them.

A knock came at the door. She got to her feet and walked slowly to open it. "Tyler?" she whispered, standing absolutely still.

"It's me. Can I come in?"

But she did not move. "I thought you would be on the train by now." She suddenly realized that she was hoping for some change in this man, but it was a very thin hope.

Tyler smiled, and he exuded an ease and a certainty that she had never seen in him before. "I was," he said. "Actually, I've already been to Paris and come back today. I've come to find out if I'm any good at all," he added.

Jolie had her eyes fixed on him. Slowly her lips grew soft and turned upward at the corners into a slight smile. "I'm glad you came back, Tyler. Come inside."

"I know you didn't expect me back," he said as she closed the door.

"I hoped you might return."

"But you didn't really think I would."

Her smile grew brighter, and her face was full of hope. "Have a seat and tell me all about it."

As Tyler told his story, he couldn't help but think, *Maybe at last I've done the right thing!*

PART TWO

June 1940

★ ★ ★

CHAPTER SEVEN

A Change of Plans

★ ★ ★

As they walked along the road that led to the orphanage, Tyler looked up and saw three military planes in formation. They were too high for him to tell if they were bombers or fighters, and he could not identify whether they were German or French. He watched them as they continued in the general direction of Paris. Even though he had returned determined to do what he could to help the Jewish children, his thoughts were confused, as he was not certain what form of help he could provide.

He had already moved back into the same room while he worked out his plan for getting the children out of the country, but Marvel's friend had consented to let him rent the room by the day. Now as he walked along, he thought about the ever-nearing war. He remembered reading something in the Bible about seeing through a glass darkly, and felt a connection with whoever had spoken it. He remembered the story in the book of Genesis about Jacob wrestling with the angel. "I guess I'm like Jacob, struggling to get something out of God and pretty sure to lose. Poor old Jake! He lost the wrestling match and got his hip knocked out of joint. I guess I can't hope for any better than one of the patriarchs."

When he entered the orphanage, he was greeted by one of the workers, a petite woman who always wore the same brown dress. She had a cheerful spirit and bobbed her head up and down as she greeted him. "*Bonjour*, monsieur, you have come to visit the children again."

"Yes, I have. I hope all of them are well."

"Yes. They are well." A shadow crossed the small woman's face, and she shook her head sadly. "But who knows what tomorrow will bring?"

Tyler had actually come to see Jolie, but as he was walking down one of the hallways, Damien Rivard came sailing around the corner, his red hair falling over his forehead and his eyes intent.

"Monsieur Winslow!" he cried.

"How are you, Damien?"

"Did you bring any candy?"

"As a matter of fact, I didn't this time." Seeing the disappointment on the lad's face, Tyler reached out and ruffled his hair. "But maybe I'll bring some next time. Have you seen Mademoiselle Vernay?"

"She is out in the garden. Yolande is helping her."

The two went through the back door and Damien at once began calling, "Monsieur Winslow is here, and he didn't bring any candy."

Before Tyler could get very far, he was met by a tiny whirlwind with blond hair and enormous blue eyes. He scooped Yolande up, and she put her arms around his neck and hugged him. He kissed her cheek and said, "Well, what have you been doing?"

"Helping Mademoiselle Vernay. You can help too, or we can go inside and have a tea party."

Jolie straightened up. She had on a pair of brown gloves and held a hoe in one hand. "Hello, Tyler," she said. "You came just in time."

"I didn't mean to interrupt anything."

"It's getting pretty warm out here. Let's go inside and see if we can find some refreshments."

"Is everything all right?" he asked as the group headed back to the building, Yolande clinging to Tyler as he carried her.

"Yes, although Rochelle is sick."

"What's wrong with her?"

"She's got a cold or something. She's a delicate child. Sometimes I worry about her."

"It's not serious, I hope."

"No, I don't think so, but it would be better if she had her full strength before you set off across the country."

"I'm still a bit worried about taking three children when I know I'm not much good with kids."

"That's not so," Damien put in. "You're good with me."

Jolie suddenly laughed. The sunshine caught the gleam of red in her brown hair, and she said, "Yes, Damien's right. You are good with him."

"And you're good with me too." Yolande put one hand on each of his cheeks and pulled his face around until their noses were almost touching. "I think I would like to be your little girl," she said solemnly.

The statement touched Tyler Winslow. He had had very little contact with children, but these three, and especially Yolande, had affected him strongly. He laughed and said, "Well, you'll have to be very good. I'll only have very good little girls."

"I am good!"

"Right you are."

They entered the orphanage, and Jolie led the way to the kitchen. She rummaged in the cupboards until she found some crackers and jam and got the children settled at a table with their snack and some milk.

As the children chattered, Tyler said, "I didn't tell you exactly what made me decide to come back."

"No. I thought you were gone for good. What changed your mind?"

"I met a Jewish family in the railroad station. A fine family," Tyler murmured, "with three children. They were talking about how Hitler was corralling the Jews and packing them into ghettos. I thought about Yolande there, and about Damien and Rochelle. I knew I couldn't live with myself if I didn't do what I could."

Impulsively Jolie reached over and squeezed his hand. She held it for a moment, and when he looked up with surprise, he saw she was smiling. "It's not easy growing up," Jolie said. "It's not always a matter of years."

Tyler was embarrassed, but he understood the truth of her statement. "Well, I should have grown up a long time ago."

"Come to supper tonight. We'll talk about what we're going to do."

"All right." He looked over at the children. "Now I think I'll go join the tea party."

★ ★ ★

The meal was nearly ready, but Marvel and Jolie stopped what they were doing and listened. As they paused, Tyler came in from the parlor, where he had been reading.

> The evacuation of British, French, and Belgian forces from Dunkirk has proved to be a modern miracle, nearly the equivalent of Moses leading the Israelites out of Egypt through the Red Sea. When the troops were pinned down on the beach, all that the Nazis had to do was take them. But for some reason, sources inform us, Hitler himself called a halt. It is believed that Göring convinced Hitler that the Luftwaffe would be able to polish off the men trapped on the beach. Göring was wrong, however, for

the RAF kept a constant stream of Spitfires flying across the Channel in sortie after sortie, keeping the Luftwaffe from striking the helpless men on the beach.

Every kind of boat imaginable, from destroyers to fishing boats, aided in the effort. The men waded out into the ocean and were carried by the smaller boats to the larger ones. It is estimated that some three hundred fifty thousand men were taken off the beach and ferried to England. There were, however, a great many casualties.

Regretfully, practically all of the Allies' equipment had to be left on the beach. This will set the effort back many months, and there is talk that Hitler may take this opportunity to strike at England when she lies practically helpless.

Marvel shook her head. "There are many who say that the British have deserted France, but that is not so. They had no choice. It's God's miracle that they got away."

"It's a pretty critical situation," Jolie said. "All that stands between Hitler and England is the English Channel. I'm afraid for England."

"That may be harder than Hitler thinks," Tyler said. When Marvel asked him what he meant, he said, "Britain has the strongest navy in the world. How would Hitler get his men across the Channel? I think Britain has a chance, but what I'm worried about is what we're going to do."

"One thing is certain," Marvel said. "You must leave very soon."

"And take at least Rochelle, Damien, and Yolande with you."

"That's why I came back," Tyler said. "But I've been giving it a lot of thought, and I'd like to convince the two of you to come with me."

"Leave my home?" Marvel straightened up. "Never."

"It won't be the same after the Germans come. You know that, Marvel."

"*I* will be the same and *God* will be the same. Someone

must stay here. One day the Germans will be gone. They will be defeated, as they were in the last war."

"I believe you are right, but still it will be a hard time for everyone."

Tyler argued as vehemently as he knew how, but neither Marvel nor Jolie seemed to be listening. Finally they sat down to eat, and immediately after dinner, Tyler went back to his place, discouraged.

It had been a long time since he had written to Caroline, and he decided it was time to be honest with her about the situation. Taking a sheet of paper and a pen, he sat down and began to write.

> June 4, 1940
> Dear Caroline,
> I'm sorry I haven't written for a while. Things have come up that are too complicated to explain, and with the way the mail is working these days, I may even be home before this letter reaches you.

He went on to write about how he had almost left France and then had changed his mind. As he wrote, he was careful to focus on the situation at hand—the German invasion and the plight of the Jewish children should the Nazis take over—but he said almost nothing of a personal nature.

When he came to the end of the letter, he tried to put into words how he felt. When he had left, Caroline had made it plain that she wanted a future together for them, and he knew she was used to getting her own way. He took a used envelope out of the wastebasket and tried to compose a sentence that would express his sentiments, but he wasn't happy with anything he came up with. Finally, feeling like a coward, he wrote:

> We will have time to talk when I get back. In the mean-
> while, I have not forgotten how you came to my aid when

I was at a low point. I will never forget you for that, my dear Caroline.

> With love,
> Tyler

He reread what he had written and, shaking his head, folded the page and put it in an envelope.

★　★　★

When Tyler arose the next morning, he turned the radio on and stiffened, for the announcer's voice crackled as he spoke, and a cold chill seemed to run over Tyler as he listened.

Early in the morning the Nazi army had struck at France with all their might along the Somme and the Aisne. From the announcer's attitude and obvious despair Tyler read into his words, the French were in utter confusion. No one, it seemed, was really in charge, and though the military said they had mobilized six million men, it was apparent that they had actually mobilized only three million. This put, the announcer said, only sixty French divisions along the Somme to oppose at least a hundred fifty Nazi divisions. The big mistake was keeping troops inside the Maginot Line instead of facing the Germans head-on. There seemed to be a stubborn density in the minds of the French leaders, who still believed that a fixed line of force could stop airplanes and tanks, while airplanes could fly over and the tanks could easily go around the ends of a line.

Tyler went at once to the Vernay house. As he had suspected, both Jolie and Marvel had heard the broadcast. They invited him to eat breakfast with them, and he tried to put a good face on the events. "Maybe the Maginot Line will stop them, and remember, the British still have some forces in France that weren't evacuated."

"It is not enough," Jolie said. "France is doomed."

"Jolie is right," Marvel agreed. "You and the children need to leave soon—while you still can."

"Will you take them right away?" There was a pleading light in Jolie's eyes. "If you don't, I will do it myself."

Her words hurt Tyler, for he had come back for no other reason. He saw that she still did not trust him and knew that the weakness she had seen in him before, especially when they were still in the States, kept her suspicious. "I'll do it, of course."

"That would take a huge load off of my mind," Jolie said. "We must plan carefully."

★ ★ ★

Tyler would have left the next day, but Rochelle's illness had gotten worse, so they were forced to wait. There was little else to do except listen to the radio. They heard that the roads were now filled with refugees streaming away from the battle zones, and one day Tyler said, "We may run into German troops somewhere along the line."

"If that happens," Jolie said quietly, "then God will have to guide you."

The three were having supper together, as had become their custom since Tyler had returned from Paris.

"You really believe that God guides people?" Tyler asked. "My folks believe that and my brother does too."

"Yes, I really do. What about you? Don't you believe it?"

"I guess I do in a sort of vague way, but the rest of my family has great faith in God." He looked down and didn't speak for a moment. "I've missed something somewhere along the line."

"You will do fine. Maman and I will be praying for you. God will be with you. But what will you do when you get them to England?"

"I've been thinking about that," Tyler said. "England is in for a rough time. It's the only nation that stands against Hitler now. I think I'd like to take the children to America. I could find a good orphanage there. Or I've even thought of taking them to Africa."

"To Africa!" Marvel exclaimed. "You mean to be with your family?"

"Yes. It's a rough life, but at least there's no war there."

When a knock sounded at the door, Jolie went to answer it.

"Your daughter says I'm a weak man," Tyler commented when Jolie was out of earshot.

"We're all weak people."

"You're not—she's not."

"Yes we are. Weakness comes out in many ways." She reached over to put her hand over his. "You haven't found yourself yet, but you will."

Tyler felt warmed by this woman's strength and by her encouragement. He had not expected to have it. "Do you know who Superman is?"

"You mean the cartoon figure? Yes, I have seen the comic book."

"She wants to marry Superman, a man without faults—and that's not me," he said, attempting to smile.

"Jolie is a very strong woman, but she has to learn that everybody has shortcomings, and we must not love people less because of them. We must pray that they will be overcome. Find God's will, Tyler. If it is His will for you to be with my daughter, He will find a way to bring the two of you together."

Jolie came back into the room. "It was Madame Colle from next door. She wanted to borrow some milk, but we're all out." She saw that the two were looking serious and asked, "What are you talking about?"

"About you," Tyler answered. "I was just saying what

a strong-willed woman you are. I'll bet you were a strong-willed child too."

Marvel laughed. "She was that, of a certainty."

"I'm no more strong-willed than you are, Maman."

The two traded several teasing remarks. "Since you've decided I'm strong-willed, I might as well be so," Jolie said with a smile that she could not hide. "But on a more serious note, I've decided to go as far as the coast with you," she told Tyler.

"Why, that would be wonderful!" he exclaimed.

"Your French is not good enough, and the children might be a problem."

"That may be the best thing. What port city were you thinking of?" Marvel asked.

"Le Havre, I think, would be the best, but if the radio reports are true, the Germans are already in some ports. They may already be there."

"If that's closed, Cherbourg might be a good option," Marvel said.

"Yes, that would be good. It's not far," Jolie said. "You could cross the Channel to Bournemouth."

"What about Rochelle? How soon will she be able to travel?"

"I would prefer to wait until she's a hundred percent healthy," Jolie said, "but I've given the matter a lot of thought today, and I think we'd better not. I think it would be best to leave as soon as possible—even tomorrow."

CHAPTER EIGHT

A SLOW START

★ ★ ★

The morning of June tenth dawned bright and clear, and Tyler spent the morning solidifying his plan in his head and saying good-bye to the friends he had made during his stay in Ambert. After lunch he walked to the Vernay house, still thinking through his plan.

Marvel answered the door and welcomed him in, and when he went inside, he found Jolie listening to the radio. She looked up and said, "Bad news again."

"More bad news? Are the Germans advancing faster?"

"No, but Italy has declared war on the Allies."

"Italy!" Tyler exclaimed. "What does that mean?"

"It means," Marvel said, "that now the Germans will be coming from the north and the Italians will be coming up from the south."

"All the more reason to leave right away, but first we must listen to Churchill's speech. They've been saying all morning that he was going to make a speech and now it's just coming on."

Churchill began to speak in his gravelly voice, which was unfamiliar to Tyler. He listened as the prime minister laid out the problems that lay ahead for the British Empire, then concluded by saying:

> "We shall not flag or fail. We shall go on to the end. We shall fight in France, we shall fight on the seas and oceans, we shall fight with growing confidence and growing strength in the air, we shall defend our island, whatever the cost may be. We shall fight on the beaches, we shall fight on the landing grounds, we shall fight in the fields and in the streets, we shall fight in the hills; we shall never surrender! In God's good time, the New World, with all its power and might, steps forth to the rescue and the liberation of the old."

Tyler listened intently and then looked up and said, "That man means what he says."

"I wish," Marvel said quietly, "that we had had a man like him in charge of our government in France."

★ ★ ★

All three of the children were tremendously excited, Tyler saw, when the car pulled up in front of the Vernays' house. One of the women who worked at the orphanage had offered to give them all a ride to the train station, and they had stopped off at the house to pick up Jolie and Tyler. Rochelle looked tired and sat fairly still in the middle of the backseat, but Damien and Yolande were bubbling with excitement, their hands flying out the open car windows. Damien pumped questions at Tyler faster than he could answer them. "Can I ride in the engine? Will it be a big train? How long will it take to get there?"

"Whoa there, young man," Tyler said with a grin, "we'll have to see about that."

Marvel had followed Tyler and Jolie outside, her face fixed in a set mold. She spoke cheerfully enough, but it was obvious that she was worried.

Jolie embraced her mother. "I should be back sometime tomorrow. Don't worry about me."

"I won't. You'll be all right."

Marvel made sure the children weren't watching and then opened her handbag and pulled out a pistol. "I want you to take this," she said as she pressed it into Tyler's hand.

"But, Maman, we can't take that," Jolie insisted. "You may need it here."

"I will feel better if you have it. Besides, you know it makes me nervous just to have it in the house."

"All right, Maman, if you're sure."

Marvel reached up and pulled Tyler's head down, kissing him on both cheeks.

"I don't know how to thank you for all your hospitality," he said.

"Don't be foolish. After this war is over you must come back. By that time you will probably be a famous painter, but come anyway."

Tyler was touched. "I will, Marvel. And I'll write you as soon as I get to England."

They put their suitcases into the car and squeezed in with the children. Jolie had packed one suitcase for the girls, along with a change of clothes for herself, and Tyler had packed his things with Damien's. Tyler had decided there was no use in trying to tote along all of his belongings. He would have enough to deal with without having to keep track of too much luggage.

As the car pulled away, Tyler looked back to see Marvel standing in front of the house. She did not wave but stood very straight. "That's a fine mother you've got there. You're very fortunate."

"Yes, I am," Jolie said. She adjusted Yolande's position in her lap. "What is your mother like?"

"She's like yours—very strong. She's the best there is . . . and so is my father. I never appreciated them before . . . but I'm starting to now."

When they got to the station, they had just enough time to buy their tickets before the train arrived. They boarded at once and got settled in their car. The only other people in the car were a middle-aged couple who both looked sad. Jolie settled Damien and Yolande on each side of her, while Tyler sat beside Rochelle.

"Do you feel better, Rochelle?"

"Yes, I think I'm getting better," she said. She did not look well, however, and Tyler fervently hoped that she would not get any sicker on the journey.

"You're taking your family out of France?"

The man, who had been seated a couple of seats away, had come down the aisle to talk to him.

"Well, yes, I am." He did not think it necessary to go into a long explanation about his companions.

The man's wife joined him in the aisle. "You have beautiful children," she said as she looked from one to the next.

"We're not his children," Yolande said firmly, "but he's a nice man anyway."

"Oh, I'm sorry," the woman said.

"We are leaving France, however," Tyler said.

"I think that's a good idea," the man responded.

The train started with a slight jerk and after it had picked up speed, Tyler said, "Have you heard any news about the war today?"

"Yes, I'm afraid so. The Germans have crossed the Seine to the north of Paris."

"That's not what we wanted to hear," Tyler said quietly.

"Everything about this war has been bad for France." The man fell silent and with a sigh, the two made their way back to their seats.

★ ★ ★

As the train passed through the countryside, it became obvious each time they passed a road that traffic was heavy. Much of it was composed of military vehicles, including trucks and even a few tanks, moving toward Paris. As was the case the last time he had been on the train, there were many cars going south out of Paris.

Before long Damien and Yolande became bored, so Jolie opened the small satchel she had brought. She took out paper and pencils and began to entertain them by drawing funny faces. She allowed them to draw too, and after a while the two younger children started playing ticktacktoe.

It didn't take too long to reach Vichy, where they needed to change trains. As the war went on, the train schedules grew increasingly erratic, and while getting from Ambert to Paris used to be easy, it was now more complicated.

When the train stopped, Tyler picked up Yolande, who had gone to sleep in Jolie's lap, while Jolie retrieved their luggage. Tyler found a bench where he and the children could sit while Jolie checked on the train schedule.

She returned quickly. "It will be two hours at least. It is late."

"I expect then that we might as well go find a restaurant and get a good meal." Jolie and Damien each grabbed a suitcase and the group started down the street. "So much for my careful planning."

It was only a small village, and there was only one restaurant. They went inside and woke Yolande up. She was cross, but when they ordered food and it came, she became quite cheerful. Rochelle ate little, although Jolie urged her, and finally when they left, there was nothing to do but go back to the station.

It was over an hour before the train pulled in, and as soon as it did, Tyler felt his heart sink. The train was loaded with soldiers, and though it did slow down, it didn't stop as it passed the station. Tyler left the children with Jolie while he went to consult with the station-master. He soon returned, shaking his head. "The army has commandeered the train. We'll have to wait for the next one."

"When will that be?" Jolie asked.

"Not until tomorrow morning." They had no choice but to find a place to stay. They were able to secure two rooms in an ancient inn close to the station. As a matter of fact, the place had almost no guests. Jolie talked with the owner, a sad-faced man who said, "I don't know what's going to happen. Everybody's leaving town. My business is ruined."

Jolie tried to offer him words of assurance, but he didn't appear to have much hope.

Jolie settled into a plain room with the two girls, and Tyler took Damien with him. The two went to bed early, and then Damien kept up a spirited conversation for nearly an hour. Tyler was weary, but he answered the boy's questions and did his part as long as he could. When Damien finally drifted off, Tyler's mind was still buzzing. *What if the train doesn't get here in the morning?* He was not accustomed to having this kind of responsibility and it troubled him. He finally managed to get to sleep, and before he knew it, Damien was nudging his shoulder.

"It's time to get up. The sun's up."

After the two washed up and got dressed, they repacked their bags and went down to the lobby. Jolie and the girls were already there, waiting in some uncomfortable-looking chairs.

"Good morning, everybody. You're looking much brighter this morning, Rochelle. How are you feeling?"

"So much better," Rochelle told him. "I slept like a rock."

"We all did," Jolie said as she stood up. "I think we'd better stop at the grocery store before we go to the train station. There's no telling what will be open on the rest of the trip."

"That's a good idea," Tyler agreed. "Let's go find some grub," he said, using the English word for grub.

"What's grub?" Damien demanded.

"It's food."

"Why'd you call it grub?"

"It's an American word, buddy. Come on. Let's go." They went to the store that they had noticed the night before and bought a good supply of bread and nuts and fruit. When they went outside, the streets were full of tanks and trucks and French soldiers marching right up the middle of the street.

"It looks like they're all headed for the battle," Jolie said.

"I expect so."

"Look at that one." She was pointing at a group of passing soldiers.

"Which one?" Tyler asked.

"Right there. Why, he can't be over fifteen years old. What a terrible thing."

"War is always terrible. You know, that boy reminds me of something. The first time I was ever really aware of what war was, I was looking at a picture book about the American Civil War. Do you know about that?"

"I've read about it. A terrible war. Brother fighting against brother."

"Yes, that's right. Well, this book had pictures of the soldiers, and one was a full-page photo of a young boy wearing a Confederate uniform. He couldn't have been more than thirteen or fourteen. He had the most vulnerable look I had ever seen. The caption said he was killed at a battle called Malvern Hill, and it scared me pretty bad."

"But it all happened a long time ago."

"I know, but suddenly it was just like I was there watching him go off to war. I could practically see his mother holding him and kissing him good-bye, telling him to take care of himself, and his brothers and sisters saying good-bye. And then he marched off to war and was killed almost at once. I thought, what if I had been that boy? And ever since then every time I think of a war I think of him."

I've never seen him like this before, Jolie thought. *It's nice to see that he actually has some sensitivity.* She stood beside him silently as he looked sadly at the soldiers passing them.

"I still remember his name. Private Edwin Jennison, killed at the Battle of Malvern Hill."

"You still remember that?"

"You know how some things are burned into your memory? I can see that picture even now. He was sitting there in his gray uniform with his brass buttons, his arms folded on his lap, staring straight into the camera. How many days was it after that photo was taken that he was lying dead on a hill?"

"Did he go to heaven?"

Startled by the question, Tyler looked down at Yolande, who had been listening to all this. Her blond hair was blowing in the light breeze, and there was sadness in her eyes. "I expect he did, Yolande."

"That's good. I want to go to heaven when I die."

"So do I," Damien said. "I'm going too," he said determinedly.

"I don't think the archangel Gabriel could keep you out, Damien Rivard." Tyler smiled and looked at Jolie. "Funny things stay in our minds, don't they?"

"You're the one with funny things in your mind," Rochelle put in.

"Come on," Jolie told the group. "Let's head over to the train station. The train should be pulling in before long."

They were just getting settled on a bench when they heard the whistle.

"There comes the train," Jolie said. "I hope we can get on it this time."

As the first cars of the train passed the platform, they could see there were some soldiers aboard, but there appeared to be plenty of room for civilians. The group boarded and got settled, and a few minutes later they were on their way.

"How long will it take to get where we're going?" Rochelle asked quietly.

"I don't know," Tyler said. "It shouldn't take too long, though." He said this with as much assurance as he could, but as the scenery flashed by outside the window, he wondered if he was telling the truth.

CHAPTER NINE

"EVERYBODY OFF"

★ ★ ★

Tyler and Damien played every game Tyler could think of on the short trip from Vichy to Varennes. The boy's attention span wasn't as long as Tyler would have hoped.

"Why are we stopping here?" Damien asked.

"To let people off or take on more passengers, I suppose," Tyler told him.

But the train stayed still for several minutes, and Tyler didn't see anyone getting off or on. A man burst through the door, calling, "Everybody off. This train will not go any farther."

"Not go any farther! But it's supposed to go to Paris!"

"Everybody off," the man called again.

"What a mess!" Tyler groaned. "What do we do now?"

"We'll have to get off," Jolie said matter-of-factly.

They gathered their things and got off with everyone else. They soon learned the military had commandeered the train. It was being routed elsewhere.

"But how can we get to Paris?" Tyler asked the ticket agent.

"You could go to Moulins. A train from Italy headed for Paris will go through there later today."

"But how will we get there?"

"I do not know, sir."

Tyler was angry and started to argue, but Jolie took his arm. "Come on, Tyler."

"Moulins. I wonder how far that is," Tyler said as the train pulled away from the station.

"It's not all that far, but it's certainly too far to walk," Jolie told him.

"Look," he said abruptly, "you stay here with the kids. I'll go try to find someone who can take us there. A taxi, a car, something."

"All right, Tyler."

At once he began his search. As he left, Rochelle whispered, "Are the Germans going to get us, Mademoiselle Jolie?"

"Certainly not. You'll soon be in England, far away from here."

"I wish you'd come with us," she said. "I'm afraid to go."

"Monsieur Winslow will take care of you. You like him, don't you?"

"Yes, but . . . I'd just feel better if you were with us."

Jolie hugged the girl tightly. "It's going to be all right. You'll see."

★   ★   ★

Tyler checked with people in several businesses but had no success until he saw a car repair shop. He found a middle-aged man there smoking a pipe and working on a car. His hands were greasy, and he did not greet Tyler.

"My name is Winslow. I'm sorry I don't speak better

French, but I'm in a bit of trouble."

"We're all in a bit of trouble. My name is Rousseau."

"Monsieur Rousseau, I am trying to get to Le Havre with three children and a young lady, but I understand I have to get to Moulins to catch a train there. I've been trying to hire somebody to drive us there."

"We have no taxis here. This town is too small."

Tyler looked at the two cars parked outside the shop. "Would it be possible to hire you to take us? I'll pay you for your time."

"These people. Are they your family?"

"No, the children are orphans and the young lady is a physician. We're trying to get the children out of the country."

"I'm not a taxi service."

Tyler argued as eloquently as he could, but Rousseau was adamant and seemed almost angry. Finally he demanded, "Who are these three children? Why would you be taking them out of the country? We can't all of us be rich and take our children out of the way of the Boche."

"As I said, they are orphans, but they are Jewish. You know what the Germans will do to them if they don't get away."

Rousseau fell silent. He looked down at the wrench in his hand and began tapping it in his palm. "Jewish?" he murmured.

"Yes. All three of them."

"I had a brother who married a Jewish woman, a Pole. He moved with her to Poland. When the Germans invaded the country, they took his wife and his little boy. When he fought to keep his family, they killed him. I don't know what happened to his wife and baby."

"I'm so sorry," Tyler said and started to walk away.

Rousseau tossed the wrench down, took the rag out of his back pocket, and began wiping his hands. "All right. I will take you to Moulins."

"I appreciate it. We'll pay you for your time and gas."

"I do not do it for money," he said. "And I will take a gun. If I see one of those filthy Germans, I will shoot him!"

Fervently Tyler hoped they wouldn't see any Germans. They went out and got in the car.

"Where are they?" Rousseau asked.

"At the station."

Rousseau drove to the station, and Tyler jumped out. "We're in luck," he told Jolie as she approached him. "This man is going to take us to Moulins." Tyler got the suitcases and the children followed him to the car.

"This is Monsieur Rousseau," Tyler introduced them as the man opened the trunk. "Monsieur Rousseau, this is Dr. Vernay."

"We are so thankful that you're going to help us," Jolie said. "I was getting worried."

"It is nothing." They put the two suitcases in the trunk and climbed into the car. Tyler sat in the front with Yolande on his lap and Damien between him and Rousseau.

As they drove out of town, the man began to talk about himself. "I was in the last war," he started.

"You don't look that old."

"I was only fifteen. I was in for the whole time."

"That was a horrible war," Tyler said over the roar of the noisy engine.

"All wars are horrible."

"Did you kill many Germans, Monsieur Rousseau?" Damien piped up.

Rousseau did not answer at once, and finally he stole a glance from the road to look at the boy. "Yes," he said, "and they tried to kill me."

Damien began to ask specific questions about how Rousseau had killed the Germans, but Rousseau shook his head and would not answer. Instead he turned his attention to Jolie. "You are a doctor, I understand?"

"Almost. I have some more training to do."

"Where do you live?"

When she told him Ambert, he said, "I have a sister who lives in your village—Yvette Villon. Her husband is Gaston. Do you know them?"

"Why, yes. Quite well. We attend the same church."

"Then you know their boy, Pierre. He's a good boy. He'll be joining the army next month."

"Perhaps the whole conflict will be over soon."

"No, I'm afraid it will be a long while before it's over."

"Where did you say you're going?" Monsieur Rousseau asked.

"We're going to Paris, and then from there it should be easy for us to get to Le Havre."

Rousseau shook his head. "Me, I do not think so."

"You think the Germans have already taken Paris?"

They passed a sign announcing they were entering Moulins, and Rousseau pulled up at the train station.

"It could be. If I were you, I would not go there."

Everybody got out of the car, and Rousseau opened the trunk.

Tyler opened his billfold and offered him some money.

"No, no, no. You may need your money."

"Thank you, Monsieur Rousseau," Jolie said. "May God bless you for your kindness."

Rousseau stared at her for a moment and then a smile broke the craggy features of his face. "And may God bless you, mademoiselle."

He got in the car then and pulled away quickly.

"I think he's a good man, but he's afraid," Jolie said.

"Well, he's like an angel to us."

"He didn't look like an angel," Yolande said, looking up. She grabbed onto Tyler's hand, her eyes wide. "He didn't have any wings."

"Not all angels have wings, Yolande."

"What do they have, then?"

He winked at her. "Come on. I'll tell you what angels look like while we're waiting."

"Tell me, please."

Jolie went to check on the train schedule while Yolande and the other two children sat listening to Tyler concoct stories about the appearance of angels. He felt the fragile spirit of the little girl and was moved and very glad that he had returned to her and the others instead of running away.

CHAPTER TEN

STUCK IN NEVERS

★ ★ ★

When the group was finally settled on the train coming from Italy, Tyler and Jolie fervently hoped it would take them all the way to Paris. They had never dreamed it could take so long to cross the country. They hadn't been under way long when the train stopped in Nevers.

Jolie looked at Tyler and sighed. "What now?" she asked.

He shrugged his shoulders and tried to smile.

She caught the arm of an employee of the railroad who was walking swiftly through the car and asked him how long they would be there.

"I cannot say, mademoiselle. The engine has developed a problem. I'm sure it will be at least a couple of hours, or it may even be morning before it is repaired. You're welcome to stay on the train, though, if you'd like."

"We may as well get off and stretch our legs—maybe find some food too," she told Tyler. "There's no use waiting here."

"I think you're right. And maybe we can hear some news while we're here."

The troublesome affair of getting off the train and keeping all the children together in the midst of all of the confusion took some time. They made their way to the platform with Jolie leading the way, pushing through the soldiers who covered the area. Some of them were laughing, but others looked totally exhausted as they sat on the dirty asphalt, resting their backs against supports or the wall of the station.

The streets were packed with trucks, military equipment, and even some horse-drawn guns. All around them the sound of heavy equipment moving through the streets drowned out the voices.

"Let's go see if we can find a restaurant that's open," Tyler suggested. "I'm sure it'll be crowded, but maybe we can get something."

Indeed, the town of Nevers was packed. They gave up on two restaurants that had long lines winding out the door but finally found one on the outskirts of town that was not completely filled. They went inside and seated themselves at the one remaining table. The waiter, a small, sad-eyed man with a dirty white apron, said, "We have roast beef sandwiches and potatoes. That is all."

"Looks like business is good," Tyler offered, looking around at the crowd. "Is there any news on the radio?"

"Yes—all bad." The man turned and left.

As they waited Rochelle said, "What if the train won't go? What will we do then?"

"It will go sooner or later," Tyler reassured her. "If this engine can't be fixed, they'll use another one." He saw that the young girl was troubled and reached over and touched her shoulder. "Try not to worry."

After they had all eaten their fill, they took their time going back to the train station, pausing to look in every shop window to kill some time. They got back to the train station and strolled through the area, reading every poster they could find and making up stories about all the people they were encountering. After a time they grew bored with their games and got back on the train.

"We might as well make ourselves comfortable," Jolie said. It was easier to do now, since most of the other people hadn't yet returned to the train.

The engine still wasn't fixed as night fell, so they did their best to settle in and made the most of it.

★ ★ ★

"Where's Damien?" Jolie asked. The group had descended from the train at the first light of dawn and found an outside faucet where they could wash up. After being assured that they had enough time to get some breakfast, they had gone back to the same restaurant where they had dined the day before and had a scanty breakfast of porridge and eggs.

"Damien? Why, he was here a minute ago," Tyler said. They were back at the train station, and now Tyler looked around with annoyance. "I'll go see if I can find him."

"You'd better hurry. I think the train is going to leave soon." Worry lines were forming on Jolie's forehead. "I'll try to find out while you're looking."

Jolie herded the children down toward the front of the train and stopped one of the employees. "The repair is almost finished, madame," the railroad worker said. He was covered with grease, and his eyes were weary with strain. "Do not go too far. There will be three blasts. When you hear them, it's time to get on the train."

"*Merci beaucoup.*"

Jolie and the children found a bench near their car and waited for Tyler. Ten minutes went by, and then twenty, before Tyler returned.

"Hasn't he come back yet?"

"No. You didn't find him?"

"I've looked everywhere!" Tyler exclaimed. "I don't know where else he could be."

"You watch the children. I'll go look."

Jolie walked to the other end of the train, her eyes searching the crowd. It was difficult to find anyone, for the area was filled with military personnel. Civilians waiting for the train to leave were now getting on board, and she began to be concerned. She went into the station office and asked if anyone had seen a young boy alone, but the stationmaster shook his head. "No. He has not been reported, I'm afraid."

Making her way back to where Tyler waited, she said, "I can't find him anywhere."

Tyler chewed his lower lip. "The train is going to pull out pretty soon."

"We won't leave him, will we?" Yolande asked anxiously. "We can't leave Damien here."

"If we miss this train, there may not be another one," Tyler said. "Why did that boy have to get himself lost?"

"I'll go look one more time."

Jolie once again hurried through the crowd, calling out the boy's name. Her voice could hardly be heard above the roar of the vehicles that passed on the street beside the station. Remembering how Damien loved to watch the armored cars and tanks, she went out into the street. There was a steady stream of military vehicles all headed in the direction of Paris but no sign of Damien.

She turned abruptly to look in the other direction when she practically ran into a man that she knew. Louis Debreaux was an old acquaintance from her own hometown. He had left the village when he was only seventeen and had become a reporter for a Paris newspaper.

"Louis," she said and saw surprise wash across his face.

"Why, Jolie! What in the world are you doing here?"

"I'm trying to get some children to the coast and then to England."

"Well, you'd better get them out at once. Things are going to pieces."

"Where are the Germans, Louis?"

"They're across the Marne."

"What about our troops? Are they holding?"

"No, they're not. They're running away as fast as they can." Anger and grief were etched on his face. "It's all over. You know that the Italians are coming up from the south now."

"I heard they declared war."

"That's right. You shouldn't be here. There's no telling when the Germans will come this way, but I have to believe it won't be long."

"What about you?"

Debreaux shrugged his shoulders. "Somebody has to write up the stories so other people can read them, and that somebody would be me. You say you're heading to the coast. You weren't planning to go through Paris, were you?"

"We were, but maybe we need to change our plans. We were hoping to cross the Channel from Le Havre. The Germans shouldn't be in Normandy."

"You're wrong there. They're going to take over the whole coastline," Debreaux said bitterly. "Look, we're getting out of here," he said, indicating another man who was leaning against a nearby car. "You'd better come with us."

"I can't do that, Louis. I've got those three children."

"We could crowd you all in somehow."

"But you're not going to the coast, are you?"

He shook his head.

"I've got to get these children out of France. That's all I care about right now."

Debreaux grinned. He was worried, dirty, and had not shaved in three days, but he gave a short laugh. "You always were the most stubborn woman I've ever known. Do you remember when I tried to get you to go out with me and you resisted my charm?"

"That was my mistake."

"Too late to make up now." The words were light, but Louis Debreaux was concerned. "The situation is going to be bad," he said quietly.

"And to make it worse, these are Jewish orphans I'm trying to get to England."

"Oh, that is a bad one. I wish I could help somehow. Do you need money?"

"No, we're fine."

"God go with you and the children."

Turning away from Debreaux, Jolie made her way back to the bench where Tyler and the children waited. She had hoped desperately that Damien had found his way back, but he was still gone. She opened her mouth to speak, but even as she did, the train gave three piercing blasts.

"You didn't find him?" Tyler asked.

"No."

The two stood there uncertainly as the other passengers hurried to get aboard. Jolie was afraid that Tyler might insist on leaving. Perhaps it would be the wisest thing to do. At least they could save two of the children.

"Well, when this train clears out, there won't be so many people to search through. We'll get the next train."

If the children hadn't been listening, Jolie would have said, *There may not be a next train.* Instead, she said brightly, "All right. That sounds like a good idea."

But when the train departed, they searched the entire area again and could find no sign of Damien.

They inquired about the next train, and the stationmaster said, "Tomorrow—perhaps."

They had to be content with the unsatisfactory answer. "I think we might be able to find a room now," Tyler said quietly.

"Yes, we'd better try. The children have to have some rest."

There was a hotel almost directly across from the train station, and fortunately there were two rooms available. After carrying the girls' suitcase to their room, Tyler said, "I'm going to get some paper and write some notices asking people to keep an eye out for a lost boy."

"Be sure to put the name of this hotel and our room number on there so that if Damien sees it, he can find us."

"That's a good idea." He hesitated for a moment, then said, "This is pretty bad, Jolie."

"I know."

"I wish my folks knew about the whole situation. I always went to them every time I was in trouble, and they'd pray me out of it."

"I'm sure Maman is praying for us already. And we need to pray too."

"From the looks of things, we're going to need all the prayer we can get."

★ ★ ★

At first light in the morning, Jolie got ready to go out again in search of Damien.

"You ought to let me go," Tyler argued.

"You stay here with the children. I'm too nervous to sit still. I'll come back as soon as I've found out something."

"Stop by the station and see if you can find out about the next train. If we find Damien, we'll need to be on it."

★ ★ ★

The next twenty-four hours passed slowly. Jolie and Tyler took turns roaming the station and going through the town asking everyone they encountered if they had seen a small redheaded boy. They got no response at all, and the train came through and left without them. Neither of them spoke of missing the train, but at the back of their minds was the knowledge that sooner or later they would have to make a decision. The news was all bad. More than one person on the street informed them the Germans were sweeping toward Paris at an incredible speed.

Evening came, and they went again to the same restaurant. After dinner, as they were approaching their hotel, Rochelle cried out, "Look, there's Damien!"

The boy was walking beside an older woman who was carrying a baby. "Damien!" Jolie called as she ran ahead. "Where have you been? We've been looking everywhere for you."

Damien's clothes were filthy and dirt was ground into his face, but he seemed all right otherwise. "I got lost," he said. "One of the soldiers took me for a ride in a tank. I got to ride in a tank!" he exclaimed.

Jolie's eyes went to the frail-looking woman, who appeared to be in her sixties, standing beside him. Her clothes were worn and the marks of poverty etched her face. She looked weary beyond belief.

"This is Madame Florin," he said. She nodded her head at them.

"When the ride in the tank was over, I didn't know where I was, and Madame Florin took me into her house. I was so hungry," Damien said. He patted the baby's head. "This is Marie. Marie Rousset."

"Come inside," Jolie said, seeing that the woman seemed almost ready to fall down. "Let me take the baby. You look exhausted."

"We walked all the way in from the farm," Damien announced.

"You are a naughty boy to run away like that," Rochelle scolded. She was relieved to see her friend, but irritation was sharp in her voice. "We missed the train because of you, and we've all been worried about where you were."

Damien looked at his shoes and mumbled, "I'm sorry. I wasn't trying to make you worried."

"I know, Damien," Jolie said, patting the boy's shoulder. "We were worried, but everything is fine now that you're here and you're safe and sound." She turned to the old woman. "Would you let me carry the baby for you?" The woman looked too weak to support her own weight, much less the baby's.

The woman nodded, looking grateful, and handed over the child.

The group trooped into the hotel and up to the second floor and then waited at the top while the woman slowly climbed. When she reached the top, she coughed vigorously and took several deep breaths. They all went to Jolie's room, and she invited the older woman to sit down. "We have some food here, and we can get milk or wine perhaps."

"No, please," the woman said. "I'm not hungry." She licked her lips and looked around at the room. "Damien says you are taking these children to England?"

"Yes, that's right."

"Please take Marie with you."

Instantly Jolie knew that she must cut this short. "Why would you ask us to do that?"

"She has no family. Her mother is dead. The father, no one ever knew who he was."

"Is she related to you?" Tyler asked.

"No, I live alone, and I cannot take care of her. What is she to do? Please take her with you," she pleaded. The woman dug into her bulging oversized pocket and pulled out a bottle and two cans of milk. She extended the items toward Jolie, her eyes imploring her.

"She's an orphan like we are," Damien told them. "She doesn't take up much room."

Jolie was almost panicked, and she saw that Tyler was

dumbfounded. Jolie took the milk and bottle. "Everyone sit down. We will talk."

After everyone was settled, Jolie asked the woman to take her time and tell her story.

"The baby's mother lived with her family on the farm next to ours. She was a wild young girl, I'm afraid, and she became pregnant." The woman pulled a hankie from her sleeve and coughed into it. "When her family grew frightened with the prospect of war, they decided to get out of the country and move in with relatives, but the girl refused to leave the area, since the baby's father apparently lives near here."

Rochelle's eyes were wide as she took the story in.

"When the child was born, the girl tried to take care of her, but because she was too weak she asked me to take her. The girl died last week." The woman's eyes looked sad. "I cannot keep the baby. I am very ill."

Jolie had already ascertained that. Based on what she'd seen, she guessed the woman might have tuberculosis. Jolie could only hope and pray the woman had taken precautions so the baby and Damien wouldn't catch it.

"Surely there must be someone. Does she have any family at all?"

"No, madame. No family. Please take her to England with you. She's only two months old."

"I will take care of her," Rochelle said quickly. "Please, mademoiselle, we cannot leave her here to die."

"I must speak with Monsieur Winslow," Jolie said. "Come outside with me, please."

The two left the room, and as soon as the door closed, Jolie said, "This is terrible."

"We'll take her with us," Tyler said firmly. "There's no other choice."

Everything that Jolie had thought about Tyler Winslow suddenly flew out the window. She had been certain that he, of all the men she'd ever known, would be the least likely to take responsibility for an infant under such terrible circumstances.

"Do you know anything about caring for babies? Do you understand the difficulties you'll encounter?"

He shrugged. "If God can get three children out of the country, He can get four."

Jolie reached out and took his hands in hers and squeezed them. "You never cease to amaze me, Tyler. Just when I think I have you all figured out, you turn into an entirely different man."

He laughed. "We may have a dozen children with us by the time we get to the coast. Let's just be prepared to do whatever we have to do."

"What will you do with the baby when we get her to safety? I mean out of France?"

"I'll find her a home either in England, America, or Africa, just like I'll do with the other children. I'll do whatever has to be done, Jolie."

She saw the determination in his face and suddenly realized they were still holding hands. She pulled her hands back and then said, "Let's tell Madame Florin the good news."

CHAPTER ELEVEN

END OF THE LINE

★ ★ ★

Tyler leaned back against his train seat the next morning and winked at Rochelle, who was sitting on the seat across from him holding the baby in the crook of her arm. "You make a fine little mother, Rochelle," he said.

"Someday I'm going to have babies of my own," she said as the train sped through the countryside. "I'd like to have six. Three boys and three girls."

"It would be better," Damien said from his seat next to Tyler, "if you had five boys and one girl."

"Don't be silly," Rochelle said gently. "Three boys and three girls is what I want."

Yolande was sitting beside Rochelle, stroking the baby's soft hair. "She's so pretty," Yolande said. "She's got blond hair just like me."

"But she's got brown eyes like me," Damien said. "And don't forget. I found her."

"Well, at least we got on a train," Tyler said to Jolie, who was sitting on his other side. "We don't have to walk to the coast."

"I can't imagine trying to walk to the coast, much less with four children in tow."

"Oh, we would have managed somehow. Yolande could have ridden on my shoulders, and you and Rochelle could have taken turns carrying the baby."

Jolie jabbed his arm playfully. She wanted to talk about their plan but could not do so in front of the children. When she looked at them her heart grew warm. "This is a good thing we're doing, Tyler."

"You know, it really is. I never thought I'd find myself a father to four children."

Damien turned suddenly and said, "I know what."

"What?" Jolie asked.

"You and Monsieur Winslow could get married. Then you could adopt all of us. That way you wouldn't have to go to all the trouble of having your own children."

Jolie felt her face grow warm, but even so, she was amused. "That's a good scheme you've got there, but it's a bit more complicated than that."

"It doesn't have to be," Rochelle said. "You like Monsieur Winslow, don't you? And he likes you. I can tell. So maybe you could fall in love and get married."

"And live happily ever after?" Tyler asked with a grin. He leaned over to bump Jolie's shoulder with his own. "Out of the mouths of babes and sucklings wisdom comes. That's somewhere in the Bible."

"I don't think I'm going to depend on Damien Rivard to pick my husband for me."

As the train moved along, there was an air of relaxation in the compartment. Outside there were men dying in battle and farmhouses being blown up—all sorts of terrible things—but for this moment, at this time, all was well.

"You know," Tyler said, "I have a friend who used to say no matter how bad things were, he was all right today. I like that philosophy. Right now we've got something to eat. We're safe on this train. I'm not going to worry about tomorrow."

"That's what Jesus said. 'Take therefore no thought for the morrow: for the morrow shall take thought for the things of itself,'" Jolie said.

"Who is Jesus?" Yolande asked as she stood up and planted herself in front of Jolie. "Is he a friend of yours?"

"Yes, He is a friend of mine, but not like you think."

"Why not? I know what a friend is," Yolande said. "You're my friend."

"My people have been hurt by Christians," Rochelle put in.

"That's true," Jolie said carefully. "Terrible things have been done in the name of religion, but Jesus wasn't responsible for that. He said we were to love our enemies."

"Even the Germans?" Damien asked with astonishment.

"That's what He said. And, of course, He loved everybody."

"Where is He," Yolande asked, "this Jesus friend of yours?"

Jolie felt a strange compulsion. She knew the two older children had come in contact with the gospel at the orphanage, but Yolande had no concept of what it all meant. Jolie told the children about Jesus' purpose in coming to earth as a baby and explained how He grew into a good man who loved everyone.

Rochelle readjusted the baby in her lap as Marie stretched. "Once a man who came to the orphanage said that Jesus was like the lambs that the Hebrew forefathers killed at Passover. I never understood that, mademoiselle."

"I remember that passage." Jolie rummaged through her bag until she found her Bible and then flipped through the pages. "Here it is. 'Behold the Lamb of God, which taketh away the sin of the world.' It's John one, verse twenty-nine."

"But I still don't understand what that means—the Lamb of God," Rochelle said.

"Well, the people of those days knew that when someone sinned, he had to sacrifice an animal—like a pigeon, a goat, or a lamb—to pay for the sin, to have the sin washed away. You've probably read about sacrifices in the Torah, Rochelle."

"Yes, I remember Papa reading to us about that."

"And all through the history of your people, one of the things they did for Passover was to kill a lamb, and to them it meant that God was looking out for them. I don't suppose they understood it, but they did it."

"I remember it said they took the blood of the lamb," Rochelle said, cuddling Marie closer, "and put it over the doors of their houses. When the angel of death came, he would pass over and not kill them. That's why they call it the Passover."

"That's right. So when John the Baptist saw Jesus, he said, 'Behold the Lamb of God.' What he was saying is that God sent Jesus to shed His blood so that we wouldn't have to die. Every lamb that was ever killed by your people, Rochelle, was pointing forward to the time when the blood of one man would be shed for all the world. And that man was Jesus."

Tyler was listening attentively as Jolie continued to talk about Jesus, although he was trying to appear uninterested. Tyler knew everything she was saying was true. Growing up with missionary parents, he had heard the gospel presented in many different ways. He had fully embraced his faith as a child, but somewhere along the way he had focused on having fun above all else. Even now, he knew he was missing out on that connection he had once had with his Lord. *Jesus*, he prayed, for the first time in years, *can you forgive me? Have I strayed too far?*

The train began to slow down, and Tyler said, "It looks like we're going to stop here. I wonder what town this is."

"There's a sign," Damien said. "It says La Charité."

"There doesn't seem to be anybody waiting to get on," Jolie said as the train came to a stop.

Soon a man in uniform came through the car, announcing, "End of the line. This train will go no farther."

"Not again! It's supposed to go to Paris," Jolie cried out.

"I'm sorry, mademoiselle. There is no way we can go any farther."

"But we must get to the coast."

He shrugged. "I'm sorry. I cannot say more."

"Well, this is another mess," Tyler said angrily. "But there's no sense in staying here. Come along." He stood and gathered the suitcases.

"Let me carry the baby." Jolie took Marie, who had been sleeping but now awoke and began to cry.

When they were all situated on the platform, Damien asked, "We're not going to stay here, are we, Monsieur Winslow?"

"No, we need to continue on our way, but I'm not sure how. Jolie, why don't you give the baby a bottle while I go check the schedule, and then we'll know better what we're up against."

He returned moments later. "There's no assurance that another train will come, I'm afraid, but the man said we can catch a bus that will get us to St. Malo."

"St. Malo? I hadn't thought of going that far west." She thought for a moment. "But it actually might work better than Le Havre, because it's so close to the Channel Islands."

"Which might make it easier for a small boat to get across the Channel," Tyler supplied, "if it had a place to refuel and rest."

"Right." Jolie nodded. "Where do we catch the bus?"

"It stops at a shop in the middle of town. He told me how to get there."

With Tyler carrying the two suitcases, Rochelle carrying the baby, and Yolande alternating between riding on Jolie's back and walking, they finally made it to the store. Tyler went inside and asked the proprietor when the bus would be coming.

"Should be here in an hour if it comes."

"Aren't they running regularly?"

The man gave him a sour look. "Is anything running regularly these days?"

Tyler shrugged.

"Do you want tickets?"

"Yes. Two adults and three children. Three children plus a baby, that is."

Tyler paid for the tickets and went back outside. "It'll be about an hour, he says. Let's hope the bus service is working better than the trains."

Fortunately, in less than an hour, a rather ancient-looking bus pulled up to the curb.

"Look at all those people," Yolande exclaimed.

"You and the children get on," Tyler told Jolie, "and I'll take care of the luggage." The driver helped Tyler tie the suitcases on top of the bus along with the luggage that was already up there, and then he got on the bus. The four children, the baby now asleep in Rochelle's lap, were squeezed into a seat built for two, and Jolie was standing in the aisle.

"Well, it beats walking," Tyler said as he stood next to Jolie.

The bus pulled out with a groan and a clash of gears, and Tyler muttered, "I hope this wreck can make it to St. Malo."

CHAPTER TWELVE

AN ANCIENT BUS

★ ★ ★

The bus was a hot box filled with irritable people. Everyone was agitated and upset, and some of them had brought some of their luggage with them, including enormous packages.

From time to time the bus would stop and let off one or two people, and after the second stop, both Jolie and Tyler found seats. The bus kicked up swirls of dust as the heavy vehicle plowed on. The road was lined with vehicles of every kind imaginable, all headed in the same direction. Old battered cars that Americans would have retired years before, trucks of various sizes, and all sorts of carts pulled by horses or donkeys traveled the same road. Traffic wasn't limited to vehicles, however. The bus passed a number of people traveling on foot, some pushing carts or baby carriages piled high with assorted belongings. It seemed as though the whole countryside was in flight.

They passed through a town without stopping, and ten minutes later the bus driver surrendered to the pleas and demands of many passengers who needed a rest stop. When the bus pulled over to the side, everyone immediately started filing off.

The area was thick with trees and bushes on both sides. By some unspoken arrangement, the women went off into the bushes on the right side of the road while the men went on the left.

Ten minutes later Tyler was walking back and forth to stretch his legs. He walked over to the bus driver and asked, "What's the next town?"

"It's a little village called Briare, but we won't stop there."

Even as the bus driver spoke, they heard the drone of distant planes in the sky. Looking up, Tyler saw three dots in the sky. At once he ran to Rochelle, grabbed the baby, and yelled, "Quick, get back into the trees!"

"What is it?" Jolie asked as she grabbed Yolande's hand and followed him.

"Planes. I don't know if they're ours or theirs."

Although a few of the other passengers on the bus followed his lead, most of them just looked at him quizzically. "Come on. Run!" He herded the children along and soon they were in the shelter of the towering trees. They lay under a huge tree, huddled close together, arms over their heads.

Noise from the aircraft grew louder. Suddenly a crackle filled the air, and dust swirled up in tiny dots along the road. He heard the sound of metal on metal as bullets struck the bus, and an old man screamed and fell to the ground.

"Enemy planes! Get out of the road!" Tyler yelled, but it was too late for some. The second plane followed the first, and small objects fell toward the earth. The first bomb struck about fifty yards from the bus, but the next one came in closer. A third fell on the far side of the road, and a number of people were caught in the explosion. The third plane dropped no bombs but strafed the area with machine-gun fire. Tyler looked up through the trees and caught a glimpse of the pilot, who was laughing as he shot over the bus.

As the planes left the area, Tyler handed the baby back to Rochelle and moved out onto the road so he could see what was happening. Jolie followed him, telling him she was going to see what she could do for anybody who was wounded. People were running in every direction as the machine-gun fire caught people who hadn't reacted quickly enough. He heard another bomb explode, and then the planes disappeared from sight.

"They're gone," he said with relief, but then he looked over and saw the bus driver, who had taken cover in the trees but now was staring at the bus.

"Looks pretty bad, doesn't it?" he said as he got closer and saw that water was pouring out of the engine.

"It's all ruined. Look." The man waved his hand helplessly. "The radiator, it's gone."

"What'll we do now?"

"We will walk. Briare is that way, maybe five kilometers."

★ ★ ★

The sun was going down by the time the small group reached Briare. Jolie had done what she could to help the wounded. Miraculously only one person was killed. A number of people had minor injuries, and one young man had taken a bullet in the leg, which Jolie had treated as well as she could. The man had managed to limp into town with the aid of a strong man on each side.

The town was full of survivors, many of whom looked dazed and disconcerted, and there was an air of uncertainty about the whole town. "Wait here," Tyler told Jolie, "and I'll go see if I can find us a place to stay."

Tyler soon discovered Briare was only a small village and had no hotel at all. He was getting desperate to find someplace to stay when a woman overheard him.

"You can stay at our place," she offered. "It's about a kilometer outside of town."

"Merci beaucoup, madame. That is awfully kind of you."

"Our wagon is parked just down the street. Is your family nearby?"

"Well, madame, they're not really my family, and they're not far at all." He sketchily explained the circumstances, and the woman stared at him.

"That is a strange situation. And you are going home to England?"

"No, actually, I'm an American."

"That is even stranger. Come, we must hurry, and later, when we get you settled, you can help me better understand your story."

★ ★ ★

Pierre Duvivier was a soft-spoken man who received them with kindness. When he listened to his wife's explanation, he motioned toward the radio and said, "Our leaders have surrendered."

Both Tyler and Jolie stared at him. "Surrendered? So soon?" Jolie whispered.

"Yes. It just came over the radio."

The news seemed to take the heart out of Jolie, and Tyler saw it at once. He said nothing but sat down and talked with Pierre Duvivier as the women got the children settled for the night.

Finally Madame Duvivier emerged from the bedroom. "These are not your children, you say?" She sat down across from her husband and Jolie at the rough table in the kitchen. It was warm and outside the crickets were beginning to sing. It seemed very quiet and peaceful, but

Tyler could not forget the bullets striking and the bombs falling.

"No, the three older ones are orphans that were at the orphanage I worked at in Ambert." She went on to explain how the baby was added to the mix.

"And you, monsieur, what are you doing in our country?" she asked Tyler.

"Believe it or not, I came to learn how to paint. I would like to be an artist. But . . . well, I got caught up in this war."

"And you will take these children to England?"

"Or to America. I'll find a place for them," he said, "even if I have to take them to Africa."

"To Africa! Why would you take them there?" Pierre asked with surprise.

"My parents are there, and I have other relatives there as well. They are all missionaries. If nothing else works, I'll take the children there."

The Duviviers were obviously puzzled by the whole situation. Pierre shook his head. "I cannot help much, but I can tell you one thing. There will be no more buses. The drivers will be afraid to travel."

"Then we'll have to walk," Jolie said tightly.

"No, no, no, you cannot walk all the way to the coast. I have an extra wagon. It is old but sound, and I have an extra horse. You will take them and go with these children."

"That's so kind of you," Jolie said with relief. "We will gladly pay you for their use."

"There will be no money involved. My wife and I would like to have a part in what you are doing."

Tyler could not speak for a moment. He cleared his throat finally and said, "That's very good of you, monsieur."

"It is very little that one can do, but we would like to help save these children from the Germans."

★　★　★

Tyler and Jolie were sitting at the kitchen table after Pierre and his wife had gone to bed. "It's a miracle that God created this way of caring for the children," Tyler said. He also realized it was a miracle that he was starting to turn his thoughts back toward God. He was surprised at how good it felt! "I don't see how we would have made it any other way."

"I know. God is good."

"Which way do you think we should go now? We're liable to find Germans on any of these roads."

The two discussed their options for a long time, tracing one possible route after another on their map. After they had come to a tentative decision, Tyler leaned back in his chair and stretched. "I guess this is a good time to find out how to trust God." He shook his head, and wonder was on his face. "I've really never had to before. I've always depended on my family or someone else anytime I ran into trouble of any kind."

"You have a large family?"

"I think I told you I only have two siblings, but I have a number of aunts and uncles and lots of cousins. The Winslows go way back. We can trace our roots to Gilbert Winslow, who was the first person in our family to settle in America."

"What was he like?"

"Well, he was quite a ladies' man in his youth, I understand from his journal, but he loved God. He left his sword to his son, and it's been passed down through the generations. I think my father has it now. But there were lots of other Winslows." Tyler told Jolie some of the stories his parents had told him of the Winslows who had fought in the wars in America, the men and the women who had found a way to serve God in hard times. Finally he said, "I've bored you enough talking about me."

"No, I wasn't bored," she said quietly.

"What about you?"

"What would you like to know?"

"Do you have other family besides your mother?"

"Just distant cousins."

Tyler was restless. He got up and opened the door and gazed out into the darkness. "Do you want to go outside with me? It's cooler out there. Or are you ready to hit the sack?"

"I'm really not sleepy yet," she said as she walked to the door. "I guess I'm on edge thinking about keeping the children safe."

The two of them went outside and stood in the yard inhaling the strong smells of the farm.

"It's so peaceful here," Jolie whispered.

"Yes, it is. Hard to think there are men dying now and women and children too. This war is terrible."

"I've been thinking, Tyler. I have a friend named Jean Clermont. We grew up together. What do you Americans call it . . . I had a 'crush' on him. Is that the word?"

"That's it. I've had several myself."

"Well, I was fifteen, and Jean was a year older. But it never came to anything."

"What happened?"

"When his father died, they moved to a small town on the coast—Honfleur—and now he's a fisherman. I've been thinking maybe we ought to go there. If we could get there, maybe Jean could take you and the children across the Channel to England."

"There's an idea. It's a long way, though, and it wouldn't be easy. Do you think he'd be willing to put himself in that kind of peril for us?"

"It's hard to say, but I think it's worth a try. What do you think? In all honesty. Do you think you'll make it, really?"

As she looked up expectantly at him, waiting for his answer, he couldn't help but notice how lovely she looked as the moonlight bathed her face with its soft silver. Her dark hair was pulled together at the back, which accentuated her smooth neck and slender figure.

He tried with some difficulty to get his mind back on their travel plans. "We'll make it," he said, "somehow." A restless desire was stirring in him now, and he said, "Have you ever been in love, Jolie?"

Startled, she looked at him, her lips parted, and she smiled. "I've always been attracted to men who were strong—physically, I mean—but he'd have to be more than that. I went with a man named Jacques for a while. He was strong and could lift heavier weights than anyone else in our village. But"—she shrugged—"he was one of the most boring men I've ever known."

"Maybe you could marry two men. A strong man to do all the heavy work and a witty one to keep you amused."

"Don't be silly." She laughed and put her hands on her hips.

A recklessness came over Tyler, and knowing he would regret it, he reached out and pulled her to him. To his surprise, she didn't pull away. He lowered his head and kissed her. She stood unmoving, her lips soft beneath his own, and he waited for her to pull away. But she did not, and he felt her respond to his embrace.

And then suddenly she did pull away. "That was a mistake."

"For you, maybe."

"For you too."

"Why do you say that?" he asked.

"We were amused at what Damien said about our getting married and adopting them all, but that could never be."

"And why not?"

"We're too different, Tyler. We've been through all this before." She shook her head. "We'd better be up early in the morning. Good night."

Tyler wandered aimlessly outside as she returned to the house. A bird flew overhead, throwing its shadow over Tyler. He glanced up quickly and saw the owl sail across the clear sky and then disappear into the trees.

"Good hunting," Tyler said before turning to go inside the house.

PART THREE

June–July 1940

★ ★ ★

CHAPTER THIRTEEN

A HORSE NAMED CRAZY

★ ★ ★

The horse that the Duviviers had loaned to Tyler and Jolie was a strange-looking creature. It was tall and raw-boned with a multicolored design that Tyler had never seen before. It reminded Tyler a great deal of a quilt that had come down to him from his grandmother, and he had started calling the horse Crazy Quilt. Rochelle and Yolande, after being informed of the origin of the title, were delighted with it, but they shortened the name of the horse to Crazy. Damien wanted to call it One Eye, for obvious reasons, but he was overruled by Yolande and Rochelle.

"We make a pretty odd-looking parade, don't we, Jolie?" Tyler asked. He and Jolie were sitting at the front of the wagon with Yolande and the baby in the back. Rochelle and Damien were walking alongside the wagon, finding it easy to keep up with Crazy's leisurely pace. The dust was thick and the lack of rain had made it so fine that the breeze lifted it in a cloud behind them.

Jolie shook her head. "The horse seems strong enough, but it certainly is a queer-looking animal."

"We were lucky to get it. I hope it holds out until we get to the coast."

"I think it will. Let's hope so, anyway."

"It reminds me of an English teacher I had in high school," Tyler said.

"An English teacher!" Jolie cocked her head. "How could a weird-looking animal like that remind you of an English teacher?"

"She was tall and lanky and wore clothes that didn't match. I think she was color-blind. She would come to school one day with a purple skirt and an orange blouse, and the next day with a pink skirt and green blouse. I don't think she could see the difference."

They stopped at noon to have a meal, and afterward they traded places with Rochelle and Damien and let Rochelle drive the horse. She was nervous about driving the horse at first, but Tyler laughed and reassured her, "Don't worry. He's not going to run away with you. I don't think he's capable of such a thing."

Before long Damien insisted on having a turn, and no matter how much the children shouted or slapped the reins, Crazy never varied his pace.

"I think he's a one-speed horse," Jolie said with a smile. "Just what we need for this trip."

As the day went by, they saw very little civilian traffic and no military vehicles. As the sun started dropping, they reached a creek that meandered across the road. "I think we'd better camp here for the night," Tyler said.

"Can't we go on to a village?" Jolie asked. "It would be good if we could buy some food."

"I don't think it would be a good idea. Look, we can pull the wagon off over there behind those trees." The banks of the creek were crowded with tall poplar trees. "They're so thick no one will ever know we're there."

"I guess you're right," she said. "We can buy food if we encounter a farmer along the way tomorrow."

Tyler jumped up into the wagon and drove Crazy

down alongside the bank. He chose a spot that was well shaded by the tall trees. The water of the creek caught the angled sun and made a pleasant sound as it bubbled over the stones.

Tyler unhitched Crazy from the wagon and took him to a grassy spot, anchoring the horse with a long rope to a tree, not that Crazy seemed to have any inclinations to run off. He patted the horse on the neck, muttering, "I guess you've got all the responsibility of getting us out of this, boy."

There was plenty of deadwood nearby, so by the time the sun had set, Tyler had built a fire. Jolie gave the baby a bottle while the children looked for thin sticks to roast some meat. Fortunately, Madame Duvivier had given them several more cans of milk, so they had enough for the time being.

The farmer had given them some chunks of beef, which they roasted on the sticks that the children had gathered. The beef was tasty, even though the children had some difficulty cooking it without burning it. As Tyler sat on the ground gnawing on a piece of the beef, he remarked to Jolie, "This is just like when I was in the Boy Scouts on an overnight camp-out, except I'm a little farther from home."

"It is nice, isn't it?" She looked up at the stars. "It's hard to believe that right now there are men lying on battlefields crying out in pain from their wounds and even dying. It's hard to think about awful things like that, but I suppose we have to face reality."

"I guess all things are relative. We're here and we're safe, for today at least. My folks always said if you had something to eat and a place to stay, you should never complain."

They sat there talking quietly, and finally Jolie said, "I'd like to read a little from the Bible if it's all right with everyone. I think if we keep the fire big enough, I'll be able to see just fine."

The children all gathered around, Marie on Rochelle's lap, while Tyler put another log on the fire and Jolie opened the Bible. Tyler sat back against a tree, his legs crossed, and watched the children, who looked eager to listen.

> "Now a certain man was sick, named Lazarus, of Bethany, the town of Mary and her sister Martha.
>
> "(It was that Mary which anointed the Lord with ointment, and wiped his feet with her hair, whose brother Lazarus was sick.)
>
> "Therefore his sisters sent unto him, saying, Lord, behold, he whom thou lovest is sick.
>
> "When Jesus heard that, he said, This sickness is not unto death, but for the glory of God, that the Son of God might be glorified thereby.
>
> "Now Jesus loved Martha, and her sister, and Lazarus.
>
> "When he had heard therefore that he was sick, he abode two days still in the same place—"

Damien piped up, "If He knew His friend was sick, why did He wait for three days? I would have gone right then!"

Jolie took her eyes off the Bible and said, "I think He wanted to show everyone that He was the Son of God. Just listen to the rest of the story." She continued to read the story, telling of how Jesus went to Judea, where Lazarus was.

> "Jesus therefore again groaning in himself cometh to the grave. It was a cave, and a stone lay upon it.
>
> "Jesus said, Take ye away the stone. Martha, the sister of him that was dead, saith unto him, Lord, by this time he stinketh: for he hath been dead four days.
>
> "Jesus saith unto her, Said I not unto thee, that, if thou wouldest believe, thou shouldest see the glory of God?
>
> "Then they took away the stone—"

"But He was dead!" Rochelle whispered. "Why did Jesus tell them to do that?"

"Because He was ready to do what He'd come to do," Jolie said. "Now, listen to the rest of the story."

"He cried with a loud voice, Lazarus, come forth.

"And he that was dead came forth, bound hand and foot with graveclothes: and his face was bound about with a napkin. Jesus saith unto them, Loose him, and let him go."

Jolie looked around at the children, her face alight. "Isn't that a wonderful story?"

"Is it true?" Rochelle asked doubtfully. "I never heard of anyone who was dead coming back to life."

"It's all true, but, of course, Jesus is God, and He can do things that the rest of us can't do."

"I have a Bible," Rochelle said, "but it's different from yours."

"Do you? Could I see it?" Jolie asked.

Rochelle got up and passed the baby to Jolie, then went to the wagon. She opened one of the suitcases, rummaged around in it, and came back with a book in her hand. She handed it to Jolie and said, "I don't think you can read it."

Jolie opened it and then looked up and smiled. "It's in Hebrew, isn't it?"

"Yes."

"Well, I can't read it, of course. Will you read some of it to us?"

"But you won't understand it."

"I know, but I would love to hear what Hebrew sounds like. I've always wished that I could read Hebrew."

Rochelle took the Bible and began to read. Tyler sat there listening, entranced by the unusual sounds. He understood not one word of it, but as the firelight flickered on the face of the young girl, he saw the beauty of womanhood that lay ahead for her and wondered what her future would be.

"Why don't you translate it for us," Jolie said.

"You mean tell you what it means?"

"Yes. Could you do that?"

"Oh yes. This is the story of the prophet Elijah. . . ." She went on to tell the story of Elijah, who had challenged the prophets of Baal and in the end had been victorious.

"That's a strong story," Tyler said. "That Elijah was some man, wasn't he?"

"He sure was!" Damien said, his face beaming. "I want to be just like him when I grow up. I'd like to call fire down on the Germans and burn 'em up!"

Tyler had to smile at this bombastic statement, but he was more interested in watching Jolie as she cuddled the baby. It made a pretty scene, and he pondered again Jolie's rare combination of beauty and strength. The firelight brought out her fine eyes, and her lips were broad and maternal as she leaned over and kissed Marie. Glancing around the small circle, he thought of how strange it was that he was at this place at this time. His life had taken a turn he would never have expected, and he suddenly realized that he could never again be the man he'd once been.

The full moon rose, and there was much chatter and laughter around the fire. Marie was getting restless in Jolie's arms, and before long her occasional pouts turned to outright cries. No amount of cuddling or cooing or jiggling would help.

"I guess we'll just have to let her cry," Jolie told Tyler. "That seems to be what she wants to do."

"Do you think it's serious?"

"No, I don't think so. She may just have some gas, something simple like that. She doesn't seem to have a fever. Hard to know about babies. You can't know how they're hurting, and there's no way they can tell you."

"Do you want me to hold her so you can go to bed?"

"No, you go ahead and sleep, Tyler. I'll walk with her a bit and see if that helps."

Tyler got the children settled in the wagon and then curled up on the ground with a blanket. He was more fatigued than he had realized and quickly dropped off to sleep. When he woke once some time later, he saw that Jolie and Marie were both asleep on the ground near the fire. *She's some woman,* he thought. *I've never known anyone like her.*

★ ★ ★

They traveled steadily the next day, and Tyler estimated they had covered about fifteen kilometers. Crazy set the pace, and there was no hurrying him, but on the other hand, he never seemed to slow down.

In the middle of the afternoon, Tyler looked at the map and then peered up ahead. "It looks like a town up there. It must be Orléans."

"Do you think we should go in?" Jolie asked. "We're going to need some more milk for Marie pretty soon."

"I think it's too risky, don't you?"

"Maybe I should just go in alone. You and the kids find a good place to camp off the road. I can go in and be back in a couple of hours at the most." She gave him a bright smile, adding, "I'll be all right, Tyler."

Tyler did not like it, but he didn't see that they had much choice, so he nodded. "But don't be too long."

★ ★ ★

Orléans was a medium-sized town, larger than many they had passed through, and Jolie easily found what she needed: fresh milk for Marie, and some fresh cheese, bread, and fruit for the rest of them. Then she spotted a drugstore and thought to stock up on some medical supplies, such as aspirin, ointment, and bandages, in case they might not be available later on.

The druggist smiled at her. He was a tall man with a full head of silver hair and kind eyes. "Are you getting ready to start a hospital, mademoiselle?"

"Oh no, just making sure I have plenty of supplies. You know how difficult it is when you run out of supplies."

"That's a good thing," he said as he nodded. "These are hard times—very difficult. We don't know what will happen next."

"What's the latest news?"

"It's always the same. The Germans are coming on faster than I could have believed. They will be here any day now." He shook his head sadly. "It's a sad day for France, indeed it is."

Jolie left the drugstore, and even as she stepped out the door, she heard the rumble of trucks. A convoy of trucks open to the sky and filled with German soldiers was coming down the street. She stepped back and stared at them.

The column stopped and a handsome officer leaped to the ground from the lead truck. He barked out some commands, and the soldiers began to disembark. From the little German she knew, she understood that he had said they would have a break. She started to walk away, but she was not quick enough. The officer came directly to her and stood before her smiling.

"Bonjour, mademoiselle," he said in excellent French. "You are out shopping, I see."

"Why, yes, Officer, I am."

"My name is Lieutenant Fritz Kaltenbach. May I ask your name?"

Jolie quickly glanced at the name of the store across the street and blurted out "Marie Thibeau" before she could give it a second thought. She didn't know if giving a false name would prove to be necessary, but it seemed the smart thing to do.

"Mademoiselle Thibeau, would you give me the honor of accompanying me into that café? You must let me buy you a drink."

"Oh, Lieutenant Kaltenbach, I couldn't do that."

"Why, of course you could! I am instructing all my men to behave themselves, and you must give me an opportunity to demonstrate how that is done."

Jolie noticed that some of the soldiers had gathered not far away and were watching the exchange. One of them called out, "That's the way, Lieutenant. Establish good relationships with the French."

Jolie couldn't understand some of the comments, but she could tell by their tone of voice and gestures that they were ribald.

"We must not pay attention to them," Kaltenbach said. "Come along. You must permit me to buy you something refreshing."

Jolie could not think of a way to get out of the situation. She walked with him over to the café, which had tables outside. He pulled a chair out for her before seating himself. When a man came to take their order, the lieutenant asked for two glasses of their best wine.

Kaltenbach turned out to be a charming man. If he had not been wearing a German uniform, Jolie would not have known he wasn't French.

"You speak French very well, Lieutenant," she commented.

"Ah, thank you. I went to school in Paris. I was a student at l'École des Beaux-Arts."

"You are an artist?"

"That is yet to be decided. While I think so and my mother thinks so, some of the critics were not so kind as she. But one day I'll go back and prove them wrong."

"Tell me about your painting."

He looked surprised. "You like painting, mademoiselle?"

"Very much, although I'm not an artist myself."

Kaltenbach began to tell her about his art, and they drank the wine. He ordered more, but Jolie refused and smiled.

Soon he began to get more personal. He leaned over and took her hand. "I must say I didn't expect to find such a beautiful woman in this little town, as well as a lover of art. I'm sure we have much in common."

As he took her hand, Jolie noticed he was wearing a ring. "I see you have a wife."

"What?"

"Your wedding ring," she said, pointing at it. "What is her name, Lieutenant?"

He reddened. "I've only been married a few months. I'm hardly used to being a husband." He laughed self-consciously and took a hasty sip of his drink.

"Do you have a picture of her?"

"Why, yes, I do." He fished his wallet out and handed a photograph to Jolie.

"She's very pretty, and she looks like a sweet-tempered young woman."

"She is. I was very lucky to get her." He gazed at the photograph. "We're expecting a baby in six months."

"Congratulations. And I hope that she will be as beautiful as her mother."

"Or if it's a boy?"

"Then as noble as his father."

Lieutenant Kaltenbach put his wallet away, then straightened up. "You are right to rebuke me, and you did it so tastefully. I'm ashamed of flirting."

"Tell me some more about your painting, Lieutenant, and about your marriage."

He described some of the paintings he had created while he had been in Paris but didn't say much about his wife. He drank the last of his wine and then glanced at his watch. "I must be going. It has been such a pleasure."

"It has been very nice. Thank you for the wine. I wish you well, Lieutenant, and I hope that your wife and the child to come will be in good health."

"You are very kind. Very kind indeed," he said as he helped pull her chair out. "Not all have greeted us so well."

"It's a difficult time for us here, Lieutenant. I'm sure you understand."

"I know. But France will be much better under German rule." He bowed stiffly and turned away. He began shouting commands and the soldiers quickly piled into the waiting trucks. When Lieutenant Kaltenbach got in beside his driver, he turned and looked at Jolie. He saluted her, and then the trucks moved out.

As Jolie watched them go, she was thinking, *He's so nice, so polite. He doesn't seem like a monster at all. I don't understand the German people.* She quickly walked out of town toward the place where she had left the others.

When she got back, she found that Tyler was anxious.

"You took a long time," he said. "What kept you?"

"I see you've started a fire. Let me warm up some of this milk for Marie and you can see what I've brought for all of you."

Tyler looked in the sack to find the fresh bread, cheese, and fruit and pulled out some of it and handed it to Rochelle to start cutting it up for their supper. He watched Jolie as she heated the milk and fixed a bottle for the baby. "You're very good with children, Jolie, but then you've had lots of practice."

"Yes, I have. It will come in handy when I have my own children, I suppose. Say, speaking of children, where are the others?"

"I told them they could go exploring if they stayed together and didn't go very far. They're right over there," he said, pointing.

She shaded her eyes and looked. "Okay, as long as we

can see them." She handed Marie to Rochelle and then turned back to Tyler. "The news isn't good. The Germans are overrunning our country faster than anyone could suppose. A convoy of German soldiers arrived when I was in town."

"Yes, I saw them along the road. They gave me a scare. I'm glad we were well off the road and out of sight."

"A young officer stopped me. He couldn't have been more than twenty-one or twenty-two, I'd guess."

"Did he harm you?" Tyler demanded.

"Oh no. He wanted me to have a drink with him, and I couldn't see any way to get out of it, so we sat down at a table outside a café."

"What did he say?"

"He was very charming, actually. Spoke French perfectly, and he's a painter like you."

"Is that what you talked about?"

"He tried to flirt with me, but when I noticed his wedding ring, he actually blushed. He has a wife and a child on the way and was quite ashamed of himself. He told me so."

Tyler wanted to hear the whole story. When she told it, he finally said, "He doesn't sound like a typical Nazi."

"You know, he really didn't. He was very nice. If I had met him out of uniform, I would never have suspected what he was." Her mind went back to the encounter, and her eyes reflected her thoughts. She looked down for a moment, then lifted her eyes to his. "He was a gentleman . . . not what I expected of a Nazi."

"They say even Hitler loves dogs, so I guess everybody has something good about them."

"I'll never understand the Germans, Tyler. Their race has produced some of the greatest artists and scientists and philosophers in the world, yet they brought one terrible war into the world and now they're beginning another. It's like they're two different breeds: the war makers and those men like Lieutenant Kaltenbach."

The two spoke for a time of the war, then Tyler said, "Someday this war will be over, but I think it'll last for a long time." He suddenly grinned and reached out to touch her cheek. "I'm not surprised the man flirted with you."

Jolie was aware of the warmth of his hand on her cheek. She wondered at her response, then drew back, saying hastily, "I'd better get started on supper. These children are always hungry."

CHAPTER FOURTEEN

ANTOINE

★ ★ ★

Although Jolie had made it her business to see that they stayed on the back roads as much as possible, they still encountered scattered traffic. Most of the refugees fleeing from Paris used the main roads, but those who knew the countryside better took the less traveled ones. Every day they saw German planes, and twice they encountered men who had seen the Germans in force moving southward.

They made little time and were anxious to be off the roads completely and concealed well before dark. Their food supply was adequate, and they stopped at farms occasionally to buy eggs and vegetables. Once Tyler mentioned that it might be possible that one of the farmers would betray them, but Jolie did not think it was likely. "They hate the Germans so much they wouldn't betray their own people."

"Most of them would not, but there are Nazi sympathizers in France, and you can't always know them."

"I suppose so—but I hate to think of that."

★ ★ ★

By the time they got to Chartres, their routine was well established. By this time the young people had become more accustomed to the dangers and hardships than the adults. While Jolie and Tyler were scanning the area and even the skies almost constantly, Rochelle, Damien, and Yolande seemed to be totally unaware of the dangers that could lie just around the turn in the road.

The day after they passed by Chartres, Rochelle and Damien were walking alongside the wagon. Rochelle looked at Crazy and said, "That horse is the funniest-looking thing I've ever seen. He's ridiculous, that one!"

"He doesn't even look like a horse, does he?" Damien agreed. "He looks like the quilt that Tyler said he reminded him of."

"But I sure am glad we have him. We'd have a hard time carrying all of our things."

The two walked on, and Damien picked up a rock and threw it at a rabbit that darted across the road. "I wish I could have hit him," he said. "We could have made a stew out of him. That would have tasted good. Maybe I'll see another one."

"Don't be silly, Damien. You couldn't hit a rabbit with a rock. Nobody could."

"I bet I could if he was close enough," he argued.

"You think you can do anything, and furthermore, you'd argue with a tree."

"Argue with a tree? Why would I want to do that?" He picked up another rock. "Girls say the silliest things."

The two wandered along, and finally Damien gave up throwing stones long enough to say, "When we get to America, I'm gonna become a race car driver."

"A race car driver? Why, you've never even seen a race."

"I don't have to see one. I know what they're like. You

get in a car, and you go around in circles, and the one that comes in first wins. I know I can do it, and that's what I'm going to be."

Rochelle smiled, for she was becoming accustomed to the boy's fantasies. "I know what I'm going to do when we get there. I'm going to go to college and become a doctor like Mademoiselle Vernay."

"You mean and cut people open and things like that? I wouldn't want to do that!"

"There's more to it than cutting people open, but I'd like to be able to help people. I talked to Jolie about it, and she said she'd help me."

The two continued to walk along sharing their dreams for a new world, but then Rochelle fell silent. She said nothing for so long that Damien finally gave her a curious look and asked, "What's the matter with you?"

"You're not going to become a race car driver and I'm not going to become a doctor. It's all nice to think about, but none of it's going to happen."

"Sure it will!"

"No it won't. Things won't turn out right. They never do."

Damien stared at her with disbelief. "I don't know why you have to talk like that. It'll turn out fine. We'll have Monsieur Winslow and Mademoiselle Vernay to look after us."

"She's not going to America, silly. Didn't you hear what she said? She's just going as far as the coast."

"Well, anyhow, Monsieur Winslow said he would give us to an orphanage."

"And you know what will happen? If we get adopted at all, it'll be to three different families. We'll lose each other."

Damien lifted his chin. "No, God's going to make it come out all right."

"He won't. I prayed to God," Rochelle muttered, "but my mother died, and then I prayed again, and my father died too. I'm not sure I believe in God anymore."

"Why, you gotta believe in God, Rochelle!"

"I'm just not so sure."

Damien was shocked by her statement and said no more, but he kept casting sidelong glances at her. Rochelle paid him no attention. She kept her head down now, paying no heed to the countryside or the clouds, and finally Damien muttered, "Well, I believe in God, and nothin's gonna change my mind! And you better think so too!"

★ ★ ★

They moved steadily ahead all day, and early in the afternoon they stopped just outside of a small village that Jolie identified as Bernay. As was now their routine, Damien and Rochelle gathered firewood, and Tyler made the fire while Jolie searched through their stores and made up a stew using a live chicken she had bought from a farmer that morning. She'd had to wring the chicken's neck, and Yolande had watched with wide eyes.

"I don't like to see that. Do you have to do that?" she asked.

"Yes, if you want anything to eat."

"We could eat bread, couldn't we? You wouldn't have to kill anything for that."

Tyler, who had been observing this, laughed. "I can see you're going to be a vegetarian."

"No, I'm going to be an American. That's not the same thing, is it?"

"Not always," Tyler said with a grin.

Once the chicken was plucked and cut up and cooked with the vegetables, Yolande lost some of her squeamishness, deciding that chicken stew smelled awfully good to her. After they'd all had their fill, they sat around the fire talking, and then Yolande asked if Jolie would tell her a story. Jolie read a story about Moses from her Bible, and then she asked Rochelle to read from her Hebrew Bible.

"I don't want to," Rochelle said.

"She doesn't believe in God anymore," Damien piped up. "I told her that was dumb."

At once Jolie went over and sat down beside Rochelle. "What's the matter, Rochelle?"

"If God wanted to, He could have made my mama and my papa live, but He didn't."

"That doesn't mean He didn't love them."

"How could He love them if He let them die?"

"It's hard for healthy people to understand that sometimes living is worse than dying."

"I don't believe that."

"I know you don't now, but you will when you're a little older. When I worked in the hospital I saw some people who had a lot of pain. They couldn't wait to get rid of it and go home to be with the Lord. It was a blessing for them to go."

"But my mama and papa weren't sick."

"No, but God knows what's ahead, and He might have looked ahead and seen that something very difficult was ahead of them, so He didn't want them to go through that."

Tyler was only half listening when he thought he saw something move in a nearby bush. At first he assumed it was a squirrel, but he grew curious when he saw the movement again. He very quietly crept, inches at a time, closer to the bushes. Then with a sudden burst of speed he made a dive. He heard Jolie cry out but paid no heed.

Jolie leaped to her feet, calling, "Children, get back here!" and gathered those she could reach close to her.

But Damien did not obey. He ran to the bush but quickly stopped when Tyler emerged holding a boy tightly by the arm.

"Let me go!" the boy cried in French.

Tyler kept a firm grip on him. "Come over to the fire and let us get a look at you."

"I wasn't doin' nothing to you!"

Everyone was standing now, and they came over to look at the boy. He was thin but rather tall and had a mop of black hair and dark eyes. His clothes were ragged, and he stared around defiantly but said nothing.

"What were you doing?" Tyler asked. "Were you spying on us?"

Jolie moved closer. "You don't have to be afraid. What's your name?"

The boy looked at her sullenly and then muttered, "Antoine Carrière."

"Why didn't you let us know you were there? Are you hungry?" she asked.

The boy named Antoine simply stared without speaking.

"We've got plenty to eat. Here. Turn him loose, Tyler. Rochelle, get Antoine a bowl for some stew."

The boy's eyes darted from person to person. When Tyler released him, however, he made no attempt to run away.

Damien approached the boy. "My name's Damien, and this is Rochelle and that's Yolande. We're orphans."

"I ain't no orphan," the boy said.

"Where is your family, son?" Tyler asked.

"They're in England."

Rochelle handed him a bowl of stew and a chunk of bread. "Here, Antoine, you can have this."

He took the bowl and bread, but he looked doubtful and suspicious.

"Come on and sit down," Rochelle said.

The boy finally sat down and began to eat ravenously.

"You don't have to choke yourself," Rochelle told him. "You can have some more."

The only sound was the crackling of the fire and the tree leaves rustling overhead in the breeze. Antoine ate two bowls of the stew and then begrudgingly said, "That was good."

"Why are you all alone, Antoine?" Jolie asked gently. "How old are you? Where are your parents?" She could hardly stop the questions from coming.

"I'm thirteen. My ma and pa went to England two months ago and left me with my uncle and aunt. My ma's parents live in London, and we're gonna move there. They wanted to go alone first so they could find a place to live. They was gonna come back and get me, but then the war got worse."

Jolie waited for him to say more, and when he did not, she said, "What about your uncle and aunt?"

"They're dead." Anger flared in his dark eyes. "The Germans killed them."

"Oh, Antoine, I'm so sorry," Jolie said.

"When did this happen, son?" Tyler asked.

"A week ago. I saw the Germans coming, and I hid. They said my aunt and uncle were spies, and they shot them just like they were dogs or something."

Jolie felt a great pity for the boy. "I'm so sorry, Antoine."

"I stayed after the Germans left. They didn't even bury them," he said bitterly. "I dug the graves and buried them myself." He looked up then, anger in his eyes. "But I'll get them! I'm gonna kill as many Germans as I can!"

"I wouldn't worry about that right now," Tyler said quietly. "What do your parents do?"

"My dad's a blacksmith. We're gypsies."

"Really?" Rochelle said. "I never knew a real gypsy."

"Well, you know one now."

"Why don't you stay here with us tonight," Jolie said. "Then you can decide where you want to go tomorrow morning."

"I know where I'm going. I'm going to England to find my ma and pa, but I'll stay here tonight, I guess."

"That's where we're going too," Rochelle exclaimed. "You can come with us."

"Wait just a minute, Rochelle," Tyler said. "I'm afraid I've got my hands full with the four of you."

The boy had looked hopeful for a moment, but now he looked at the ground.

"We're all tired," Jolie said. "Let's get settled in for the night and we can discuss this tomorrow." Jolie found a blanket for Antoine and he went off a short distance away from the rest of the group and quickly went to sleep.

The children were too excited to sleep, but they did get settled in the wagon and then stayed awake whispering for a long time. Tyler and Jolie stayed by the fire, discussing Antoine as they poked at the fire with long sticks. Before long Damien climbed out of the wagon and approached the two.

"We've got to take Antoine with us. We're going to England anyway. It wouldn't hurt for him to join us."

"We can't do that," Tyler said.

"Why not?"

"We can't be responsible for him."

"You're responsible for me, and for Rochelle and Yolande—and for Marie too."

"Go to sleep, Damien," Jolie said.

"It wouldn't hurt anything," Damien argued, but grumbling as he went, he returned to the wagon.

"I just don't think it would be a good idea for us to take the boy with us," Tyler said.

"Everything's so hard," Jolie said. "It was hard enough before, and now this comes up."

Tyler was surprised. She was usually so upbeat that it was odd to hear her sounding defeated. "Well, we'll see tomorrow. I'm going to go to sleep. You'd better see if you can get some sleep yourself. You look tired."

"I guess we're all tired. Not as tired as we will be, though. We still have a ways to go. Good night, Tyler."

Tyler watched as she picked a grassy spot and rolled up in her blanket. He continued poking idly at the fire, thinking about Antoine's predicament. Finally he sighed deeply and tried to get comfortable on the ground. It wasn't easy to calm his thoughts, though, and it was a long while before he dropped off into a fitful sleep.

★ ★ ★

By the time breakfast was prepared and consumed the next morning, Damien, Rochelle, and Yolande had all made a plea to take Antoine along with them. Antoine himself said nothing but watched carefully. Finally it was Jolie who called Tyler aside and said, "What do you think? Have you changed your mind?"

"I feel sorry for the boy, but we've got too much on our plate."

Jolie bit her lip, then said, "Whatever you think, Tyler."

Tyler turned and walked over to where Antoine was standing. He saw that the boy was looking at him with anxiety and knew that he wasn't going to take it well. "Son, I'm sorry, but we just can't take you with us."

"Why not? I won't be any trouble."

Tyler saw that there was no way to reason with the boy, so he said firmly, "It sounds hard to you maybe, but I just can't take on the responsibility of another child. I'm sorry."

At once Rochelle said, "Please, Monsieur Winslow— let him go!"

Damien added, "He won't be any trouble. Please let him go with us!"

"There's no use arguing," Tyler said. "It's going to be hard enough without taking someone else. You can stay with us today, Antoine, but you can't go with us all the way to the coast."

Antoine's face reddened but he said nothing. Tyler saw that the other youngsters were looking at him with expressions that left no doubt as to their feelings. "Come on, let's get going," he said roughly.

★ ★ ★

Antoine did not speak to Tyler or Jolie all day, and that evening he suddenly trotted down the road and then disappeared in the distance.

"He's a strange boy, isn't he?"

"Yes, he is. Have you ever known a gypsy before?"

"No. I've seen them, of course, but I've never known any personally. Have you?"

"No. They've got a pretty bad reputation."

"Hitler hates them. He's had them killed in every country he's taken over, along with Jews and others."

They continued in silence for a good distance.

"We're going to have to stop soon for the night," Tyler said. "I don't know where that boy has gotten to. Maybe he's decided he doesn't want to go with us after all."

But this proved not to be the case, for not ten minutes after they had stopped, Damien cried out, "Look, here comes Antoine!"

"What's that he's got in his hand?" Jolie asked, shading her eyes against the setting sun.

"It's chickens," Damien said. "He's got two chickens."

They watched as Antoine approached carrying a dead chicken in each hand. "I brought supper," he said tonelessly.

"Where'd you get those chickens, Antoine?" Rochelle asked.

"From a farm."

"Did you buy them?" she asked.

"Buy 'em? No. I just took 'em."

"Why, that's stealing!" Rochelle exclaimed.

"If they don't keep their chickens locked up better, they don't deserve to keep 'em."

"Next time, Antoine," Jolie said quickly, "we'll buy the chickens, as well as any other supplies."

"But that would be silly. They were right there and nobody was looking."

"I don't think now's the time to discuss ethics with Antoine," Tyler said. "Let's get these chickens dressed. We got anything to fry them in?"

"Fry chickens? We don't fry chickens," Jolie said.

"We do in America. If we have some grease, I'll show you what good fried chicken tastes like."

★ ★ ★

The fried-chicken cook leaned back, nibbling on one of the drumsticks. "Not as good as Aunt Maude used to make, but not bad, considering what we had to work with. Wish I could have made some biscuits to go with the chicken."

"It was good," Jolie agreed. "Where'd you learn to cook?"

"Oh, I don't know. I'm not really a cook," Tyler said. "I think I just watched my mom cook and some of my aunts. Men don't cook much in America."

"They do in France. Some of the best cooks are men," Jolie said, then gave him a sharp look. "You're not one of those men who are afraid to do women's work, are you?"

"Why, you just saw me cook, didn't you? Of course I'm not afraid of women's work."

Rochelle had been sitting beside Antoine during the meal, and they had been sharing a quiet conversation.

"Tell me what it's like to be a Jew, Rochelle," Antoine asked as he licked his fingers, one after the other.

She laughed aloud. "That's a hard question to answer. What's it like to be a gypsy?"

"It's pretty bad sometimes."

"Why is it bad?"

"Well, people think we're thieves."

Rochelle giggled. "Aren't you?"

Antoine looked at her with disgust. "Stealing two little chickens does not make me a thief. People think we steal horses or anything that's not tied down. That's not so. Like I told you before, my pa's a blacksmith. He works for a living. He wants me to be one too, but I'm not gonna be a blacksmith when I grow up."

"What are you going to be?"

"I've got something on my mind, but I'm not telling anybody about it."

"I do too," Rochelle said, "but I won't tell you what it is if you won't tell me."

Antoine grinned. "I'll bet I find out what you're going to be before you find out what I'm going to be."

"I'm gonna be a race car driver," Damien said as he joined the conversation. "It's not a secret either. I don't care who knows it."

Jolie was enjoying watching the young people talk, and finally she said, "What'll we have tonight, a song or a story?"

"Let's have a story," Damien said.

"No, I want a song," Yolande said. She loved music and could never get enough of the songs that Jolie sang for them.

"How about if we have both," Jolie suggested. Without waiting for an answer, she starting singing an old French folk song, and when she was done she said, "All right, it's your turn to tell a story, Tyler."

"All right. I'll tell you about the time I had a run-in with a lion in Colorado."

"There aren't any lions in America. They're all in Africa."

"That's not exactly right, Jolie. There are mountain lions out west in America. They're not as big as the kind in Africa, but they could make a good meal of you, I suppose." He plunged into the tale of how he had gone hiking with a friend in Colorado during a school vacation and ended up killing a mountain lion when it had cornered his friend.

The children listened in amazement as he built up the suspense in his story.

When he was through, Jolie said, "That was quite a story. Now let's read an incredible story from the Bible." She pulled her Bible out and read the story from the Old Testament of the three young Hebrew men who chose to be thrown into the fiery furnace rather than obey Nebuchadnezzar.

After she finished the story, Antoine asked, "Is that true or just made up?"

"Why, it's in the Bible," Damien said. "Of course it's true. You ought to know that."

"You mean they got thrown into a furnace and they didn't burn up?" Antoine was incredulous. "Why not?"

"Because God kept them from burning up," Jolie said.

Antoine fell silent as he considered this. "I don't know why the Germans want to kill all the gypsies and all the Jews. What's the matter with those Germans?"

"It's not all of them," Jolie said quietly. "There are many good Christian Germans, but they got the wrong man in as leader. And the Germans have a bad habit of listening to strong men no matter who they are."

"Do the Germans kill Jews and gypsies in America, Monsieur Winslow?" Rochelle asked.

"No, they don't, and they know better than to try it. Why, we wouldn't put up with it for a minute!"

"Why don't you stop 'em from doing it in France?" Antoine demanded.

"I think it's going to come to that, Antoine. Americans are a bit slow to get started, but we'll be in this war before long, and I think that'll be what puts an end to Hitler's madness."

Yolande said, "I want another song."

"You always want another song," Jolie said. "Come along. Get in your blanket, and then I'll sing you a song."

"Bedtime for everybody," Tyler said. "We've got to get an early start in the morning."

"I want to go with you," Antoine said suddenly. "I can get food for us and keep a look out for the Nazis."

"We settled that earlier, Antoine," Tyler said gently. "We just can't take you."

Antoine glared at him, then turned away and stood stiffly staring into the darkness. Rochelle went to him and said something, but he didn't answer.

"Everyone get to bed," Tyler said. He wished the boy had kept going when he had left earlier that day, and he could see trouble ahead. Tyler ignored the protests of the youngsters, and soon they were all in their usual sleeping places.

After Jolie had given Marie a bottle and rocked her to sleep, she came to sit beside him. "Are we going to make it, Tyler?"

"Why, of course we are!" Tyler looked at her, noting the fatigue in her features. He was a little shocked, for it was the first sign of weakness he'd seen in her. "You're just tired, but you'll feel better tomorrow."

"I hope so. But it all seems so impossible."

"Nothing's impossible with God." He smiled. "That was what my folks said over and over. I guess it didn't mean much to me then, but it does now." He ran his hand through his hair, then added, "Funny how things like that stick with you. I find myself wishing I'd been a better son—like my brother."

"It's never too late to start. Maybe the purpose of this whole ordeal is to give you a new start."

"I suppose that's possible. But what a way to get a new start!"

Jolie picked a leaf off the ground and slowly began

tearing it apart. "I . . . I'm glad you're here, Tyler. It would be hard to be alone."

"Two are better than one. The Bible says that, I think." She didn't answer and he asked, "Are you sleepy?"

"No, not a bit."

"Come on. I'll make some coffee and tell you the story of my life."

Jolie smiled at him and took a deep breath. "All right, then if we're not sleepy yet I'll tell you all my adventures too."

Long after the children were asleep, they sat beside the fire talking in hushed voices. Jolie had been worried, but Tyler had a way of telling stories that was amusing, and she started feeling better.

"Thanks for the stories, Tyler. For some reason I'm a little more hopeful about the outcome of this whole affair now." She stood up. "Good night. Next time I'll cheer you up."

Tyler watched as she went to her blanket and rolled up in it. He looked into the fire for a long time before finally lying down, but he still couldn't sleep.

What in the world brought me to this place, he wondered. *I came to France to study art, not to get into a dangerous cross-country trek with a beautiful woman and several orphans.*

He tried to will himself to sleep but finally gave up. He opened his eyes and stared up at the stars. They spread across the sky like diamonds, and he thought of how much his father loved the stars. He had even made a primitive telescope, and Tyler remembered how the two of them had stayed up late many nights, looking at the sky. He could almost hear the sound of his father's voice naming off the stars.

Well, Dad, I wish we could do it again! The thought stayed with him, and he lay there naming the stars until he fell asleep.

CHAPTER FIFTEEN

"Get Off the Road!"

★ ★ ★

The tension in the group was even more pronounced the next morning as they all sat near the fire eating breakfast. Antoine did not speak a word but sullenly sat off to one side. When Rochelle said, "Come on, Antoine, and eat breakfast," he just glared at her.

"Don't be angry, Antoine," Jolie said. "It's just that—"

"Who needs you? I can get to England by myself." Before anyone could speak he stood up and ran away.

Rochelle called after him, "Come back, Antoine!"

He stopped and shouted back, "I hope the Nazis get you all!" before sprinting down the dirt road.

"I'm sorry he took it like that," Tyler said.

"I feel sorry for him," Yolande said.

"So do I, but we can't take everybody."

"He's not everybody," she said. "He's just one little boy."

Rochelle was looking at Jolie with a hardness in her face that Jolie had not seen. Rochelle burst out, "Would Jesus have done a thing like that?"

Jolie was completely silenced by the question. She

looked helplessly at Rochelle, who got up and walked away, her back stiff.

"Let's get everything packed up and get going," Tyler said hurriedly. It was a bad situation and he hated it. As he went to hitch up Crazy, Jolie approached him.

"I think we should have taken him, Tyler."

"I'm starting to feel the same way. Maybe we'll catch up with him on the road or maybe I should run ahead and catch him."

"No, don't do that. I don't want to be left alone with the children."

"I made a big mess out of the whole situation, Jolie. I'm an expert at doing things like that."

She gave him a sad smile and left him to hook up the wagon. When everybody was ready, he said, "Rochelle, why don't you drive for a while. I feel like walking."

Rochelle did not answer, but she got up on the seat and took the reins when he handed them to her. "Yolande, you get in with her," Jolie said. She lifted the girl up and then took the baby from Damien.

Rochelle had become a good driver, and she slapped the lines on Crazy's back. She sat stone-faced with her back straight as the horse stepped out.

"Are you mad at me, Rochelle?" Yolande asked.

"Why, of course I'm not mad at you. Why would you think that?"

"You look mad."

"That's because I think we should have taken Antoine with us to England."

"I think so too."

Usually as they walked along or rode in the wagon, there was a great deal of joking and laughing and talking. But it was very quiet this morning. The sun rose and began to heat the earth, and Jolie walked on the opposite side of the wagon from Tyler. She was occupied with the scene that had taken place during breakfast and had seldom felt as unhappy with her choice as she felt this day.

She went over and over it again and found no consolation in the way that it had turned out. More than once she looked ahead hopefully, willing Antoine to come back, but there was no sign of him.

In the middle of the morning the silence was suddenly broken by Damien, who shouted, "Look, there comes Antoine!"

"It is," Tyler said, "and he's running like the devil's after him." He ran ahead to meet the boy. Antoine's elbows were flailing, and he was gasping for breath. "What is it, son? What's wrong?"

"It's the Germans. They're coming. Get off the road!"

Tyler ran quickly back, grabbing Crazy's bridle and leading the startled horse off the road, urging him on. "Come on, Jolie," he shouted, "we've got to get out of sight."

Fortunately there was a copse of trees with thick underbrush nearby. They had barely managed to get everyone hidden before they heard the sound of the trucks coming. Tyler had a tight hold on the harness, but Jolie moved to the edge of the trees. "I can see them," she whispered. Yolande held on to Rochelle, who put her arms around her, and they all froze as they waited. The trucks roared by one after another, at least twenty of them.

They all remained where they were until the sound faded away. Tyler drew a deep breath. "Well, that was a close one." He turned to Antoine and saw that the boy looked terrified. "Thank you, Antoine. You saved our necks."

Jolie joined the two and put her arms around Antoine, hugging him hard. "I'm so proud of you, Antoine. That was a brave thing you did."

Damien was jumping up and down and pulling at Antoine. "You came back! I knew you would, and you kept those old Germans from getting us."

Rochelle crowded in close too and put her hand on

Antoine's shoulder. "Thank you for coming back and saving us, Antoine."

The boy was startled. He had regained his breath, but as they all continued to tell him how grateful they were, he didn't know what to think.

"We were all sorry you left feeling upset as you were," Jolie said, "and it was my fault. The children were right, and Monsieur Winslow and I were both wrong. We'd like very much if you'd go to England with us."

Antoine could not speak for a moment. He swallowed hard and muttered, "I guess it'd be all right."

"Good," Tyler said, coming over and slapping Antoine on the back. "You know, I think sometimes God works things out even when we make a mess of them. He makes things happen the way He wants them to happen even when we get in His way."

Antoine was looking at him with his head cocked to the side.

"I'm mighty glad you came back to pull us out of the fire."

"Come on, Antoine, you can drive Crazy," Rochelle said.

Tyler and Jolie watched as the youngsters all piled into the wagon, talking happily and laughing.

"I think this was a good thing, Jolie. I guess God pushed us around a bit to get us where He wanted us. Come on. Let's get on the way. We won't get to England standing here."

This time the two of them walked together as the wagon moved along. Tyler suddenly reached down and took her hand. She looked at him, startled, and said, "What are you doing?"

"Holding your hand."

"Why are you doing that?"

"I always do that when I walk with a pretty girl. I hold her hand and tell her how pretty she is. It's an old Winslow tradition." He grinned slyly and said, "We have a few more traditions about how to treat women. I'll be letting you in on them from time to time."

"I'm afraid you Winslow men are like all other men. Ready to take advantage of a young woman."

"We Winslows never take advantage of young women." He squeezed her hand, then lifted it to his lips and kissed it. "There, another Winslow tradition. Come on. I'll tell you more about this as we walk along."

CHAPTER SIXTEEN

STORIES OF AFRICA

★ ★ ★

All the next day Tyler was edgy. He spoke little but kept scanning the road, watching for another convoy. When they didn't see any Germans by late afternoon, his nerves started to grow calmer.

When he and Jolie decided they should stop for the night, he led the group to a grassy area near a tiny creek that trickled through the meadow. He unhitched Crazy from the wagon and tied him to a tree by the stream, even though there was little danger of a horse like Crazy running away.

The animal munched on the grass while Tyler watched, his thoughts going back, for the first time in several days, to Caroline. He had somehow managed to make a box and put the memory of her in it and keep it tightly closed. Now, however, as the twilight moved across the land, the sun easing down behind some high hills to the west, the memory escaped from the box.

From far off in the distance came the tinkling of some bells, probably tied to a farmer's goats or cows, as was often the practice in France. The tinkling made a comforting musical sound. He watched the horse send his long tongue into the stream. "I wish I didn't have any more worries than you do, old boy, but sooner or later I'm going to have to face the music with Caroline."

He had known for some time that there could never be anything between the two of them but didn't know how to tell her. He had been the one who had accepted her generous offer of paying his expenses in France. Before he left, she had spoken of his return and their future life together. Even though he had never thought they would have a future together, her offer seemed too good to pass up. Now as he sat in the grass, his legs crossed, he wondered why he had let himself get into such a frightful mess.

I'll have to write to her as soon as I get to England, or maybe even call her. But he knew what he had to say to her should not be said in a letter or over the phone. It would be hard enough to say it to her face, but he knew it had to be done.

"The kids are getting hungry. Do you want to eat soon?"

Tyler turned to see Jolie walking toward him. He did not get up, and as she came over and sat down, he said, "Is there enough food to put a meal together?"

"We've got enough to make some sandwiches. We'll have to try to find some more food tomorrow."

The two of them sat quietly watching the horse crop the tender green grass and listening to the tinkling of the bells in the distance.

"Those bells make me feel like I'm far from civilization. But I guess you know what it's like to live in the country. What was it like living in Africa?"

"Well, it was the only life I knew. Sometimes it wasn't easy."

"Did you live in a town?"

"We had a mission station, but we moved around a lot

to the tribes in the interior. Sometimes we lived right with the natives."

"That must have been exciting."

"It was pretty hard. When you're used to living in a progressive country, you have no idea what it's like to live without the modern conveniences. Out in the African jungle, they don't have any sewage, of course, and they never take baths. Until you get used to it, the smell is almost overwhelming."

"Tell me more."

Tyler found himself telling her about his life growing up in a way that he had seldom shared with anyone. *I never told Caroline much about my childhood,* he thought, *but then she never asked.*

"What about wild animals?" Jolie asked. "Wasn't it dangerous?"

"Yes, it was."

"Which animal were you most afraid of?"

"Well, the elephant, of course. They're amazingly quiet for such a huge animal, but there's no way to defend yourself if you upset one."

"Did you ever have a problem with one?"

"One time I was hunting wildebeest, and I was sitting very quietly waiting to get a shot. Suddenly I had a feeling something was behind me, even though I hadn't heard a sound. I turned around slowly, and there stood one of the biggest elephants I'd ever seen! He had his ears out, which they do when they're about to charge. There wasn't anyplace to hide, and I knew I couldn't outrun him. I was a dead man."

"What happened, Tyler?"

He grinned. "Why, he killed me."

"Oh, you fool!"

"I don't really know what happened. He was twitching and staring at me with his beady little eyes, and then another elephant called from off in the distance. The elephant just turned around and walked away."

"What did you do?"

"I nearly fainted when it all caught up with me. I was so weak I couldn't even move."

"So the elephant's the most dangerous beast?"

"I think leopards kill more people than any other animal. They'll come right into your house at night and take a child away."

"How terrible!"

"One almost got me once." He went ahead to tell the story, touching the scar on his forehead. "He left me this one big gash. If Dad hadn't shot him when he did, the animal would have killed me. I still remember it as if it happened yesterday. I guess you never forget a thing like that."

"Tell me about your family."

"Well, a distant relative of mine, Barney Winslow, is a missionary in Africa. He once killed a lion with his bare hands."

"How in the world did he do that?"

"I think it was a very old lion—maybe sick. Barney got around behind him. The lion clawed him pretty bad, but he got his arm around him and choked him to death. He was a very strong man. The Masai called him the Lion Killer after that."

"I can't imagine being that close to a lion!"

"I have all kinds of relatives who did crazy things. Barney's dad, Mark Winslow, was a gunman in the Wild West."

"Really? Did he shoot anybody?"

"I'm sure he did. He had a hand in bringing the first transcontinental railroad across the United States. He became very wealthy."

"What a wonderful family you have."

"Except for me. I'm the black sheep."

She reached over and squeezed his arm. "You're not that, Tyler. Look at what you're doing for these children."

Tyler was moody and feeling down. "Yes, and I had to

be backed into a corner before I would do it. No, I'm not much of a Winslow, Jolie."

"I think you are."

He put his hand over hers. "Well, that's nice of you to say. Maybe I'm a work in progress."

★ ★ ★

Antoine was relaxing in the grass by the stream when Rochelle came by, carrying a bucket. She suddenly let out a scream and dropped the bucket.

"What is it?" Antoine yelled.

"A snake—it's a snake!" she screeched as she jumped back.

Antoine got up to check it out. He reached down and picked the animal up, letting it squirm in his hand. "It doesn't have no poison," he said. "Look, it's just a grass snake."

But Rochelle was trembling all over. She sat down, pulled her knees up to her chin, and buried her face against them.

Antoine stared at her in disbelief. He stroked the snake and then walked several paces away before putting it in the bushes. He sat down beside Rochelle. "It's okay. It's gone now." When she did not respond, he reached over and put his arm around her. "Don't be afraid," Antoine said, squeezing her shoulder. "It wasn't gonna hurt you."

Her only response was sobs.

He let her cry for a minute and then said, "Look, everybody is afraid of something. My uncle Theo, I thought he was as brave as they come. He was a hero in the last war."

Rochelle stopped crying and looked at Antoine.

"He came back alive, but one hand got shot off in the war. We were out hunting once and a spider got on his other hand, and you know what? He fainted. Passed right out. Yes sir, and it wasn't even a bad spider, the kind that kills you. Just a tiny wood spider."

Rochelle wiped her tears with the back of her hand. "What are you afraid of?"

"Me? I don't know." He suddenly realized his hand was still around her shoulder and he removed it.

"You said everybody was afraid of something, so that means you're afraid of something."

Antoine hadn't known Rochelle very long, but he already trusted her enough to tell her something he'd never told anyone else. "Well, there's one thing I'm afraid of. I'm afraid I'll never really do anything."

"Do anything! What do you mean by that? Everybody does something."

"I mean I'm afraid I'll never do anything important. That I'll just live and die and that'll be the end of it."

"That's what everybody does."

"No it's not. Some men make a difference and some women do too. But if I do what I want to do, I'll make a difference."

"I'll tell you what I want to do if you'll tell me what you want to do."

They made a joke of refusing to tell the other their dreams, but now in the quiet of the evening as they sat close together, he said, "I'll tell you what. I want to do something that no gypsy I ever heard of has done. I want to be a doctor."

Rochelle sat up straighter and stared at him.

"What's the matter? Why you lookin' at me like that for? You wanted to know and I told you. I guess you think it's impossible for a gypsy to become a doctor."

"No I don't. You can do it if you want to."

"I don't know. I don't have much education. Just a little bit here and there, along with what my folks and my aunt and uncle taught me. Doctors have to go to school. I never heard of a gypsy that went to college and became a doctor."

"I bet you can do it, though."

"Well, okay I've told you. Now, what do you want to do? Ride a horse bareback in a circus?"

"No. I want to be a doctor."

"You're makin' fun of me."

"No I'm not. I've always wanted to be a doctor, and then when Mademoiselle Vernay came to help us at the orphanage, I asked her tons of questions about it. She says she'll help me."

"Wow! What a coincidence."

"I know. I've never met anyone else before who's wanted to become a doctor."

"Don't tell no one, though, Rochelle."

"Why not?"

"They'd make fun of me."

"No they wouldn't, but I won't tell. I'm sure you can do it, Antoine."

"It takes lots of money, and you have to have a good education. I don't have either one."

He saw Jolie approaching, calling, "Rochelle, what are you doing?"

"I'm sorry," she answered as she got up and retrieved the bucket. She dipped it into the stream. "I saw a snake and got all flustered and forgot what I was doing."

Jolie smiled and walked with the two of them back to the others.

When they got there, Damien demanded, "Why have you been gone so long?"

"We've just been talking," Rochelle told him.

"About what?"

"About grown-up things," she said. "You wouldn't understand."

"You ain't grown-up."

"I'm more grown-up than you are."

"What's she been telling you, Antoine?" Damien asked.

"Oh, nothing important." He winked at Rochelle, and the two smiled at each other.

CHAPTER SEVENTEEN

GERMANS!

★ ★ ★

"What town is that up ahead? Can you tell from the map, Jolie?"

Jolie was trying to walk and read the map at the same time. The wind fluttered it, and she stilled it. When it happened again, she stopped and laid the map flat on the ground and knelt down so she could lean over it. The wagon passed them as she traced her finger across the paper.

"I think that's Pont-l'Évêque up ahead, although I've never been on this road before."

"How far is that from Le Havre?" Tyler asked as he looked over her shoulder.

"It looks like maybe twenty kilometers."

Folding the map, Jolie stood up and watched as the wagon lumbered along, Crazy's multicolored hide catching the glints of the sun. "I think I'd like to go into town and get some more fresh fruit and cheese."

"I don't want you to run into any more German officers," Tyler said.

"I'll just have to be more careful to avoid them if I can.

We'd better hurry. We don't want the children to get too far ahead of us."

The two walked faster until they caught up with the wagon. Damien was driving, Rochelle was sitting on his left holding Marie, and Yolande was on his other side. Antoine was far ahead, his figure looking small in the distance.

"Antoine takes his duties as a scout seriously," Tyler remarked.

"Yes, he does. He's a good boy. I hope he'll be able to make something of himself someday."

"Well, when he gets with his parents he'll be all right." Tyler glanced over at Rochelle and saw her cuddling the baby. "Rochelle's got a strong mothering instinct. She holds that baby every chance she gets."

"I'm afraid it's going to be quite a jolt for her when they're separated."

Tyler did not argue, for he had already foreseen some problems. He knew the children thought they would be adopted by a single family, but he knew that was highly unlikely. Most families did not want to adopt two orphans, much less three.

"It's going to be hard to place those three, Jolie. I suppose it'll have to be a Jewish family."

Jolie had been thinking about that herself, and she trudged silently, contemplating the possibilities. She thought of her friends Jack and Irene Henderson and their big, mostly empty house in New York. How wonderful it would be if the children could end up in a home like theirs. "We'll just have to trust God, Tyler. We're doing the best we can."

"I don't think I'd like—"

"Look," Damien cried out. He was standing up and pointing. "Antoine is running. I bet he's seen some Germans."

"Quick, get the wagon off the road," Tyler directed.

He tried to grab Crazy's lines, but the horse must have

been spooked by all the sudden activity and reared up before surging forward. The jolt threw the children back, Yolande falling over backward with a cry. Tyler struggled to grab the lines, but Crazy seemed determined to run away. Tyler chased after the wagon and soon managed to grab hold of the lines up close to Crazy's jaw.

"Whoa there, Crazy," he said as he started to lead the horse off the road.

"It's the Nazis," Antoine cried as he got close.

Tyler looked ahead and saw an open car crest the hill and knew it was too late to hide. "Everybody take it easy."

Jolie was paralyzed by the sight. They were caught out in the open, and she watched helplessly as the black car slowed down. There were four soldiers in it, she saw, two privates in the front seat and two officers in the back. The car came to a stop next to the group, and the officers got out, the younger one pointing his Luger.

Jolie glanced at the children to make sure they were all right after almost being thrown out of the wagon, and she saw Rochelle pull Marie tight against her chest.

"Stop where you are," one of the men ordered in very bad French. "What's your name?" he asked Tyler.

Tyler and Jolie had discussed several days ago what they would do if they were caught. The only papers Tyler had were his own, which showed him to be an American citizen, so he spoke in English. "My name is Tyler Winslow."

"You are . . . an American?" the older officer asked with almost no accent.

"Yes."

"Your papers."

Tyler fumbled in his pocket and pulled out the papers. He wished ardently that he had Marvel's pistol in his pocket, but it was in the wagon.

The senior officer took the papers and studied them. "What are you doing in France, Mr. Winslow?"

"I am a painter. I came to France to study art."

"I am Major Hermann Dietrich. This is Lieutenant Werner Braun." Dietrich looked down at the papers again and at the rest of the group. "This is your family?"

"No, we're not related," Jolie said. "My name is Jolie Vernay, and my home is here in France. In Ambert."

"And these are your children?"

"They are orphans, Major," Jolie said. "I was a physician at the orphanage in our village."

"They're obviously lying, Major Dietrich," the lieutenant said. There was a hardness in him and a chill in his blue eyes.

"They probably are."

"I'm an American citizen," Tyler insisted. "All I'm trying to do is get back to America."

The man studied Tyler critically and then turned his attention to the children. "We must take them in for questioning," he told the lieutenant. "I do not like this."

"Yes, Major," Lieutenant Braun agreed. "But how will we arrange it?"

"I will leave you here, along with Krupke. The driver and I will go on ahead. There are trucks at our rendezvous up ahead. I will send one of them back for you and the prisoners."

Braun laughed. "Perhaps they will try to escape."

"Now, Werner, none of your tricks." Dietrich smiled and then turned to speak to Krupke, barking a crisp order. The soldier got out of the car carrying a rifle.

"It should not be too long, nephew," Dietrich said to the lieutenant.

The major turned to leave but then stopped abruptly. "Why did you leave Ambert with these children?"

"The orphanage is closing," Jolie said, thinking fast, "so we are trying to find homes for all the children. We're taking this group to stay with a relative."

"What relative is this?"

Jolie made up a name. "Their uncle, Philippe Cordon, and his wife."

"Where does he live?"

"On the coast in the village of Fécamp."

"That will be easy enough to check." He holstered his pistol. "Watch them carefully, Lieutenant."

"Yes, Major Dietrich."

Dietrich got into the car and snapped an order, and the car pulled away at once.

The lieutenant looked over at the soldier and winked. "Keep your rifle ready, Hans. You may need it. They look like dangerous characters to me. Maybe spies."

The soldier, a heavyset man with a broad, brutal face, grinned. "*Ja*, Lieutenant Braun. I wish they would try it."

Braun walked up to the wagon and said, "What is your name?" speaking to Rochelle.

"Rochelle."

"Rochelle what?"

"Rochelle Cohen."

"Cohen." Braun stared at her and lost his smile. "You are a Jew?"

She shot an agonizing glance at Jolie, and when Rochelle did not answer, Braun grabbed her arm. "Answer me. Are you a Jew?"

"Yes," Rochelle cried. She was still holding the baby, and Braun kept his grip. "Are the rest of you Jews too? Speak up, boy!"

"Yes, I'm a Jew," Damien said defiantly.

"So you are taking Jews to a place of safety," he accused.

Braun released Rochelle and went to stand in front of Jolie. "What did you say your name was? It's Cohen, I believe."

"No, my name is Jolie Vernay, as my papers will prove."

"Well, if you're a physician, I must say you're a pretty one. But I do not believe anything you French say."

He grabbed Jolie's dress and pulled her away from the group. "You come with me. We know how to treat you French girls."

She cried out and tried to hold her dress together, but Braun only laughed.

When the lieutenant saw Tyler start to run after him, he waved his gun and said, "Shoot the man if he moves again, Private."

"Yes, Lieutenant."

Jolie tried to fight him, but the German was many times stronger than she was.

Tyler threw himself at the lieutenant but wasn't prepared for the force of the butt of the rifle in his back. He fell to the ground, face in the dirt, choking for breath.

He heard the private laughing, and when he caught his breath, he saw Jolie being dragged by the powerful lieutenant straight toward the trees. Tyler sprang to his feet and grabbed at the soldier's rifle, yanking it from the man's hands.

Taken off guard, the private yelled, "Lieutenant!"

Tyler whirled and leveled the rifle, but even as he did he saw that Lieutenant Braun's Luger was pointed in his direction. Tyler dove to the ground and immediately heard the bullet strike the German private. The man uttered a single coughing moan as he fell to the ground next to Tyler.

Tyler scrambled onto his knees and took aim at the lieutenant, but Jolie was in the way. "Get out of the way, Jolie!" he shrieked.

As she threw herself to the ground and rolled away from the German, Tyler wasted no time pulling the trigger. He heard the explosion and felt the recoil of the rifle, but at almost the same time felt a horrible pain in his forehead and fell to the grass.

Jolie saw the lieutenant fly onto his back, his arms flailing, and cried "Tyler!" as she saw him fall as well.

"Stay here," Rochelle told the younger children, who

had crouched down in the wagon when bullets had started flying. Marie was screaming at the top of her lungs. Rochelle and Antoine ran quickly to where Tyler lay still.

"He's dead!" Antoine whispered.

Jolie ran to join them, panic filling her, and knelt beside him. She put her ear to Tyler's mouth and was relieved to feel hot breath and see his chest rise and fall. "No, he's alive," she breathed.

"He's hurt pretty bad, isn't he?" Antoine asked.

Jolie gently wiped the blood from Tyler's forehead so she could examine his wound. "He's a very lucky man. It looks like the bullet just grazed him. Still, he's going to need stitches to stop the bleeding."

"What will we do?" Rochelle asked.

"First of all, we need to try to stop this bleeding. Do either of you have a clean handkerchief?"

Rochelle pulled one from the pocket of her dress.

Jolie showed Antoine how to hold it gently but firmly to Tyler's forehead.

"They'll be coming back," Antoine said. "If we don't get away quickly, they'll shoot us all."

Jolie was trying to think. She got up and walked over to Private Krupke. She knelt down and probed for his pulse but shook her head when she felt nothing. She repeated the procedure with the other German. *The major called him "nephew." That's strange that two family members would be working together.*

Her mind was swimming as she returned to Tyler's side. She checked his wound again. "He may be unconscious for a long time. It's hard to tell."

"We can't stay here," Antoine said urgently.

"I know. We've got to leave right away."

"Right now!" Antoine insisted.

"I know we must hurry, but I don't know what to do." She looked up and said, "We must pray to God for guidance."

Antoine stared at her. "I don't believe in God."

"I do," Yolande said.

Rochelle summoned a smile, although she knew her hands were unsteady and her heart was beating fast. "I do too," she said.

Damien beamed a huge smile at her. "You do, Rochelle?" he asked.

"I do now," she affirmed.

"Damien, will you pray with me?" Jolie asked.

He nodded his head.

"And you, Rochelle?"

She nodded her head also.

"All right. Let's pray." The three children dropped to their knees around Jolie as she bowed her head and began to pray aloud. "Lord, we are helpless, but you can do all things. I ask that you help us find our way out of this frightening situation. Give us the wisdom to do the right thing, and deliver us from this evil! We pray in Jesus' name. Amen."

She opened her eyes. "Now," she said firmly, "we will believe and trust in God, our Deliverer!"

CHAPTER EIGHTEEN

A PLACE TO HIDE

★ ★ ★

Jolie's heart had been filled with doubts and her mind had been swept with confusing thoughts. But as she prayed, an inexplicable peace had come over her. "We have to get Tyler into the wagon and leave at once," she told the children.

"Yes, that is what we've gotta do," Antoine agreed. He ran over and untied Crazy and then led the horse, still pulling the wagon, back until the rear of the wagon was even with the wounded man. "He's a big man. I don't know if we can lift him."

"Together we can," Damien said. "I'll help and you too, Rochelle. Give the baby to Yolande."

Jolie directed them all to positions around Tyler, with Rochelle and Damien on his legs and Antoine with Jolie on his upper body. "Be very careful to keep him level and not bump him into the wagon. I don't want to make his head wound any worse."

The four of them leaned over and Jolie said, "When I say go, everyone lift. Are you ready?" She waited for their assent, then took a deep breath. "All right—go!"

Jolie had not realized how hard it would be to lift an inert man. But somehow they managed to get his upper body onto the wagon, and then she quickly went around to help the two younger children push Tyler's legs into the wagon. He uttered a grunt during the shift and then grew still again.

"Quick, let's go!" she cried. She was troubled at the sight of Tyler's pale face, but there was no time to do anything else. "Everyone into the wagon."

"But where'll we go?" Antoine asked. "The truck might be back any minute. The soldiers will find us."

"We have to hide someplace very quickly." A plan leaped into her mind. "They'll be expecting us to head for the coast, but we won't. We'll go back from the direction we just came, toward the south."

"But we might run into other Germans," Rochelle said faintly. "What will we do then?"

"If we hear any vehicles coming, we'll pull off and hide until they pass us, and we'll stay there until dark."

"They'll be searching everywhere for us," Antoine said.

"I know, but God will help us."

Expecting every moment to see German vehicles coming down the road, Jolie drove Crazy with all the speed she could get out of him.

As she drove, she kept turning around to check on Tyler. After they had gone a couple kilometers, she pulled over to the side and jumped into the back. "Rochelle, we need to use a couple of those blankets for Tyler. Can you move off them for a minute?"

Rochelle, with the baby on her lap, had found the stack of blankets made a comfortable seat. Jolie grabbed two of them and quickly arranged them under and around Tyler's head to protect him from the constant motion.

"Even with this extra cushioning, I'm a little worried about jolting Tyler around like this. The next time we see a place to hide, I'm going to take it."

About a half hour later, Antoine said, "Look, there's a house over there. See that little road that leads to it?"

"We'll take that." Jolie turned Crazy down the lane. Darkness was falling, for which she was thankful, but she knew they couldn't assume these people would help them. There were Nazi sympathizers in France, she knew that much. Not many, but it only took one.

"What if they won't help us?" Rochelle asked, fear in her voice.

"I think we have to take our chances."

"What if they won't hide us?"

"Then we'll keep going."

"If the Germans stop here, they might betray us," Antoine said.

"We have to trust them," Jolie insisted.

As they got closer, they could see a man was sitting on a chair leaning back against the house. There was a barn behind the house, and over to the right a field where sheep were grazing in the gathering darkness. It was a peaceful, idyllic-looking place, but there was nothing peaceful in Jolie's spirit, for she knew they were in a desperate situation.

The man stood up and watched the wagon approach, and Jolie told the group, "None of you say a word, you understand? Let me do the talking."

She pulled up in front of the house, and the man came slowly toward them. He had a pipe in his mouth and wore the roughest of clothing, including an old hat that had seen much bad weather.

Even before Jolie could speak, a woman came out of the house wiping her hands on her apron. A younger woman followed her out of the house.

"*Bonsoir*," she greeted. "Who are you? What are you doing here this time of the day?"

"My name is Jolie Vernay," she said. "My friend and I are trying to get these children away from the Nazis.

They caught us and my friend was shot. We need a place
to hide." She saw shock run across the man's face and she
prepared herself to hear a rejection.

"He was shot?" the man asked. He came forward and
looked over the edge of the wagon. "Is he dead?"

"No. I'm a doctor, and I can treat his wound, but the
Germans will come looking for us."

"How did you get away from them?"

"We had to kill one of 'em," Antoine said importantly.
"The other one was already dead—his friend shot him by
mistake."

Jolie wished that Antoine had obeyed her order to
keep silent, but then she thought, *It might be just as well to
tell the whole truth.* "These children are from an orphanage
in Ambert. If the Germans catch them, their lives will be
in danger. Will you help us in the name of God?"

The younger woman came over to the wagon and
peered at the children huddled on the seat and in the
back, taking in each face methodically. The attractive
woman was in her late twenties or early thirties, Jolie
thought.

She turned and said to the older couple, "We must
take them in."

The two had a quick conversation and then the man
nodded. "We will help you all we can, but you realize
this is a dangerous situation, don't you? For all of us."

"I'm very sorry to put you in this situation. You
understand if the Germans find us and know you've
helped us, they will execute you. They will have no
mercy on you." She watched their faces and saw no fear
in them.

"The filthy Boche will do anything," the man said. "I
fought them in the last war, and I will fight them again.
If they come for you, we will tell them nothing."

The young woman appeared to be thinking hard. "We
must take them to the old house."

"Yes, Annette," the man said at once. "That is good.

You will have to hide the wagon too."

"Where is the old house?" Jolie asked.

"We used to live in another house about half a kilometer back there," the young woman said as she pointed. "We built the new house closer to the road."

"I can't even see the other one," Jolie commented. "It sounds perfect."

"Yes, the area is overgrown now. No one would think to go back there. The roof leaks, but it's sound enough. I don't think the Germans will go that far into the woods."

"Quickly," the young woman said. "We must go."

Without another word, she headed off behind the house. The older woman called out as Jolie urged the horse after her. "We will bring you something to eat and our first-aid supplies for the sick man."

"Merci, madame," Jolie cried out.

As the wagon caught up to the woman who was striding quickly through the pasture, she turned to Jolie and said, "By the way, my name is Annette Fortier."

"And my name is Jolie Vernay. We are so grateful to you and your family."

Yolande was bouncing as the wagon ran over the uneven ground, but she cried triumphantly to Antoine, who was holding her to keep her from falling out, "Didn't I tell you that if we prayed, God would help us?"

He grunted but made no other comment.

Nature had definitely taken its course on the land between the new house and the old house. Weeds had grown knee-high, and bushes and saplings had taken over much of the land. As the wagon bumped over the little-used lane, Jolie again worried about Tyler's head bumping but hoped the blankets would give it adequate protection.

The small house was nearly hidden by brush and dwarfed by two huge trees in front of it. Jolie pulled the wagon as close as she could to the door and then called Crazy to a stop.

Annette opened the door and put a brick in front of it to hold it open. Jolie instructed the children to take all the food and blankets into the house and then to return to help with Tyler. The children quickly tumbled from the wagon, their arms full of supplies.

Rochelle left Marie inside the house with Yolande and then the older children helped Jolie and Annette carry Tyler inside. Carrying him was much easier this time, with two adults helping.

"I will hide the wagon deep in the woods and tie the horse out there as well," Annette told Jolie after they had Tyler settled on a bed.

"Why are you helping us like this, Madame Fortier?" Jolie asked.

"My husband was trapped on the beach at Dunkirk and escaped on an English ship. The Germans are evil. I know that much. My husband will fight wherever he can until this country is free of the filthy Germans!" She took a deep breath and looked at all the children, who were peering at her. "I won't be long. Do you have milk for the little one?"

"Only a little."

"I'll bring some when I come back."

"Will the Germans find us here?" Yolande asked as Annette left.

"No, God has brought us this far. He won't abandon us."

★　★　★

Tyler groaned at the pain in his head. He felt buried in blackness, as if he were wrapped in a huge black bunting of wool.

Gradually the darkness lifted, and he felt hands touching his head. He tried to push away whoever was hurting him, and his hand struck something soft.

"Be still, Tyler. You're all right."

Consciousness came rushing back, and when Tyler opened his eyes, he saw Jolie's face above him. An oil lamp threw a yellow corona of light over her, giving her hair a reddish glow. She was looking at him strangely, her lips soft and maternal.

"You're all right," she said. "You were shot, but it's not serious. I had to put a couple of stitches in."

Tyler tried to remember what had happened and suddenly he did. He tried to sit up, but Jolie put her hand on his chest and held him down. "Don't try to move. You'll feel better if you lie still."

"The Germans. What—"

"They were both killed. The lieutenant's first shot hit the soldier, and then your shot killed the lieutenant. But his bullet grazed your head."

Suddenly Damien's face appeared to Tyler's left. "Does it hurt? Did you know the Germans are both dead and we're hiding in this house because Madame Fortier says it's all right?"

"Hush, Damien," Jolie said with some irritation. "Go to bed as I told you."

"I'm not sleepy."

"Then get sleepy."

Damien went away grumbling and intimidated by the determined set of Jolie's features. "They've all been terribly worried about you," Jolie told Tyler.

"Where is this place?"

"It belongs to a family named Fortier—an older couple and their daughter-in-law."

"But how did we get here?"

"We put you in the wagon and hauled you here. We knew the Germans would expect us to go north, so we came back south."

"Jolie, they'll be searching every house in the vicinity."

"I know, but we traveled a pretty good distance before

we stopped here, and this house is completely hidden from the road. The Fortier family has another house closer to the road. That's where they live. If the Nazis quiz them, they'll tell the Germans that nobody has passed by this way."

"What about Crazy and the wagon?"

"They're well hidden. Don't be concerned."

A movement across the room caught Tyler's eye. A woman was standing across the room by a fireplace, apparently cooking something. She now brought a bowl over and said, "You must eat. This will be good for you."

"I must thank you, madam, for your kindness."

He felt dizzy as Jolie gently helped him to a partially upright position and then put her arm around his shoulders. "Perhaps you could feed him, Annette, while I hold him."

"I feel like a stupid baby!" he muttered. "I never did like to have to be taken care of."

"It will teach you humility," Annette said, and a trace of a smile touched her broad lips. "Some Americans can use a little extra humility."

Yolande appeared at Tyler's side, her face troubled. "Oh, you're awake. I was afraid for you."

"I'm all right. Don't worry. I'll be as good as new first thing you know."

"Could I lie on the bed beside you?"

"Sure you can. It's a big bed." Tyler tried to be patient while the woman fed him the soup, but he felt a weariness creeping in on him. "My head's swimming, and . . . I seem to see two of you." He blinked and the illusion didn't go away, which was a bit frightening. "I hope this isn't going to be permanent."

"You probably have a concussion, Tyler. You have to rest and be very still. Now, let me help you lie down."

Tyler lay back, his head pounding, and closed his eyes. Yolande moved in closer and he clasped her small hand in his.

"Maybe I can pray for you to be well," the little girl said. "We prayed for God to bring us somewhere where the Germans wouldn't catch us, and He did."

"I think that would be very good, Yolande."

Tyler lay very still and listened to the small voice as the child prayed the simplest kind of prayer for him. But as she was praying, extreme fatigue came over him and a warm blanket of darkness enveloped him.

PART FOUR

July 1940

★ ★ ★

CHAPTER NINETEEN

House-to-House Search

★ ★ ★

Lieutenant Bernard Scharmann felt the perspiration coating his forehead but did not dare move. He held his hands down at his sides, his back straight as a ramrod, as he stood in front of Major Hermann Dietrich. He had served under the major long enough to recognize the danger signals, and he was well aware of the dangers that beset him now. He would not be the first aide that Major Dietrich had demoted back to the rank of private and thrown into an infantry spearhead division, where the odds of death were all too good.

The two were standing in the library of a local pastor whose house they had commandeered as a temporary headquarters. The walls were lined with shelves containing books of all sorts, some of them very old, some new, some paperbacks and others exquisitely bound in expensive leather. Sunshine poured in through a window to Lieutenant Scharmann's right, illuminating the face of Major Dietrich and emphasizing the flush that discolored his cheeks.

From outside drifted in the noise of vehicles roaring

by—motorcycles, trucks, and staff cars—and overhead the hum of aircraft scored the heavens. Desperately Scharmann racked his brain trying to think of some way to pacify Dietrich, but absolutely nothing came to him.

Ever since the death of Lieutenant Werner Braun, Dietrich's nephew and the pride of his life, it seemed to Lieutenant Scharmann that Dietrich had stepped out of rationality and reason into mindless rage. Lieutenant Scharmann had been present when the news of the death had arrived, and it had seemed as if all other rational and reasonable powers of thinking had left Dietrich, and he had thrown himself into a tornado of activity. He seemingly had forgotten his duties of sweeping across France to nail down the critical checkpoints and had given up sleep in a furious search of the countryside for the murderers of his nephew.

"Why are you just standing there, Lieutenant? Do I have to do everything myself?" A vein throbbed in Major Dietrich's forehead—a certain sign Lieutenant Scharmann had learned to recognize. When that vein throbbed, Dietrich was capable of any sort of violence.

"Sir, I'm sending more men out to search for these murderers, but it is—"

"Why do you not go yourself? Our men need a good officer, and somehow, Lieutenant, I think you are not the one. Perhaps you would serve more efficiently as a private!"

Scharmann felt beads of perspiration coalescing and running down his face. He had long known that there was no way to argue with Major Dietrich when he was in this mood. Everything he might say would be seized upon and used as another opportunity for provocation. It was best to remain silent, and he did so by holding himself rigid while Dietrich marched back and forth, his legs moving stiffly as if he were a robot.

"Look at this area, Scharmann," the major said as he pointed to the map on the wall. "It's a small area. We have enough men to search every house and every business. Did you order them to look in the cellars and in the attics?"

"Yes, sir, I did. I followed your orders explicitly, passing them on to the men. They all understand how important this is, and—"

"They understand nothing! They are stupid and will do anything to get out of performing their duties." Dietrich banged the map with his fist. "If you do not find these people within twenty-four hours, you will regret it, Lieutenant."

"I will go at once to talk to those making the search. I will make the matter plain to them!"

"You may threaten them in my name. If they do not find these dogs, they will all suffer for it!" Major Dietrich glared at the pale-faced officer and snapped, "Make it plain!"

"I will tell them, sir." Scharmann saluted, but Major Dietrich gave him a withering look of disdain. Wheeling, Scharmann left the room, and as soon as he had closed the door behind him, he pulled off his hat, fished in his pocket for a handkerchief, and with an unsteady hand wiped the perspiration from his face. Under his breath, he cursed the fate that had brought him under the authority of a man like Hermann Dietrich. He remembered sourly how happy he had been when he was appointed to this position, for serving as Dietrich's aide was an almost certain route to promotion. Now, however, he would have changed places with almost anyone in the Third Reich.

He's gone crazy! He doesn't care about the war and doing his duty for the fatherland. All he wants to do is find these people. And Braun was never such a great a man either. He was spoiled rotten and a poor soldier, but nevertheless he was Dietrich's nephew, and if we don't find his murderer, we may all wind up being shot.

★ ★ ★

Sergeant Franz Holbein pulled a bottle from his hip pocket, unscrewed the cap, and lifted the bottle to his lips. His throat worked like a snake swallowing a frog, or so it seemed to Adolf Müller, who watched with a sour expression. "Save some of that for me," he complained as the other drank.

The two were marching along, rifles slung over their shoulders by the straps. Holbein handed him the bottle. "Don't drink it all. That's all I've got. And there's no telling when we'll be able to get our hands on more of it."

Müller took a long drink and gasped as the fiery liquid hit his stomach. "That's good stuff." He burped heartily. "These Frenchmen keep some pretty good wine— even peasants. Maybe we'll liberate some of it, eh, Sergeant?"

"If we don't find this American that killed the major's nephew, we'll be needing more than liquor to keep us going. You heard what the lieutenant said."

They had been searching all day long, and now the sun was starting to go down and the heat seemed to be passing away from the earth. Both of them were weary of the search and longed to get back to their regular duties.

"We can't search behind every bush and every tree," Müller complained.

"Why don't you go explain that to the major?" Holbein said bitterly. "Lieutenant Scharmann bawled us all out like we were the enemy." He let out a string of curses. "What do they expect us to do? We need to be conquering France, not looking for a bunch of kids and some American. Sometimes I think Major Dietrich has lost his mind!" He kicked viciously at an empty bottle, sending it rolling off the road and into the bushes.

"I think they must have gotten away. These people hate us. You can see it in their faces."

"I wouldn't doubt it. Did you expect them to love us?"

"It wouldn't be too hard to hide a wagon and a horse with all the trees around here, and if they split those kids up, they'll disappear like a puff of smoke."

The two men trudged steadily on until they came upon a lane that led to a small house. "We'll search this house and then we'll take a rest," Holbein said.

"Keep your eye open for some of that wine—maybe something even stronger."

The two men stepped up to the cottage, and Sergeant Holbein beat on the door with his fist. "Open up in there," he yelled loudly. "Come out!"

The door opened and the man said, "Yes. What can I do for you?"

"You can get out of the way. We're searching your house." Holbein shoved his way in, closely followed by Adolf Müller. Two women were inside—a middle-aged woman standing beside the stove stirring something in a pot, and a younger woman who was watching him steadily.

"We're soldiers of the Third Reich, and we're searching for a man and a woman with some children. Have you seen them?"

Holbein saw the man glance over toward the woman. "There's been nobody like that come by here today."

"Müller, search the house while I interrogate these people. Look in the attic and in the cellar, if there is one." He winked and added with a crude grin, "And keep your eyes open."

Sergeant Müller grinned. Keeping his rifle at the ready, he moved out of the main room of the house, which consisted mostly of a cooking and a dining area. He went past the dining table and down the hall.

Meanwhile, Sergeant Holbein peppered the family with questions. "What is your name, old man?"

"Henri Fortier. This is my wife, Bertha."

"And who are you?" Holbein asked the younger

woman. He moved closer to her.

"Annette Fortier."

"You are their daughter, then?"

"My husband is their son."

"Where is he?"

"He is in the army."

"The French army, I assume."

"Yes, Sergeant."

"You understand the penalty for concealing fugitives?"

"We have concealed no one."

"If we find any evidence that you are lying, you will all be shot."

"I have not seen the people you speak of." She kept her eyes fixed on him. "Who are they?"

"Three of the children are Jewish. The man is an American. You could not mistake him. The woman, they say, is French."

Annette Fortier's expression did not change. "We have not seen anybody like that. It would be impossible for them to pass without our notice."

"I know that." He stepped closer and put his hand on her arm. "A woman must get lonely without her husband," he said as he lifted his hand and held her chin. "Maybe we will come back after we find these people. Would you like that?" He grinned at her.

"No."

There was a coolness in the woman's eyes, and all the frustration that had built up in Sergeant Holbein seemed to explode. He slapped her face with his open hand and saw that her expression did not change.

"Stupid pig!" he shouted.

Müller reentered the room, a bottle of wine in each hand. "They're not in the house," he declared, "but they've got a good wine cellar."

Holbein was exhausted and his anger at the woman faded as he contemplated, with a great deal of concern, having to face his superiors. He turned again to Henri Fortier and said, "Don't forget that your women will be shot, as will you, if we find out you are hiding these people."

"There's no one here. You're welcome to look all you please," the farmer said as he shrugged.

Holbein cursed them all and then walked out the door, followed by Müller. As soon as they were outside, he said, "Give me one of those bottles."

"Sure, here you go."

Holbein took a corkscrew from his pocket and opened the bottle, then handed the tool to his partner. When the two men had drunk deeply, Holbein said, "It's going to be dark soon. We'll try to get to one more house. This motley group can't have gone far with all those children in tow."

"Pretty good-looking wench, that younger one back at the farm." He tilted the bottle and took a long drink. "Maybe I'll come back and visit her."

"Keep your mind on your business, Müller. If we don't find these people, both of us will wind up being cannon fodder in a frontline division."

". . . and they threatened to come back," Annette said. "We may have to find another place to hide you. It won't be safe for you to stay here. I thought they would have given up by this time."

"No, we'll have to get away," Jolie said. She was seated at the kitchen table across from Tyler. Jolie was thrilled at Tyler's quick recovery. He still had a slight headache and the wound itself was tender, but he was feeling much more like himself already. He wore a bandage around his head, and Jolie thought with a chill that if the bullet had gone directly into his skull he would probably be dead.

Annette had come to the old house to deliver the news about the two German soldiers searching for them.

"Did they have good descriptions of us?" Jolie asked.

"They knew you were an American, monsieur, and they knew that three of the children were Jewish. They described your group well enough that anyone would recognize you from it."

"It's a miracle they didn't come back into the woods," Jolie said. "That would have been the end of us."

"They'll probably do that sooner or later," Tyler said. "They know we couldn't have gotten far. They're searching the houses now, but I'm afraid when they don't find us, they'll bring as many men as they can spare and look behind every tree." He touched his wounded head. "I'm well enough to make a move now—and we've got to do it."

Annette Fortier did not understand the American man's part in this at all, but after spending a little time with Jolie Vernay, she understood how attached the woman had become to the children while working at the orphanage. She was holding the baby, Marie, and looking down at her face. The baby suddenly smiled, and Annette remembered someone saying that babies this young couldn't really smile but probably just had gas. She smoothed Marie's fine, soft hair with her fingertips as Tyler and Jolie wrestled with the problem before them. She had cared for the baby almost constantly since the two had come.

"I must proceed with my original plan to go into Honfleur and find my friend Jean Clermont," Jolie was saying. "It's our only hope. That was my plan from the first. The only problem is that I don't know where he lives. I only know the name of the town."

"If you get on the road with these children, they'll pick you up at once," Annette said quickly.

"No, I will have to go alone to find my friend."

"I don't see how that can work," Annette said slowly. "It would be too dangerous."

"Why?" Jolie asked.

"You do not know the back roads, and if you stay on the main roads, you will certainly be picked up and taken in for questioning, anyone fitting the description as closely as you do."

"But I've got to get to Honfleur!" Jolie said. "Jean is the only one who can help us."

"Then I will go with you. We'll take your horse and go together."

Jolie looked up with a slight shock. "But, Annette, you know how dangerous it is."

"Just being alive is dangerous in these times." She smoothed Marie's hair and rocked her gently. She was holding the baby as if she were a priceless treasure.

"I don't think you should go, Annette," Jolie said. "It's not your problem."

"Your problem has somehow become my problem. I will go with you, but you must disguise yourself."

"I could do that, I suppose."

"My parents live in Deauville. It's a very small village only two or three kilometers from Honfleur. Everybody knows everybody in those two villages." She shrugged. "If your friend lives in Honfleur, my parents will know him or at least know somebody who knows him."

"I'd feel better if you didn't go alone, Jolie," Tyler said quickly. "Annette is right."

"But what about Marie?"

"It won't take you too long, will it? Rochelle and I can take care of Marie."

Jolie hesitated but saw no other way. "All right," she said. "We need to go as soon as possible."

"Yes. We should go tonight," Annette said. "The Germans won't be familiar with the back roads that we'll take, so we should be all right."

"I'm ready," Jolie said and got to her feet.

Annette looked down at Marie again, kissed the top of her head, and came over to hand her to Tyler. "You take good care of her until we get back."

"I'll do my best. And you take good care of my favorite doctor there."

"If God wills, we will be back very soon. But first I need to go to the other house and get a few things. I also need to let my husband's parents know that I will be gone for a time."

★ ★ ★

Jolie slipped the ragged dress over her head and looked down at the rough shoes that Annette had provided. They were worn, and Annette had already removed the laces that had originally come with them and tied them together with pieces of string. Jolie reached up and touched her hair, which was now stiff with dirt.

"Hold still," Annette said as she spread some dirt on her face. "There. That looks better. Pull this hat down over your ears."

Jolie put on the floppy hat. "How do I look?"

"A lot better, but remember you're a half-wit. If anybody stops us, don't talk at all. Just slobber, I suppose. Make sounds as if you want to speak but can't. Keep your eyes down. Don't even look at them. I know it'll be humiliating, but this is dangerous. If we make one mistake, that would do it."

"What about my papers?"

"If anyone asks for them, I'll give them mine. I'll ask you for yours, but you'll moan and cry and say you lost them."

"I think this will work, Annette." Jolie put her hand on the other woman's arm. "Why are you doing this for us?"

"For two reasons. One, I hate the Germans, and two, I think God wants me to help you escape."

"You're a good woman. I hope all goes well with your husband and that he will be back with you very soon."

She leaned toward the mirror and smudged some of the dirt on her chin. "Have you been married long?"

"For four years." Annette hesitated and then said, "I come from a large family. All I ever wanted was to have a husband and my own children about me."

"I'm sure that will happen very soon," Jolie smiled. She knew she looked grotesque with her dirty face and stringy hair, but she was sure Annette would understand her sincerity anyway. "You will have your own family someday, and it won't be long."

"I'm not so sure. God has not given us a child yet." She shrugged her shoulders, and the two went into the main room to join the others.

"What happened, mademoiselle?" Damien asked. "You look awful."

"It's just part of my disguise, Damien." Jolie grinned at him. "Rochelle, you take very good care of little Marie."

Rochelle looked down at the baby in her arms. "I wish you didn't have to go. I'm afraid for you."

"I'll be all right." Jolie kissed Rochelle on both cheeks and passed her hand over the baby's head, holding it on her forehead for a moment. "I'm so glad she's doing well, but it's so important that she stay healthy. I pray that God will keep her from any sickness until we reach England." Jolie was well aware that a baby's constitution is delicate, and being exposed to the elements as they were day by day, she could only pray that Marie would remain healthy for the rest of their travels.

"Let me go with you," Antoine said quickly, his eyes bright. "Maybe I can help."

"No, they'll be looking for young people. It's something we need to do alone. You stay and help take care of the children." She hugged him and then kissed him on both cheeks, laughing at his shocked expression. "I hope you don't mind the hug too much. I've grown rather fond of you."

Antoine cleared his throat. "It's all right. I didn't mind."

Jolie knelt down beside Yolande. "Are you going to be a good girl?"

"Oui."

Tears were forming in the girl's eyes. "Why, you shouldn't be crying."

"I'm afraid."

"Afraid of what?"

"Afraid you won't come back."

"Oh, I'll come back," Jolie said with more confidence than she felt. "And then when I come back, you'll go on a ship, and it will take you far away from here, where you'll be safe."

"All right," Yolande said, but her lips were quivering. "You help Rochelle take care of Marie."

"I will."

"And be sure Damien behaves himself."

"I always behave myself," he said indignantly. "You know that, I hope!"

Jolie kissed the girl and put her hand on her head as she stood up.

"Damien, I was just teasing," Jolie said. "I expect you to take care of things while I'm gone."

"You won't be too long, will you?"

"We'll be back as quick as we can." She kissed him as well. "Now, you all be good children."

Tyler walked the two women outside, but Annette quickly went back inside to retrieve the coat they had forgotten. It was meant to be part of Jolie's disguise.

As soon as she disappeared, Tyler said, "I wish you didn't have to do this."

"It'll be all right."

"You take care of yourself, now," he said. She saw that he was nervous.

"If I don't make it, I know you will take the children to safety."

Tyler reached out and took her hand. He lifted it to his lips and kissed it and then imprisoned it in both of his. "I guess this is no time to mention it," he said slowly in a voice that seemed tight and strained, "but I love you, Jolie."

She could not speak. She knew that her own heart was somehow tied up with this man who had come into her life so abruptly, but something seemed to turn over inside her heart. She freed her hand and put it on his cheek. "You're not the man you were when you first came to France." She put her arms around his neck and pulled his head down. She put her lips against his and held him tightly. When she pulled away, she said, "We will talk when I come back."

Annette came out of the house holding a coat. She glanced at the two and grinned. "Put this on, Jolie."

She put it on and followed Annette out into the darkness.

Tyler watched them until they disappeared. He felt something touch his leg, and he looked down to see Yolande standing there. He reached down and picked her up.

"I'm afraid," she whispered.

"You mustn't be afraid."

"Will God bring her back?"

Tyler peered into the darkness and knew that he was asking that same question in his own heart. "Yes, Yolande. He will."

He could feel the tension in her body. She was so small and fragile that he thought he could feel the beat of her heart. "You mustn't be afraid," he whispered again.

"But what if they don't come back?"

"They will come back. Jesus will help them."

"Do you think so—really?"

"Yes, I do," Tyler said and as he spoke, he found that he believed what he was saying. "Yes, Yolande, Jesus will bring them back to us!"

CHAPTER TWENTY

JEAN CLERMONT

★ ★ ★

A thin line of light appeared in the east announcing the coming of the morning. Annette and Jolie had ridden together on Crazy throughout the night, but they could not go quickly in the darkness. Also Annette, being the tougher of the two, soon noted that Jolie was not used to riding, and they had stopped for a rest every two hours.

An hour before sunrise, Annette had said, "This road bears off to the west and will not get us to Deauville. We will have to get back on the main road, but we're not far now. We'll be there soon. And so far we've not seen any Germans."

The earth was awakening now from the night's sleep as the trio trudged along. A small symphony came from overhead as a flight of birds flew over. Jolie looked up and saw them outlined against the sky. They seemed almost like a band of pilgrims headed for a happy shore somewhere in the distance. *I wish I were as certain that all of us would find our way as those little birds seem to be, but then birds don't have as many worries as people do.*

A light rain had fallen some time shortly after midnight, and now the smell of the moist earth rose like incense, thick and sweet-smelling but at the same time musty. In order to rest the horse, the two women were walking now, leading the horse by the reins. The dust of the road underfoot had been settled by the light rain and now was only slightly mushy.

The oversized shoes that Jolie wore were uncomfortable. She had put on heavy socks but still could feel a blister forming on her left heel. There was nothing she could do about it, so she did not mention it to Annette.

"How long is it that you have known Monsieur Winslow?" Annette asked.

"Not very long. I met him when I was studying in America, and not long ago he came to our village."

"He came all the way from America just to see you? That's unusual."

"He's a painter, and he wanted to study art in Paris. When that didn't turn out exactly the way he'd planned, he decided to go farther south and do some painting in the mountains." Even as she spoke, Jolie knew she was not telling the complete truth. For some time now she had been aware that Tyler had indeed come to see her. She saw that Annette was puzzled by all this, but she didn't want to make the effort to make it clear to the woman.

"He is not like I thought Americans would be."

"How did you think they would be, Annette?"

"Oh . . . loud, boastful, selfish."

"Some of them are."

"But he's not. He's risking his life for those children. It's not what I expected."

"But you're doing the same thing, Annette," Jolie responded. "I think we find goodness in people if we look for it."

"That is true. It is also true," she said with a sharp, bitter tone, "that we find evil in some people whether we look for it or not."

"That's the way it has always been. And most of us are not all evil or all holy."

Annette laughed. "That is what my husband always used to tell me."

"What is his name?"

"Alain. He always used to say, 'You want everything to be black and white, but life is not like that. There are many shades of gray in between.'" She laughed. "Then he would grab me and say, 'I'll leave it up to you to tell me what shade of gray I am right now!'"

Jolie laughed. "I think that's sweet. I know you miss him very much. It must be so hard to have him so far away."

"I do miss him. I didn't ever expect to have a good husband for some reason, but he came along and surprised me. I think about him all the time."

"I'll be glad when this horrible war is over and he comes back to you. Then you can get on with your lives."

"That will be a long time, I think."

Jolie had exactly the same feeling.

As the women came to the crest of a hill, Annette whispered urgently, "Quick, we must hide. There are soldiers ahead!"

Jolie had also seen the truck that was pulled over to the side of the road, and she immediately recognized that the soldiers were German. "It's too late," she said. "They've seen us. Look."

One of the men was pointing up at the two women and shouting something to the other soldiers. "It's too late to run," Annette said quietly. "Don't forget you're a half-wit. Don't say anything at all—just act your part. We'll get through this all right."

Jolie wished that she had as much hope as Annette, but as the soldiers approached them, she let her shoulders slump and tried to put an idiotic expression on her face. The best she could do was to stand there slack-jawed and roll her eyes from time to time. She looked down and saw that her hands did not fit the part. Her face was smeared and begrimed and her hair stiff with dirt, but her hands were clean. She was wearing a long sweater that was too big for her, and now she pulled the sleeves down so that only the tips of her fingers showed. She quickly put her fingertips in her mouth and reached over to smear them with dirt. Before the soldiers were halfway up the hill, she settled into a round-shouldered posture.

"Who are you? Where are you going?"

The sergeant who came up to them was a massive man with blunt features and fingers like sausages. He held a rifle in his hands, but the other four soldiers who were with him were watching with what looked more like curiosity than anything. They all looked weary and bored with their work.

"I am Annette Fortier, sir. This is my sister Alice."

"Let me see your papers."

Annette took a pouch out of the saddlebag and retrieved her papers.

"Where do you live?" he asked after he had studied them. "Close by here?"

"On a farm near Pont-l'Évêque, sir."

"And your papers," he said to Jolie.

Jolie knew that if she did not perform well, all would be lost. She made a gurgling sound with her throat and rolled her eyes and then let her jaw sag loosely. She even allowed a little saliva to roll down her chin.

"What's wrong with her?" the soldier demanded. "Give me your papers, woman!"

"She . . . she has never been quite right," Annette said quickly. "Let me talk to her." She bent her head down so she could look up into Jolie's face. "Alice, give me your papers." She began to search Jolie's pockets, complaining loudly.

Jolie began to fumble at the sack that Annette was carrying. She continued making the gurgling sounds in her throat and then somehow managed a creaky giggle that sounded insane even to her!

"What's she doing?"

"She always wants sweets." Annette reached into her bag and got an apple. "Give me your papers, and you can have the apple."

Jolie tried to reach for the apple, and when Annette held it back, she began to sob. "Apple," she said in a creaky voice.

"Give me your papers."

Annette continued to ask, and finally she gave Jolie the apple. Jolie ate it with great gusto while Annette continued to look through her pockets. "Where are your papers, you fool?" Annette searched her thoroughly and then turned to the sergeant and said bitterly, "She's put them somewhere. I should have known better than to let her carry them."

The soldiers were watching the whole scene with some amusement. Jolie continued to smack and chew and swallow the apple, holding it with both hands, making as much noise as possible. When the officer stepped forward, she cried out and held the apple in a protective position.

The man spoke to the others in German. They responded by shaking their heads and snickering. Then in rough French he said, "All right. Get on your way."

With a voice filled with disgust, the sergeant threw Annette's papers back at her.

"Quick, get on the horse," Annette said. She helped Jolie get on and then leaped up behind her. She kicked Crazy in the side, and the animal ambled on.

They went past the truck full of soldiers, and not until they were a hundred meters down the road did Jolie start to relax. Her muscles were so tense she felt as if she had been holding some huge weight at bay, barely keeping it from crushing her. "I thought we were gone that time."

"So did I, but the good Lord was with us."

"Can't we go faster?"

"That would look suspicious, but Deauville isn't far now. We'll be there soon." Annette suddenly laughed. "You did well. I think you've missed your calling. You should have been an actress rather than a doctor."

Jolie smiled and shook her head. "I hope I don't have to do that again."

★　★　★

"Sergeant Dent is back with his squad, Major."

Major Dietrich looked up expectantly at Lieutenant Scharmann. "Well, what did he report? Don't just stand there, man!"

"No success, I'm afraid, sir, but—"

"No success? Is that all I can get out of you?"

"We're trying to cover a big territory, sir. I'm sure the men are doing the best they can. "

"The best they can! These people can't have vanished into thin air. They've got to be *somewhere*." He waited for an answer. "Well, what did they see?"

"Nothing, sir, worth reporting."

"I'll decide what is worth reporting! What did he say?"

Scharmann looked over the paper and read off a list that the sergeant had given him. He ended by saying, "That's all, sir, except a pair of peasant women."

"Peasant women? Where were they from?"

"From Pont-l'Évêque, at least one of them. The other looked like she was retarded. She had lost her papers."

Major Dietrich stared hard at Scharmann. The air was still, and from outside there was a sound of a radio playing somewhere. "I will talk with the sergeant."

"Yes, sir." Scharmann was glad he was not the source of the look of lethal fury on the major's face. That had come to be his almost normal expression. Scharmann followed the major out of his office and said, "There he is over there. I told them they could get some sleep. They were out nearly all night."

Ignoring Scharmann's comment, Major Dietrich walked over. The sergeant had his back to the two officers, but when Dietrich's voice rang out, "Sergeant!" he moved very quickly.

Whirling, his eyes flew open, and he came to attention and saluted. "Sir!" he said.

Dietrich gave him a parody of a salute, then said, "Tell me about these two women the lieutenant tells me you saw."

"The two women?"

"Do you have a hearing problem, Sergeant?"

"Oh no, sir. Well, they were just two poor women, you know. You see them on the road all the time."

"What did they look like?"

"One of them was larger than the other, not a bad-looking woman. But the idiot was disgusting."

"Tell me what she looked like."

"Why, she wore old clothes that were too big for her—her sleeves came down over her hands just like that. Her face was smeared with dirt."

"Did she say anything?"

"I don't think she could talk, Major. She just gurgled, sort of, you know, like an animal."

"But she had no papers."

Dent shook his head. "No, sir. The other woman said she had let her carry them and she lost them."

"What else can you tell me about her?"

"Well, she was all dirty; her clothes were filthy. She had on a pair of old men's shoes."

"How old was she?"

"At first I thought she was older, but then I watched her eat an apple. You know how old women's hands are. Well, this one's hands were smooth and strong looking." The sergeant grinned. "If the rest of her looked as good as her hands, I might have been interested."

"I'm not interested in your foolishness! Is that all?"

"That's all."

Dietrich turned away in disgust.

"The old horse they rode looked as bad as they did," the sergeant added as an afterthought.

Instantly Dietrich whirled. "Horse? What about a horse?" He stared at the man with a hard look in his eyes.

"They were riding an old horse—a one-eyed horse."

Scharmann was suddenly aware that Dietrich had frozen. Something in the sergeant's words had kept him absolutely still.

"What color was the horse?" Dietrich asked, his tone clipped and without expression.

"Well, that's the odd thing, sir. It was every color I could think of, you know, sort of mixed-up, like you see cats sometimes. We used to call them calico cats. Why, this horse was red and brown and he had some white—"

"Idiot! Idiot!" Dietrich screamed. The sergeant took a step backward. "Sir—" he began to plead, but the major cut him off.

"That's the woman! She's the one we've been looking for!"

"She was just a retarded girl."

"A retarded girl with beautiful hands? Didn't you have sense enough to know that she was in disguise? I want her found!" Dietrich turned and shouted at Scharmann, who leaped with shock at the intensity of the major's voice. "She's headed for the coast, Lieutenant. She's looking for a boat. That's obvious. How many towns are there up ahead—towns on the coast, I mean?"

"Sir, there's Honfleur, Trouville, Deauville . . . hmm . . . and Villerville. That's about all that are close."

"Those murderers are headed for one of those fishing towns! I want to throw a cordon around them so tight they can't possibly get through. They're probably already there by now. How far were you from the coast when you stopped them, Sergeant?"

"No more than a few kilometers."

"They're probably already there, then, but they won't get away. We've got them in a trap. Now, pull every available man and begin to search the area—houses, businesses, streets, alleys. . . . I want those people found!"

★ ★ ★

Annette's parents, Robert and Élise Séverin, were surprised to see Annette. But that was nothing compared to their shock when she introduced them to Jolie. They were polite enough, but Annette said quickly, "We need to get inside. Something very bad is happening."

The Séverins let the two women into their home, which was simply a cottage built on the outskirts of the small village. The village itself contained no more than a hundred houses, all old and weathered, with one main street.

After the women were seated on the couch, across the tiny living room from Annette's parents, Annette quickly explained the situation and then let Jolie continue.

"A childhood friend of mine moved with his family from my village, Ambert, to Honfleur. I used to hear from him now and then, but I haven't heard from him in several years and have lost track of his address."

"What is his name, mademoiselle?" Monsieur Séverin asked. He was a short man with gray hair and blue eyes.

"His name is Jean Clermont. He's a fisherman."

"Oh, Jean! Yes, we know him well!" Madame Séverin exclaimed.

"Yes indeed. He lives alone in a small house that he bought perhaps three years ago. You remember, Maman, from the old butcher. What was his name?"

"That doesn't matter, Papa," Annette said quickly. "We must find him."

"Annette, you know the old house where the carpenter Monsieur Moreau lived?"

"Yes. I remember it."

"That's where Jean lives."

"I must go to him at once," Jolie said. "He's our only hope. Tell me where the house is."

"He may be out fishing right now," Annette's mother said.

"Not with weather like this," Monsieur Séverin said. "There's quite a wind out there. Jean would have better sense than to go out in it."

"I'll take you to his place," Annette said as she stood. "Come. We don't have time to dawdle."

Her parents got up as well, and Annette embraced each of them. "We'll probably come back here after we've spoken to Jean."

"Be careful. The Nazis have been everywhere!"

★ ★ ★

"That's the house right there—the one with the blue shutters."

Jolie slipped off of the horse and said quietly, "Let me go in alone, Annette."

"Very well. I'll keep watch out here. If I see any Germans, I'll come and get you, although I don't know where we could run to. Be as quick as you can."

Jolie rapped sharply on the door.

"Jean!" she cried when the door opened, relieved that she had found her friend.

But Jean Clermont was staring at her. "What do you want?" he demanded roughly.

After seeing the confusion in his eyes, Jolie realized

what she looked like. "It's me," she cried, "Jolie Vernay. Don't you know me?"

"Jolie?" He peered at her intently. "Is it really you?"

"I had to make myself look like this. The Nazis are after me. Can I come in?"

Instantly Jean opened the door wide and then closed and locked it before leading her to the kitchen. "What's this all about?"

Jolie sat at the kitchen table and pulled off her hat. She had always loved the feeling of cleanliness and despised her filthy hair and body. "I'm trying to get five children out of France, Jean, and I think it will have to be in a boat." She quickly gave him some of the background of her story.

Jean listened silently until she stopped. "How did you get here?"

"We came in a wagon."

"Was it pulled by a crazy-colored horse—many colors?"

"Why yes, it was. How did you know?"

"The Germans have been searching for two women and a horse like that. Not here but in the next village—Trouville. A friend of mine just came from there. They're searching every house from top to bottom. It's a wonder they didn't see you. Where's the horse now?"

"Outside with Annette."

"They'll be here soon," he said. "Why did you come to me?"

"I was hoping you could take the children and the American across the Channel in your fishing boat."

Jean stared at her with shock. Then he laughed. "You don't mind asking for much, do you? But you always were bold. Why don't you just ask for the moon?"

Jolie's throat suddenly felt thick. She had not seen Jean for a long time, and although he had usually been open-hearted, she remembered there was a trace of selfishness in him.

"The children will die if the Nazis get them. You know what they're like."

Jean cleared his throat. "I'd like to help you, but they're watching the coast all the time, Jolie. You can't imagine how they watch the boats. When a fishing boat goes out, they send a small boat with soldiers in it."

Jolie realized she could not beg this man to do something that might mean death to him. "I'm sorry. It was just an idea, Jean."

She stood and suddenly his hand closed on her arm. "Wait a minute. You always were too impulsive. I didn't say I wouldn't do it." He laughed and said, "Do you remember when I tried to kiss you when we were on that picnic, and you broke the bottle of wine over my head?"

"Yes, I do remember," she said as she sat down again.

"I've still got the scar up here." He put his hand on his head and pretended to grimace. "If I do this for you, maybe I'll get a kiss out of it."

Jolie smiled. "Maybe."

"You're still not making promises. Now, listen. There's bad weather coming in."

"Yes, it's already awfully windy."

"We expect the storm to hit tomorrow and be really bad the day after that. Now, the Nazis won't expect a small fishing boat to go out in that. It's risky, Jolie, because the storm may be more dangerous than the Nazis. But if you think it's worth the risk—if you think this is the only way—I'll try it."

Jolie reached out and grasped his hands. "Thank you, Jean. That's so like you."

"No, it's not like me. I usually look out for number one."

Jolie pulled her hands back. "I'm trying to figure out how to get the children here. The roads are being watched constantly. Do you have a truck or a car?"

"Yes, I have a truck. I use it for hauling fish to the villages inland."

"My friend Annette knows all the back roads that you could take without being seen."

"So she lives nearby?"

"Yes, she lives near Pont-l'Évêque. Her name is Annette Fortier."

"Oh, she's the one who married Alain. We were good friends. I'm afraid it may not be well with him. I heard he was at Dunkirk." He frowned and added, "He may be dead."

"She's terribly worried about him."

"Why don't you go get her and we can work out a plan."

Jolie went to the door and called out for Annette, who came riding up on the horse.

"Let me get that horse out of sight," Jean offered. He at once led the horse into the shed behind the house and was back soon.

"I'll put you all in the back of my truck and surround you with my empty fish barrels. Then I'll put the tarp over the back. But will the children be able to stay quiet if the truck is searched?"

"We'll make them understand how important it is."

"How can you tell a baby that?" Annette asked.

"A baby? You have a baby?"

"Yes, she's only about three months old."

"That's a bad one." Jean frowned. "We'll have to think of something. I'll go and find a better place to hide your horse, and then you can show me the back roads."

★ ★ ★

Tyler was the first to hear the truck. He snatched up the pistol and turned to say, "All of you stay inside and away from the windows."

"Let me go with you," Antoine entreated but knew it was hopeless.

"No, you stay here. Don't come outside and don't make any noise."

Tyler ran outside and hid behind one of the big trees. As the truck came closer, he took the safety off the gun. But then he saw Jolie and Annette get out along with a man.

They must have found the friend. He breathed a sigh of relief and put the safety on. He jammed the gun inside his belt.

"You're back," he said. He wanted to reach out and embrace Jolie, but he did not.

"Yes. I want you to meet my good friend Jean Clermont. Jean, this is also my good friend, Tyler Winslow."

The two men shook hands, assessing the other as they did. Jean laughed. "Jolie always had a way of getting the best-looking men to do what she wanted. First she had me and now she has you."

"Don't be a fool, Jean!" Jolie exclaimed, her face reddening.

"Listen quickly," Annette told Tyler. "You and Jolie and the kids will hide out here for another day and a half. Then Jean will come in the middle of the night and get you all. He'll take you to his boat and get you across."

"That's probably the worst plan anybody ever made," Jean said with a grin. He stared at Tyler for a moment, then lifted one eyebrow. "I've heard all Americans are crazy. I suppose we French are too. Listen, I'll come at ten o'clock. Pray for terrible weather." He turned to Jolie. "Don't forget my reward if this crazy idea works."

"I won't forget."

The three of them watched as Jean got back in the truck, turned it around, and left with a cheerful wave of his hand.

"It pays to have old sweethearts around," Tyler said.

"Oh, it was nothing serious."

"What's this reward that you promised him?"

Jolie grew flustered, and Tyler lifted his eyebrows. "We'll talk more about that later."

CHAPTER TWENTY-ONE

A PRAYER ANSWERED

★ ★ ★

Captain Otto Breit, commander of the naval forces stationed in France, had received Major Hermann Dietrich in his office and now sought to make himself as pleasant as possible. He had nothing but disdain for officers of the armies of the Third Reich, for his whole life was built around fighting ships. It was his greatest disappointment that he had been unable to make Hitler or any of the higher-ranked Nazis realize the importance of naval forces. All the fools could talk about was divisions and airplanes!

"Make yourself at home, Major," Captain Breit said in an amiable voice. He was a massively built man, well over six feet, bulky with muscle and a face weathered by seas and winds. He was standing beside a window glancing out at the sea, where a destroyer was being readied for a nightly patrol. As always he studied the outlines of the destroyer, wishing the designers would listen to him instead of whichever idiots they were listening to. He let nothing of this show in his face, however.

"I wish to congratulate you on your sweep through

France, Major," Captain Breit said as he sat in a chair across from Dietrich. "It was a masterful piece of action." What he did not say was that without the navy, all of it would be useless. He had to watch his remarks carefully, for he had the reputation of a man with tunnel vision who could only see naval factors in a war. He could not resist saying now, "If our navy had not taken over the action in Norway, of course, the army would not have been able to sweep into Belgium."

"That is true enough, I suppose." Dietrich spoke more carefully than was usual. He wanted something from the captain and forced himself to be amicable, which was not easy for him. "I have always admired our navy, and so has the führer."

That's two lies, Captain Breit thought, but he did not let the opportunity pass. "I'm afraid men not bred to the ways of the navy do not understand the problems that can only be solved by ships. It's natural enough, I suppose."

"Problems such as what, Captain?"

"Rumors are circulating that since we have conquered France, our next step will be to capture England. This will involve a naval invasion, as you know."

Indeed Major Dietrich had heard such himself and not rumors. He had heard it from none other than Hermann Göring, a close personal friend. Göring had more or less botched the annihilation of the English army at Dunkirk, but he was absolutely confident that his Luftwaffe could clear the skies over England.

"I think an invasion is highly likely," Dietrich said. "That should please you."

"Please me? Why should it please me? It's impossible, totally out of the question!"

Dietrich stared at the massive man. "I don't understand you, Captain," he said stiffly. "Why should it be impossible?"

"How would you propose to invade England if you

were in charge?" Breit asked with a brittle smile.

"Why, I would clear the air of the RAF and send troops across to attack."

"You have two rather dangerous propositions there. One, you are assuming that the Luftwaffe can defeat the RAF."

"Why, we all understand that's the truth."

"You may understand it, and Herr Göring may understand, but I don't think the English do. Their Spitfires are every bit as good, I am told, as our own fighter planes. There's a saying that the bombers always get through, but it should say *some* of the bombers get through. What chance would a heavy bomber have against a Spitfire?"

"That's what our fighter planes are for. They will escort them over, of course."

Breit turned and crossed his arms and smiled pityingly at the major. "And how far, Major, do you suppose our Me-109s go without refueling?"

"Why, I'm afraid I don't know."

"I can tell you. They can fly to England, and they will have exactly ten minutes of fighting time, and that will leave them enough gas only to get back to France if they don't have any trouble. Ten minutes! That's all they'll have and then the bombers will be on their own. But that's not the big problem."

"Well, what is the big problem, if I may ask?"

"How would you transport your army across the Channel?" The captain's eyes were filled with contempt as he asked the question. He had asked it of others, even generals, and discovered that none of them had the answer.

"Why, in ships, of course."

"I hope you have the ships up your sleeve, Major, because the navy doesn't have them."

Dietrich stared at Breit. "But I see ships all the time! The Channel is full of them. You have many ships."

"We have a few destroyers. Not enough. What will

happen when these destroyers meet the battleships and cruisers of the British navy? It seems to be a fact generally overlooked at headquarters that the British have the finest navy in the world. If we start across the Channel with a group of destroyers, we won't last ten minutes. They'll blast us out of the water!"

Breit stood and strode to the window. "And as for transports, we have none. We have never been permitted to build up what it takes to make an invasion by sea." Anger swept across Breit's face and he started pacing the floor. "I understand they propose to take your army across in flat-bottom boats. What will happen when you're midway across the Channel and a storm strikes or when one cruiser gets in the midst of that flotilla? Would you like to be in one of those ships down to the gunnels in a rough sea with a cruiser bearing down on you with all guns blazing?"

Major Dietrich stared at the captain and said stiffly, "I'm sure you have a point here, Captain, but I don't see what it is."

"My point is that we will not be able to invade England. We have no means to destroy her navy. We do not have the ships to make an invasion, and I am not at all certain that the Luftwaffe can win the battle for Britain in the air."

These sailors are dense fellows indeed, Dietrich thought. He kept his voice on a pleasant tone. "It will be interesting to see who is right about this. But I've come to ask you a favor."

"What sort of favor, Major?" He stopped by the window again.

"I'm convinced there will be an attempt to escape from France in a small boat to cross over to England."

"It would not be the first time. We usually manage to catch such fellows."

"I would appreciate it very much if you would put every available ship in the area around Honfleur."

"What makes you think there will be such an attempt?"

"We've heard from informants."

Breit shrugged his shoulders. He turned to look out the window. "Look at that sea, Major." He waited until Dietrich came to stand beside him. "There will be no small boats leaving France until this storm blows over."

"Perhaps, but these are desperate people. I would like to ask that a sharp lookout be kept."

"Very well, Major, if that is what you wish. Even our own small ships won't go out in this weather, but I'll have my destroyers keep a close watch."

"Thank you, Captain. I very much appreciate it." Dietrich picked up his hat, settled it firmly on his head, and left the office.

As soon as Dietrich left, a lieutenant came in. "Can you guess what the major wanted, Hauptmann?"

"Who knows what a soldier thinks," the man said with a grin. He understood his captain's contempt for any service other than the navy.

"You're right. These landsmen. Why don't they leave sea duty to men who know what they're doing?"

Hauptmann grinned broadly, enjoying the captain's disgust. "They don't know much for a fact, sir."

"Well, he's convinced that there will be an attempt to escape from France in a small boat. Have the captains on patrol for the next few days keep a sharp lookout."

"Nobody will be crossing in this weather."

"I know that, but the major doesn't. But at least this way I'll be able to tell him that we cooperated to the extent of our ability." He stared out at the sea that was now moaning and crashing upon the beach with a grim ferocity. "Invade England? In what?" he snapped. "Rowboats?" He brought his fist down on the window ledge with a crashing blow and forgot at once about the major.

* ★ *

Arnaud Heuse stared up at the sky with considerable aggravation. He turned his gaze to his boat, which was bobbing up and down like a ball on the waves that crashed into the shore. He moved to get a better view of the sea. "I tell you, Jean, you're crazy. You'll never get across in this kind of weather."

Jean clapped his hands on the smaller man's shoulders. The two had become very close after years at sea together. They were co-owners of *Leota* and fished together practically every day. "What's life without adventure, Arnaud?"

"It's staying alive. That's what it is."

"I suppose I'm crazy, but I've got to get these people across."

Heuse laughed. "Well, I'm crazy too. I'll go with you. You'll never make it without me."

"Did you talk to Pascal and Garland? Will they go with us?"

"Oh yes, they think it's all very romantic. They're just young and crazy enough to go along with your scheme. Now, tell me again about this insanity."

"I'll leave in time to get the party here by midnight. You and the rest of the fellows will have *Leota* all ready to go. Be sure you have enough gas." His features grew intent as he continued. "Be ready to go the instant we get here."

"You're taking the truck?"

"Yes. I'll load everybody in the back and then surround them with the empty barrels and put a tarp over them."

"If you get stopped, the Germans will find them."

"I'll just have to be careful not to get stopped. I don't expect to find many Germans out in the storm. There's a back road that leads to Annette's place."

"The destroyers will be out once we get them to the boat. This storm won't bother them. If they see us, it's all over."

Clermont looked up into the darkening sky. "It will be very dark tonight with the thick cloud cover. They won't see us."

"All right. We'll be ready. You know, it might not be a bad idea just to stay in England until this war blows over."

"It's not going to blow over, Arnaud. It's going to be a long, hard fight. I've got a feeling all of us will be involved in it before it's over."

★ ★ ★

Rochelle looked over at Antoine. The two of them were sitting in the kitchen of the small cottage. Rochelle was, for once, not holding Marie. "Why are you so quiet? Are you afraid?"

"I told you once I'm not afraid of anything."

Rochelle shook her head. "Everybody's afraid of something."

Antoine's mouth was twisted in a strange, wretched grin. "Well, it was a lie. I'm scared of the sea."

"How come?" she asked. "I've never even been on it, but I'm not afraid of it."

"You don't have a grandmother like mine."

"What does your grandmother have to do with it?"

"She told me once to beware of the sea."

Rochelle turned her head to one side. The wind was whistling outside, moaning like a huge beast, and rain was pounding down on the roof. "Is she a fortune-teller? You don't believe in that stuff, do you?"

Antoine looked down at his hands. "Sometimes I do— like now. She sometimes got things right."

"Well, we've all got to die sometime."

He laughed. "Well, that makes me feel better! Why didn't I think of that?"

Rochelle was instantly sorry. "I didn't mean to say that. We're going to be all right."

"Now *you're* telling the fortune."

"No. It's really going to be all right. We're going to get to England and you'll join your parents, and someday you'll be a famous doctor."

"And then what happens?"

"Then I'll get sick and you'll get me all well. Then you'll fall in love with me, but I'll already have a fiancé. . . ."

Antoine laughed and reached out and squeezed her hand. "That's about as crazy as anything I ever heard in my life, but keep on with your fairy tales. It's better than thinking about being in a boat and going out on the ocean."

Tyler and Jolie had been conversing quietly in the living room. Damien and Yolande were asleep, and Annette was rocking Marie in one of the bedrooms. The adults had talked their plans over until both of them had absolutely nothing new to say.

Tyler saw that Jolie had circles under her eyes. She had slept little for the past two days. The Germans had come up and down the main road. They had questioned the Fortiers again, but the couple had been able to keep up their appearance of ignorance.

"You're worried about the way things are going, aren't you?" he asked.

"I'm worried about Marie."

"What's the matter with her?"

"She just has some sniffles. I think it's only minor, but who knows what we're getting into? I can't believe a ship would go out in a storm like this. Jean may have changed his mind."

"I don't think so. He seemed determined to do this for

us. By the way, you were going to tell me how you were going to reward him for getting us out of here."

Despite her fatigue and anxiety, Jolie smiled. "Once, when we were out on a picnic, he tried to kiss me, and I broke a bottle over his head. It was bleeding all over the place. I thought I'd killed him. It scared me to death!"

"I'll have to be careful," Tyler said with a grin. "I didn't know you were so violent."

She jabbed his arm playfully. "Anyway, he didn't get his kiss, so when I begged him to help us and he agreed, he said he'd have to have that kiss that he missed. Just a foolish game. I think we were both about sixteen—no, I was just fifteen."

Tyler reached up and touched the bandage on his head. "This itches," he said.

"Well, leave it alone. Don't be scratching at it." She reached up and pulled his hand down. "You'll just make it worse if you keep clawing at it like that."

Tyler studied her by the flickering light of the lamp. The amber light threw her eyes into darker shadows, and he could see the lines of fatigue along with fear on her features. "Look, I've been thinking about this. Why don't you keep Marie here with you? Then after I get clear—"

"I'm going with you."

"What! What does that mean?"

"You heard me. I'm going with you."

"When did you decide all this? Going with us, I mean."

"It's been on my mind since a few days into our journey." It had been just a vague notion at first, but it had grown, and now as she sat across from Tyler, she said firmly, "I've got to go with you."

"But what about your mother? She must be worried sick. You were only going to be gone one night."

"I've written her a letter telling her I'm going with you. Annette mailed it for me."

Tyler could not take it all in. "I don't know what to

say." He reached over and took her hand. "I'm glad you're going. I'd hate to leave you here."

She dropped her eyes and then Annette suddenly entered the room, holding Marie in her arms. She spoke almost harshly. "You can't take Marie out into this storm."

Jolie and Tyler exchanged glances. "But what else can we do?"

Tyler and Jolie had both noticed before that Annette always looked a little sad, and they had wondered if she had endured a tragedy of some sort. "My husband and I love each other very much, but we haven't been able to have children."

She stopped for a moment, and the wind seemed to be creeping around the house like a beast trying to get in. It moaned and keened and seemed to claw at the windows. Annette paid no attention to it. "We want children more than anything, but so far, no success." She looked down into the face of the sleeping infant. "But now this one has come. I want to keep her, and I know my husband will be happy with my decision when he comes home. We may never bear children of our own, but we will have Marie. Please leave her with me."

"But, Annette, are you certain that's what you want?" Jolie asked. "It's not something to do lightly."

"I have never been more sure of anything in my life. I have prayed since I was married for a child. I believe that God has sent this little one to me."

Jolie felt tears come into her eyes. She had seen the care that Annette lavished on the baby, and now she turned to Tyler. "What do you think?"

"I think Annette will be very good to her. We couldn't do better than to leave her with you."

Annette gave a short intake of breath, and tears were rolling down her cheeks. "I will be a good mother to her. I promise."

"It will be best if you keep her, then." Jolie got up and

went over to put her arm around Annette. "I think you're right that God is in this. He brought us to your house and little Marie to the one person in the world who will give her a mother's love."

Annette turned with the baby and walked away, unable to contain her sobs of joy.

As soon as she disappeared, Tyler took a deep breath. "I really believe this is of God. It would have been criminal to take that child out in weather like this."

"Yes. If He sees the sparrows fall, He can surely put a motherless child into the arms of a childless woman."

★ ★ ★

The children, and especially Rochelle, took it hard about leaving Marie. Jolie had taken her off to one side and explained the situation. Rochelle had begun to cry, but Jolie had explained patiently how good it was that Marie would have a mother and a father one day. She also explained how dangerous the crossing would be. "What would you think if we took her with us and she got sick and died because of what happened? Neither of us would ever forgive ourselves."

She had spoken quietly and comfortingly to Rochelle, and the girl had finally sniffled and wiped her face. "Yes, you're right. She'll have a good mother."

"That's right. She'll have a home and parents."

The other children had been less emotional, and by the time Jean pulled up in the truck, they were saying good-bye to her. As each one came to give Marie a kiss, Annette promised, "She will have a good home."

They said good-bye to the Fortiers, who had come to the cottage to spend the last couple of hours with the group. When they went outside, they found the rain had weakened to a drizzle.

"Get up between the barrels, and then I'll put a tarp

over you and the barrels. No matter what happens," Jean said sternly, "don't make a sound."

"That will be easier now that Marie's not here," Jolie said.

The group huddled together as Jean drew the canvas over them. Rochelle was sitting next to Antoine, and she leaned over in the darkness and groped for his hand. "Don't be afraid," she whispered.

He held on to her hand tightly. His eyes were closed despite the fact that he could not have seen even if they were open. All he could think of was his grandmother telling him to stay away from the sea.

Jolie was holding Yolande on her lap. Yolande pulled Jolie's head down and whispered, "Are you afraid?"

"A little bit."

"Don't be afraid," Yolande whispered. "Jesus can walk on water. He won't let us drown!"

"Are you sure about that?"

"Yes. You told us about it."

"You're right. I'm glad you're not afraid."

Yolande was quiet for a while, and then she drew Jolie's head down again to whisper in her ear. "I am afraid, a little bit. Is that bad?"

"No, sweetheart, it's not bad at all." She hugged the child and wondered what would happen. In all truth she was very afraid, but there was no turning back now.

CHAPTER TWENTY-TWO

DESPAIR

★ ★ ★

Staring down into his glass of brandy, Major Dietrich was aware that his senses were numbed. Ordinarily he was not a drinking man, but ever since his nephew had been killed—murdered, actually—he had been drinking steadily. He downed the burning liquid and set the glass on his desk, aware that the sound seemed dull and softened by the alcoholic haze that surrounded him. Dietrich despised drunks, and since he rarely drank, the brandy had gone to his head much more readily than he had anticipated.

Outside, the wind moaned, reminding Dietrich of something he could not quite place. The sound was eerie, at times rising to a high-pitched keening, like the scream of a banshee, although he did not actually know what a banshee would sound like. Other times it would drop down and moan, like a voice coming up out of the earth and roaming the land seeking a victim to devour.

Looking down, he saw the letter he had written to his sister. It was intended to comfort her on the loss of her son, but it had degenerated into a rage that had found its way onto the page. He wadded up the letter and threw it across the room. It struck the wall and fell to the floor. Dietrich stared at it and then poured more brandy into the glass.

Finally he rose and walked over to the window and stared out. The darkness was complete. The storm had brought with it shreds of fog, which seemed to drape over the buildings built close to the shore. A tiny flicker of lightning lit up the sky far off to the north, and he remembered Captain Breit's words: *"Not even our own ships will be going out. A small boat would have no chance at all."*

For a long time Dietrich stood there, and then his immobility became insufferable. He was a man of action and could not bear to be still while there was work to be done. He drank the rest of the brandy and walked over to the coatrack. He pulled his raincoat off, calling at the same time, "Scharmann—Scharmann!"

Lieutenant Scharmann burst through the door and stopped abruptly while Dietrich put a rain protector over his billed cap. He was wary, never knowing what the major had in mind. "Yes, sir?"

"Get the car ready, Lieutenant. We're going down to check the docks."

Scharmann let nothing show on his face, but he thought, *He's gone crazy, but I can't argue with him.* However, he did observe mildly, "Surely no one in his right mind would be stirring on a night like this, Major."

"Put on your rain gear and come with me."

The two men left the shelter of headquarters, plunging out into the darkness of the night. The keening wind raised its voice, and both men had to lean against the driving force of the powerful blasts that shook them. They got in the staff car, slamming the doors against the force of the wind, and without comment started toward the dock.

* * *

Jean peered out into the darkness, edging the truck along. He left the lights off and thus far had seen no patrols.

"They're all asleep or drunk—or both," he muttered, grinning into the darkness.

The truck was rocked constantly by blasts of wind, and the question that kept returning to his mind was, *If it can push a truck around, it can push a ship around too.* He was not a man, however, given to nursing his fears, so he concentrated on moving along. Finally he pulled up at the dock and saw the bare outlines of *Leota*'s mass. Leaving the engine running, he leaped out and was joined at once by Arnaud.

"Everything all right?" his friend asked.

"Sure. Why wouldn't it be? I've got them here. Are you ready to shove off?"

Arnaud shook his head. "Pascal and Garland are in the boat, but we'd better think twice, Jean. It's awfully rough out there. I've never been out on a sea like this. And you haven't either, have you?"

"No. But there's a first time for everything. Help me get the canvas off."

The two men struggled to untie the canvas and pull it back. They removed two of the barrels, and Jean leaned forward in the darkness. "We're here. Get out."

He helped the children down as they emerged from the dark. When they were all off, he said, "Arnaud, take these kids on board. And send Pascal out to hide the truck."

"Right!"

Jean helped Jolie get out and then stepped aside as Tyler came to the ground.

"Have you ever been out in a ship in weather this bad?" Jolie had to raise her voice against the wind.

"No, but we can make it. I never start something I can't finish." He grinned.

Tyler braced himself. The rain had now stopped, but it seemed even windier than before. "Will it get better at sea?"

"It'll probably be worse, but we don't have much choice, do we? It's now or never."

"I hate to put you and your men at risk, Jean," Jolie said. "It's not even your problem."

"We're old enough to know what we want to do. Come on."

Pascal jogged up to Jean.

"Take the truck back to my place and park it in the shed. Take the keys out of it and put them over the right front tire. And hurry up, will you?"

"Right." The man got into the truck and drove off at once.

"Come on," Jean said, turning his attention to Jolie and Tyler. "Let's get on the boat."

No sooner had he spoken than twin beams cut through the gloom of darkness, centering directly on the figures that stood there, suddenly helpless. All of them involuntarily glanced at the lights and then, unable to meet their brightness, dropped their heads and waited.

"Stay right where you are," a voice came. "Shoot anyone who moves, Lieutenant."

Jolie knew the blackest form of despair she had ever known in her life. *To come so close and then to lose it,* she couldn't help thinking. She had been filled with a fierce sense of satisfaction, believing they were going to make it, but now she knew that all was lost.

The three of them stood there, and Jean said mildly, "I hate that we didn't even get a chance at it."

A figure came into the headlights, and Jolie recognized the officer as Major Dietrich. He came forward holding a Luger in his hand, and behind him another officer was similarly armed.

Tyler edged his hand toward the pistol in his belt, but instantly Dietrich pointed his weapon straight at Tyler.

"That man's reaching for a gun," he barked with a harsh tone that left no doubt about his intentions.

"Should I shoot him?"

"If he doesn't drop it, yes."

"Drop the gun, Tyler," Jolie said. "They'll kill you if you don't."

Tyler plucked the pistol out with his thumb and forefinger and dropped it on the ground.

"Back up now." The three backed up, and Dietrich picked up the pistol. He now had one gun in each hand, his forefingers on the triggers. He stepped closer, and there was a thin smile on his face that Jolie could see by the faint light. "So," he said, "we meet again." He swung one of the weapons in Jolie's direction. "Did you kill my nephew?"

At once Tyler said, "No. I did."

Dietrich swung the Luger in Tyler's direction, and Jolie cried out, "No, please don't shoot!"

"I will not shoot as long as you obey, but you will pay for murdering my nephew."

"Lieutenant, take the car back to the squad room and get some backup over here at once."

"But, Major—"

"I will take care of this." Dietrich's voice was triumphant. "Go now. That's an order."

"Yes, sir."

"But first bring me the flashlight from the front seat."

"Yes, Major."

Scharmann brought the flashlight back. Dietrich turned it on and slipped the extra weapon into his pocket. "Now, go get the squad. Don't worry. I'll be all right here. I'll be very well indeed." He seemed pleased, and there was cruelty in his smile as he stared at the prisoners.

Scharmann ran to the car, leaving the group in the

single beam of light that came from the flashlight.

"Stay very close together," Dietrich commanded. "I would not mind killing any of you. But I must warn you. You are all going to hang. If you'd rather be shot, I'd be glad to accommodate you."

Jolie said quietly, "I'm sorry, Jean—and you, Tyler, for getting you into this."

"We knew what we were doing," Tyler said.

"You knew what you were doing when you killed my nephew."

"He was attempting to assault this young woman," Tyler said evenly. Death was very close, and for some reason he felt no fear. He had always wondered what he would feel if he knew he was going to die, and now he knew. All he felt was a great disappointment. The children were on the boat, but Jean's friends couldn't leave with the major standing so near. It was all over—all finished and all for nothing.

A sharper blast of wind and a rising volume of sound rocked all of them. Dietrich kept his balance, and the light in his hand was steady. "You fools would have drowned even if I had not caught you. You American. What's your name?"

"Tyler Winslow."

"I suppose you thought because you were an American we would not dare to execute you. Rest assured, we have no fear on that score."

"I'm sure you can handle it," Tyler said.

Jolie listened as Major Dietrich spoke, venom dripping from his words. He was cursing and pointing out in exact terms what waited for them, but even as he spoke, Jolie caught a fleeting glimpse of a movement over to her left. She saw a form of a man, dressed in dark clothing, come slowly out of the water and up onto the dock. As she watched, Major Dietrich moved over and cut off her view. She knew she must keep Dietrich's attention on her so that whoever was on the dock would not be seen or heard.

"Major, I beg you to let these children go. Let the crew take them to England."

"And what about you, Doctor?"

"It doesn't matter about me, but they're only children."

"Don't worry. I will see that they find a place."

"Please let them go."

Jolie could not see anything but the bright ring of the major's light as he held it steadily. She continued to shout against the wind, begging him to have mercy.

"You're an educated woman. You should have better sense. I suppose the American gave you the idea for this mad scheme. Americans all think they are heroes like Buffalo Bill."

"No. I'm the one who talked him into this plan."

"Then he is a fool!" Dietrich laughed sharply. "You love him, I suppose."

Without a pause, Jolie said, "Yes, I do love him. Let him go, at least."

"Let him go? He murdered my nephew!"

"To keep him from attacking me." She was desperate now. "If anything happens to him, the Americans will find out about it."

"The Americans will not come into this war. They're smart enough to take care of their own problems." Dietrich glanced over his shoulder, evidently looking for the car, and for a moment fear grasped Jolie. Then suddenly the light disappeared. It spun crazily, casting its single beam upward and then downward before falling to the ground.

At once Jean leaped forward and shouted, "Is that you, Arnaud?"

The flashlight suddenly rose from the ground and Arnaud Heuse held it to his own chin. He was laughing wildly, and then he pointed it down at the crumpled body of the major. "I have captured the German army, Jean. You must see to it I get a medal."

"Quick, everybody get on board," Jean said. "They'll be back soon."

"What about the major?"

"He's a prisoner of war." Jean picked up the major's pistol and stuck it in his own belt. Then he grabbed the major under the arms and started to drag him. "Give me a hand here, guys. Jolie, get aboard. We've got to get away from here."

"What about the soldiers—the other men that are coming?" Tyler demanded.

"Unless they can walk on water, which I doubt, they'll never catch us. Come on."

Jolie scrambled to get on board while the men carried the limp body onto the boat. Jean let the major's head drop onto the deck and then called, "Is Pascal back yet?"

"There he is," Tyler said as Pascal flew toward the dock.

As soon as the man had jumped aboard, Jean called, "Let's get out of here!"

Arnaud looked down at the major, his hair dripping on the man. "Is he dead? But no, I suppose my luck couldn't be that good."

. Jolie bent over and took the major's pulse. "No. Just knocked out."

"Too bad," Arnaud laughed before disappearing.

Jean came to stand over the fallen officer. "I wouldn't have shed any tears if Arnaud had killed him, but he'll do well enough in a British prisoner-of-war camp." He turned to the wheel. The engine was already started. He watched as the men cast off the lines and jumped back aboard. At once he shoved the throttle forward. *Leota* began to pitch and buck, but he patted the wheel, murmuring, "Come along, my lady, you can do it."

"Where are the youngsters?" Tyler asked.

"Below on the lower deck. Pascal and Garland are

with them. They'll be all right."

Tyler moved over and put his arms around Jolie. There was only a small green light inside the cabin, and Jean was peering intently into the darkness. A sudden pitch of the *Leota* threw them roughly to one side. Tyler fell with his back against the wall of the cabin, but he did not release her. He could feel the trembling in her body.

"So you love me. You came out and admitted it to that Nazi."

"I always get more romantic under pressure." Jolie put her head down on his chest and was grateful for the strength of his arms around her, for she wasn't at all sure she could stand unaided. All the strength that had built up within her began to fall apart, and she simply clung to him.

Jean glanced back and then laughed. "Why don't you two go on below. You're distracting me up here!"

CHAPTER TWENTY-THREE

LEOTA

★ ★ ★

Jolie was sitting on one of the built-in benches holding on as the boat pitched wildly. The young people were all sitting on the floor and appeared to be as calm as the situation would allow. Even Yolande was calm. She was holding Rochelle's hand, and as the ship bounced around, though her eyes were big, she did not seem terribly disturbed.

Tyler was sitting with the children, one arm around Rochelle and the other around Antoine. Tyler was whispering something to Antoine that made the boy summon a ghost of a grin. Jolie could not imagine what it was, but she was glad that Tyler had noticed that the boy who had seemed so fearless on land was petrified by being in a storm at sea.

She tried to judge if the storm had lessened any, but it did not seem so. The three hands were evidently up in the wheelhouse with Jean, and none of them had come below for the past hour.

"I think it's letting up just a bit," Tyler called out. The electric light emitted a faint glow, casting stark shadows over the inhabitants of the belowdecks cabin, and she saw that Tyler looked relaxed. She envied him, for she was still tense over the scene at the wharf. She knew she would never forget the hopelessness that had seized her when the major caught them there.

"I can't tell if it is," she called back, raising her voice over the wind. "It seems bad to me."

"Well, if this boat holds together, we'll be on friendly soil soon," Tyler said. "Just hang in there."

A slight sound caught Jolie's attention, and she looked down to see that Major Dietrich was moving his arm. Two of the deckhands had tied his arms and legs and moved him down to the lower deck after they were under way so Tyler and Jolie could keep an eye on him. Quickly she stooped beside him and checked his pulse. It was strong. His eyelids fluttered and then he opened them, staring up at her wildly. When he tried to get up, he discovered that his feet and his hands were tied. He slumped back onto the deck.

"You took a rough knock," Jolie told him. "You'll be fine, but right now you need to be still."

For a moment Dietrich lay perfectly still; then he struggled again and this time managed to get into an upright seated position. He looked around at Tyler and the youngsters across the cabin sitting on the floor, and as the ship rolled, he could not catch himself because his hands were tied. Jolie caught him and said, "Here, back up against this bulkhead. It'll be better if you don't move around. You really should lie down."

Dietrich's face was pale, and his lips were drawn together in a tight line. Very rarely was he in a situation he did not control, but as he looked about him, some of the authority that was so obvious in him as a rule seemed to drain away. "This ship will never make it to England," he whispered hoarsely. "Our naval vessels will catch you, you can be sure of that."

"Oh, I think we'll get to England," Jolie said. "And

you'll be there in a prison camp until the war is over."

"You have violated international law. You are non-combatants."

Tyler laughed. "I'll tell you what. Why don't you sue us, Major Dietrich?" He was highly amused at the German's preposterous attitude.

Dietrich glared at him but said no more.

As much as she detested what he stood for, Jolie felt that she was responsible for his health. She watched him carefully, for he had taken a terrible blow to the back of the head. She came forward and looked at his eyes carefully, studying the pupils. "I think you're all right, Major. Just try to be calm."

Jolie went over then and joined the group on the floor. It was easier sitting there than trying to cling to the narrow bench while *Leota* was being tossed in several directions. She sat down and put her arm around Damien, and he leaned against her. "You'll have a story to tell people when we get to England, won't you, Damien?"

"Yes," he agreed. His eyes were glowing, and he began to speak rapidly about the possibility of finally being adopted. Jolie let him go on, preferring his chatter over the oppressive silence. She looked over and saw that Rochelle was holding Antoine's hand. The boy looked pale and sick, and from time to time Rochelle would whisper something to him.

She could not hear it, but it seemed to help the frightened boy, for he got some color in his face.

"We're going to get there," Rochelle told Antoine confidently.

"I-I'm scared."

"So am I."

Antoine swallowed hard. "I've never told anyone else that I was afraid."

"It's better to tell," Rochelle assured him. "It's not good to keep things like that to yourself."

"We may die."

"I guess so. It's possible."

Antoine looked over at Jolie. "She's not afraid of dying, is she?"

"No, I wish I was like her. She risked everything to save us. She's such a good person."

"So are you, Rochelle, but I'm not."

She shushed him. "Don't be foolish. We're going to be all right. Your grandmother was wrong."

As the ship continued to toss, the major finally gave up trying to sit up and lay flat down on his back again.

Tyler got to his feet. "I'll go up and find out how we're doing."

"Come back quick," Yolande called out.

"I will, sweetheart."

Tyler moved carefully along, balancing himself as the boat pitched. When he opened the door, the roar of the sea was loud, and then it was muted again when he shut it. Holding carefully to the walls, he climbed the ladder and found Jean and the other three members of the crew staring out into the darkness.

"How we doing?" Tyler shouted.

"All right. She's holding together."

Tyler watched for a few moments as Jean struggled with the wheel.

"Do you believe in God?" Jean asked Tyler.

"Yes."

"Then you'd better pray, American."

"I've been doing that already," Tyler said. "What about you?"

"Yes, me too."

Even as Jean spoke, Arnaud shouted, "Jean, look out!"

At first Tyler could not believe what he was seeing. The darkness was intense outside, but there before them rose an immense gray wall. For a split second he could not imagine what it was, and then he knew—a ship. "We're running into a ship!"

Jean let out a cry and pounced on the wheel. Tyler stood there petrified, unable to move. There was nothing to do but watch. They were headed straight for it. He felt the churning of the engine and saw that the bow of *Leota* was making headway in turning, but the ship still loomed like a mountain. Tyler found himself holding his breath, and finally the wall of steel passed to the side of the fishing boat.

"It's a destroyer!" Jean yelled.

"They'll blow us out of the water!" one of the men cried. "We don't have a chance!"

But the encounter was over almost before it had begun. *Leota* must have been at the stern of the vessel, or almost so, for suddenly the ship was gone and they were in darkness again.

"Did she see us, Jean?" Tyler asked. He felt his pulse racing and forced his panic down.

"I doubt it, but we'll know soon enough. If they did, we don't have to worry about navigating to England. She'll just ram us."

The four men held their breath and stared out of the glass. Tyler found, to his surprise, that he was thinking of those below instead of himself. The children were so vulnerable, and he could not bear the thought that Jolie might perish after all they'd been through. He found himself praying constantly, *God, take care of us!*

"It's all right now," Jean yelled, and the men began to shout and dance around even though the boat was still lurching from side to side. "We've got to be pretty close to the line," Jean said. Relief softened the lines of his face, and he was able to smile.

"What line?" Tyler demanded.

"Oh, it's not a line you can see, but British ships patrol the Channel. The Germans are careful not to get too close. They know they'll be sunk if they do. We may have even crossed it already."

Tyler released his breath. "So you think we made it, then?"

"If she holds together, I think so. And if this storm doesn't sink her, nothing will!"

"I'll go down and tell the others," Tyler said. "They'll be glad to hear it."

"What about the major? Has he come to yet?"

"Yeah. He's going to sue us," Tyler said with a grin. "Doesn't that scare you a lot, Jean?"

The men all laughed, and Arnaud said, "I'd like to throw him overboard as shark food."

"I'd rather keep him," Tyler said. "He'll be pretty valuable to some folks in England."

He went down to the lower deck. As soon as he stepped inside, he shut the door and grinned. "Jean says we're probably close enough to England that no German ship can get at us now."

The youngsters all began to cheer.

"That's wonderful," Jolie exclaimed. "We're going to be all right."

Damien got to his feet and walked over to where Major Dietrich was lying flat on his back. He stared down at him, and the German struggled to sit up again.

"What do you want?" the major muttered. "Go away from here."

"Why do you hate Jews?"

The cabin suddenly was quiet. The wind outside still blew, and the chugging of the engine was audible, but no one spoke or even moved.

Dietrich's eyes opened wide and his lips moved as he tried to answer. Finally he shook his head. "I don't hate Jews." His voice was a mumble, and he cleared his throat and looked down.

"Yes you do," Damien said. "If you didn't, you would have let us go. You were going to do something bad to us. Why would you do that? We never did anything to you."

Dietrich was silent, and it was Jolie who said, "I'd like to hear your answer, Major. I think we all would."

The man struggled with his bonds, but he was well tied. He glared at Jolie and then at Tyler before sitting back against the bulkhead and closing his eyes.

"I don't think you need to worry about your profession anymore, Dietrich," Tyler said. "You'll sit in a prison camp until the war is over. When you get out, Germany will be smashed. The Third Reich and all you believe in will be dead."

Dietrich began to scream in German.

When he finally stopped, Rochelle said, "You are a bad man, and God will be your judge."

Little Yolande walked over to stand beside Damien. Looking Dietrich in the eye, she asked, "Why don't you be a good man?"

As they waited for an answer, everyone noticed that the boat was not rocking so violently. Arnaud Heuse burst through the door. "We're almost there," he declared. "Come up and see England."

Instantly everyone rushed to the door. Tyler and Jolie let the children go first, and then they followed them up.

"You see," Rochelle told Antoine as they went up, "I told you we would be all right."

"You were right," he muttered. He turned to her and then found a smile. "I will never be afraid of water again."

Before the small boat was able to get too close to land, a naval cutter came out and challenged them. An officer came aboard, and Tyler answered all the man's queries in English. The officer listened without saying much as Tyler explained the whole story.

"You have a German major as a prisoner?" he asked, incredulous.

"Yes we do. He's tied up down below."

"That will be good news." He turned to Jean and said,

"Take her in, Captain. You'll get a warm welcome, I assure you."

The man returned to his own vessel and Jean navigated the fishing boat slowly toward the dock.

"Are you going to leave us now, Jolie?" Damien asked.

"Not until I find you a good home."

"Do you promise?" Yolande asked solemnly.

"I promise."

Tyler scooped Yolande up and gave her a kiss. She tasted salty, for they had all been sprayed with sea water. She held him tightly, and he could feel her trembling. "We'll be eating a good English breakfast in no time," he told her.

When she did not answer, he whispered, "Are you all right, Yolande?"

"I don't want to lose my friends and you and Jolie."

Tyler pulled her closer. "We'll just have to ask God to take care of that."

★   ★   ★

Colonel Lionel Simons listened while John Hastings of the State Department did most of the talking. Tyler and Jolie had been brought to Whitehall, and these two officials had heard their story several times. Jolie was disturbed. "Do you think we're spies?" she demanded.

"No, indeed, mademoiselle," Mr. Hastings said. "But we're very interested in how you managed to get here."

"Yes," Colonel Simons agreed, "and how you managed to take Major Dietrich prisoner."

"But we've explained all that to you."

Hastings laughed. "This is all like a Gilbert and Sullivan musical or a very bad movie."

"No," Jolie said with a smile, "like a very good movie."

"I think you're right," Simons agreed. "We've got an

excellent captive, a Nazi major. He'll be very valuable to our people. You may be sure we'll take good care of him."

Hastings carefully put the top on his pen and slipped it into his briefcase. "What is your plan from here?"

Jolie looked at Tyler, and he knew that she wanted him to speak. "First, we need to find the older boy's parents. They came to London from France to find housing before they brought Antoine over with them. His mother's parents live here."

"It shouldn't be too difficult to find them if you have the grandparents' full names," Hastings said. "I'll take care of it personally."

"Oh, thank you, Mr. Hastings," Jolie said. "Antoine will be so happy to hear that. As for the other children, we want to take them to America and find good homes for them."

"Not in England?" Simons asked. "We might be able to help you if you wanted to do that."

"I don't think it'll be too safe in England," Tyler said. "Not for a while, at least."

"I'm afraid you're right about that," Hastings said ruefully. "It's going to be very hard."

"Well," Hastings said with a smile, "we owe you a favor for bringing Major Dietrich to us. I'm sure the American embassy will be very glad to help with temporary passports for the children. I'll hurry them up a bit." He got to his feet and said, "As a matter of fact, I'm sure we can find room for all of you on a ship that is taking some of our people to Washington tomorrow. Can you be ready by then?"

"I don't see why not. That would be wonderful, Mr. Hastings," Tyler said.

"But what about you, mademoiselle?" Simons asked as an afterthought. "Do you want to go back to your home in France?"

"I promised the children I wouldn't leave them until I found a proper home for them."

"That may take some time," Simons said, lifting his eyebrows.

"I will take as much time as I need."

When Tyler and Jolie explained to the children that they were going to America, they were all ecstatic—except Antoine. He had grown attached to his new friends. He said little, but Tyler went over and put his hand on his shoulder.

"We're going to miss you, Antoine. You've been a good friend to the children and a great help to Mademoiselle Vernay and me."

The boy just looked at his shoes.

"Are you sure you wouldn't like to go to America with us?" Tyler asked teasingly.

The boy finally grinned. "I would like to see America . . . someday. But right now I just want to find my parents."

Jolie joined the conversation. "Mr. Hastings is working on finding them as we speak, Antoine. You should be with them and your grandparents before the day is over."

"Really?" His face glowed. "I can't believe it!"

The other children had started chatting about the adventures that awaited them on the ship when the door burst open.

"Good news," Mr. Hastings exclaimed as he entered the room. He scanned the children and then walked straight up to Antoine. "You must be Antoine."

The boy nodded his head.

"We've already reached your parents, and they will be here within the hour!"

The boy's mouth dropped open as his eyes grew big. "You're not kidding me, are you?"

"Oh no. I wouldn't do that. Why don't you go ahead and say your good-byes, and then you can come with me and get cleaned up a little before they get here."

Antoine was smothered with hugs and good wishes

as the others congratulated him and said good-bye.

"I'll write to you," Rochelle told him, "and you must write back to me."

"My writing isn't very good, but I promise I'll write back."

"Are you ready?" Mr. Hastings asked.

"Let's go!" Antoine exclaimed.

The others followed the pair to the door, shouting more good-byes and promises to write.

★ ★ ★

The ship was full of officials on their way to America. Tyler had learned that the officials were going over to try to persuade President Roosevelt to give arms to England. The plan was that America would donate used naval vessels and munitions. "England's going to have a hard time," the man had told Tyler, "but with America's help we can pull through."

Jolie and the children were lined up along the ship's rail, fascinated with being high above the water as it rushed by. The children had charmed some of the statesmen, who were talking with them, and Tyler took the opportunity to talk to Jolie.

He pulled her aside and asked if she would sit with him for a few minutes.

"Sure, Tyler," she said as she sat down in a chair next to him. "I wanted to tell you about my idea."

"What is it?"

"I've been trying to figure out where we can go once we get to the U.S., since neither you nor I have family there."

Tyler had been so consumed with his need to tell Jolie about Caroline that he hadn't considered that they would have no place to go when they arrived. "Did you come up with something?"

"I think I told you about my friends Jack and Irene Henderson?"

"Yeah, I guess you mentioned them."

"Well, they live in a big house in New York, and I'm sure they would let all of us stay with them until we can get the children into a foster home."

"Really? Do you think they have room for all of us?"

"I know they have at least two or maybe even three empty bedrooms. When I was working at the hospital, Jack was always offering his place to families who needed a place to stay while their loved ones were in the hospital."

"That sounds like the perfect solution, Jolie. I just hope they don't have any visitors staying with them right now."

"It's certainly a possibility, but we'll just have to find out when we get there."

"Okay. That sounds like a good plan." He took a deep breath and held it for a few seconds before letting it out. "I've got to tell you something, and it's not going to be easy."

A tremendous seriousness came across her face. "I think I know what it is."

"Why, you can't!"

"You're married, aren't you?"

"Married!" Tyler was shocked. "No, of course not! What makes you say such a thing?"

Her face suddenly relaxed. "I knew that you'd been trying to tell me something for a long time, and that was the most obvious thing. You looked so worried."

"No, it's nothing that complicated, but it is a difficulty, and it's something I should have told you about long before."

"Just tell me what it is, Tyler."

"All right. I'm not proud of myself, but this is what happened." He spoke slowly, not sparing himself. He told Jolie about his partying and drinking too much and about flunking out of school. He told her he had disappointed his family and everybody else, for that matter. When he got to the part about Caroline, he spoke even more slowly. "While I was in New York, I met this young woman, whose name is Caroline." He could not face Jolie but looked down at his hands, which he clasped together. "She's a very wealthy woman and attractive, and we had lots of fun together."

Jolie listened as he continued his story. Finally, when he got to the end of it, she was silent for a moment. He still had not looked at her.

"So she thinks you're coming back to marry her."

"I'm afraid so." Tyler straightened up and looked at Jolie. "Pretty sorry, isn't it?"

"Do you love this woman?" she asked quietly.

"No, I don't—and I'm pretty sure she doesn't love me either."

"How could you know that?"

"I think she likes the idea of being in love more than she feels all that affectionate toward me."

"You were right," Jolie said. "You should have told me long ago. Why didn't you?"

"Well, at first it didn't really matter. I had no idea that I'd ever feel anything for you. Then when I began to fall in love with you it became harder, and the more I loved you the harder it got. Then when we started on this journey with these children, there was a chance we wouldn't make it and I wouldn't have to tell you. Maybe I'd be dead."

"You should have told me, Tyler. People should trust each other."

"But how did I know that I'd fall in love with you?"

Jolie was staring at him in an odd way. He noticed that her features were still, but her back had grown stiff. She said quietly, "You will have to go to her."

"And do what?"

"And be an honorable man, Tyler. I could never love a

man who didn't honor his commitments to women."

Jolie got up and took her place at the rail next to Damien again. As she looked down at the water, Tyler leaned back in his seat, feeling about as miserable as he ever had. As the ship moved across the ocean, Tyler Winslow knew he was not going to talk his way out of this problem, as he had in times past.

CHAPTER TWENTY-FOUR

ON AMERICAN SOIL

★ ★ ★

Tyler woke up to a combination of scents he hadn't smelled in a long time. Coffee, bacon, eggs, and toast. He inhaled deeply, wondering how he had survived his time in France without a good, hearty American breakfast. He quickly got dressed and made his way down to the kitchen.

He was the last one to get up, he quickly realized as the children ran to him, calling out his name. He smiled at Jolie and the Hendersons as he scooped up Yolande and put his arm around Rochelle. Damien threw his arms around Tyler's neck and hugged him with all of his might.

"Good morning to you too," he told the children. "And to you, Jolie and Jack and Irene."

"Good morning, Tyler," Jolie said. She was sitting at the kitchen table sipping her coffee.

"How did you sleep?" Mrs. Henderson asked as she turned the bacon in the frying pan.

"Like a rock."

As soon as the group had arrived on American soil

the day before, Jolie had contacted her friends and explained their predicament. Without any hesitation, the Hendersons had told Jolie that the whole group was welcome to stay with them for as long as necessary. Jolie had assured Irene they wouldn't stay long—just long enough to find a foster family that would take all three of the children.

Just as quickly as they had attacked him, the children returned to their places at the table, where they had started breakfast. Rochelle was sitting next to little Barbara, who was in her high chair. Barbara opened her mouth wide as Rochelle fed her a tiny spoonful of oatmeal.

"Well, everybody," Jolie said, "how do you like your first taste of an American breakfast?"

"It's very good," Rochelle said.

"But I want to have a hot dog," Damien piped up. "All Americans eat hot dogs, don't they?"

"Well, we usually don't have hot dogs for breakfast," Jack said with a grin.

"If you play your cards right," Tyler said, "maybe we'll take you to a ball game and you can have all the hot dogs you want."

Irene joined the others at the table, and the couple asked endless questions about the war and Jolie's life in France.

Tyler took one last sip of his coffee and said, "Thank you for that delicious breakfast, Irene." He wiped his mouth and stood. "I'll see you all a little later. I've got an errand to run. It'll be all right with you, won't it, Jolie?"

"Of course."

Tyler was rebuffed by Jolie's cool reply. She was not smiling. In fact she had not smiled at him since he had told her about Caroline.

"Where are you going?" Damien piped up.

"I have a little business to take care of. I won't be long."

"Take all the time you need," Jolie said. "We'll be fine."

He asked the Hendersons if he could use their phone to call a cab, and all the way out to Caroline's house he slumped in the seat, wondering how he could possibly break the news to Caroline that their relationship was over.

★ ★ ★

"Miss Caroline's out back in the tennis court with Mr. Robert," the maid said. "You can go through the house or you can go outside and walk around. There's a pathway. You'll probably hear them."

"Thanks a lot," Tyler said. He chose to leave by the front door, and as he walked around the palatial mansion, he was making up speeches in his head. He was also throwing them out as quickly as they came, for he could think of no way to tell Caroline what had happened to him. His thoughts, as he followed the flagstone pathway through the beautiful flowers, were a jumbled mess.

I took your money and promised to marry you, and now I've come back to tell you that I don't love you, I've spent your money, I don't have any way to pay it back, and I'm in love with somebody else.

A grimace twisted Tyler's lips, and he muttered, "I don't think that will go over very well. Maybe I can think of some better way of putting it."

An old memory flashed before Tyler as he reached the edge of the house and heard Caroline's voice punctuated with the ponging noise of a tennis ball being hit. He remembered an old friend of his, Bax Buckley. Bax had been quite a ladies' man and had held forth to a group of freshmen, including Tyler, expounding on the subject of how to get rid of a girl that you no longer cared about. He could almost hear Bax's voice saying, *"Don't fool around with tact or gentleness or any of that stuff. You're out to get rid of the girl, and she's going to know it no matter what you say. Just march in and tell her something like, 'Well, we've had fun, baby, but it's all over.' She may cry a bit, but it's better to set things right on the front porch."*

Tyler remembered asking, *"But isn't it better to do it gently, a little at a time?"*

"No, it's not. You're just prolonging the pain. March in, give her the news, pat her on the back when she cries, and get out of there. Nothing you say is going to make it any better for her."

"Well, Bax, I hope you knew what you were talking about," Tyler said and took a quick deep breath.

Tyler passed beyond the hedge that shielded the tennis court and saw Caroline dressed in a white tennis outfit running back and forth volleying with a tall bronze man with tawny hair and a grin on his face. Obviously the man was a much better player than Caroline. He was toying with her, and finally she missed a shot and said, "Shame on you, Bobby."

"You're doing fine, Caroline. A few more lessons and you'll be ready for the big time."

The young man ran forward, cleared the net with an athletic leap, and put his arm around her. She turned her face up and he kissed her lightly. "Now, about that backhand," he said.

Tyler cleared his throat, and Caroline and the young man jerked their heads around. Shock and amazement swept across Caroline's face. "Why . . . Tyler, you're here!"

"I guess I am." He walked across the court and saw that the man was observing him carefully. Caroline was clearly trying to regain her composure.

"I'm sorry I didn't call first. I don't know what I was thinking."

"Oh, that's fine. It doesn't matter," Caroline said.

"Bobby, this is Tyler Winslow, an old friend of mine. Tyler, Robert Harper."

Harper stuck his hand out and smiled. "Glad to know you, Winslow."

"Good to meet you." Tyler turned to Caroline and said, "I can come back at a more convenient time."

Caroline's face suddenly changed, and a determined look caused her to compress her mouth in a straight line. "No, this is fine. Tyler has been out of the country," she told Robert. "I need to talk to him for a few minutes if that's all right."

"Why, sure."

"We'll go in the house. Bobby, would you have Eloise make us some drinks?"

"Sure thing. Good to meet you, Winslow."

"Same here." Tyler followed Caroline into the house, through the kitchen, and into the study.

"When did you get in?" Caroline asked after she closed the door.

"Just yesterday."

"Sit down. I want to hear what you've been doing."

Tyler took a chair, and Caroline seated herself across from him. "I don't want to keep you from the game," he said. "Have you known Harper long?"

"Oh, heavens yes! We were in school together, college that is. We dated a bit." Her face grew slightly rosy. "We've been renewing an old acquaintance." She crossed her legs. "I haven't heard from you in so long I was starting to wonder about you. The news has been terrible. I thought maybe you were trapped somewhere in France. . . ."

"It's kind of a long story, but I'll cut out some of the details." Tyler recounted his entire story and even told her about his relationship with Jolie. "So Jolie and I are sort of responsible for three youngsters."

"This woman. Is she older—middle-aged?"

"No, she's about your age."

"Is she overweight, unattractive?"

Tyler was amused. From the moment he had seen Caroline kiss Robert, he knew that his basic problem was over, but Caroline would always be the same. She had found a bigger fish than poor Tyler Winslow, but still she couldn't stand to lose.

"She's a very beautiful young woman, highly educated. A doctor, as a matter of fact. I met her when she was working at the hospital right here in New York, by the campus. I don't think I've ever known another woman with more courage."

"Well"—Caroline's tone was bitter—"it seems you've done very well for yourself."

"I think you've done well too, Caroline. It's pretty obvious that you and Bobby are more than just friends."

She lifted her chin. "Yes, we are. When you stopped writing, I was very lonely and worried about you. So when I began seeing Bobby, I realized you and I—" She stopped abruptly. "That is, I knew we couldn't ever—"

"You're right. We couldn't."

"Well, things have changed. I can tell you're different, and you're obviously in love with that woman, that doctor."

"Jolie Vernay."

"Whatever. But I might as well tell you, Tyler, that Robert and I have come to mean a great deal to each other."

"I hope you'll be very happy, Caroline. I think it's great."

"You're not grieving over me much, are you?"

"I guess I'm grieving about as much as you are," Tyler said with a grin. "Come on, Caroline, we had some good times together, but I would have made you miserable."

She smiled. "I think you're right, Tyler. I'm sorry I was so terrible about your girlfriend."

"I'll try to pay you back the money you gave me as soon as I can, but it may take a while."

"No. Forget about that. Were you able to develop your skills as an artist over there?"

"Well, I found out that I can paint a little and I maybe could be good if I gave it all the time it needs. Only time will tell."

"Keep in touch, Tyler," she said as she stood. "I really would like for you to do well."

"Thanks. I want you to do well too."

She walked him to the front door. "Good-bye, Caroline." He kissed her on the cheek, and she patted his shoulder. As he walked out of the house, he straightened up and took a deep breath of fresh air. The world seemed brighter somehow, the sun more brilliant and the flowers more colorful.

★ ★ ★

Jolie was walking through Central Park watching the antics of a pair of dogs that an older man was trying to walk. They were strong animals. She had never seen any like them before, and the man had his hands full.

He saw her watching and said, "They're stronger than I am."

"They're very beautiful. What are they called?"

He noted her accent and smiled. "They're dalmatians."

The man was telling her how wonderful the dogs were when suddenly she heard her name called. She turned back and saw Tyler loping along the pathway waving his hand.

"Excuse me," she said.

"Is that your young man?"

"I . . . don't know. He may be." She waited for Tyler to catch up while the man went on his way. Tyler came up to her, his cheeks flushed with the exercise.

"Caroline threw me out. Best day's work she ever did!"

"What do you mean she threw you out?"

"Well, she didn't really throw me out, but she had another fellow there who will be much more suited to her." He laughed and took Jolie's hand. "I had my speech all made up. I was going to try to be tactful and break it to her gently, but she beat me to it." He went on to tell her about how he had seen them playing tennis and when he saw them kiss he knew his problem was over.

"So all the cords are cut with her?"

"Yes." He put his arms around Jolie and drew her close. "You know what, Jolie Vernay?"

"What?"

"This is your lucky day!"

She laughed. "You are the most egotistical beast I've ever known!" She would have said more, but he drew her closer and kissed her thoroughly.

When he lifted his head, he said, "Well, I belong to you until you decide to dump me. I hope it's when your hair is silver and I've lost all my teeth."

"What are we going to do, Tyler?"

"We're going to live together for fifty or sixty years and enjoy every second of it. We're going to find a home for those kids, a good home where they can stay together. If we can't, I'll ask you to marry me, and when you finally say yes, we'll adopt them. If I can't make a living painting, you can support us while I stay at home with the children. Or we could always go back and sponge off your mother and live in France for the rest of our lives."

"That sounds wonderful to me. Come on, let's go tell the children that no matter what, they'll always be together."

G

Looking for More Good Books to Read?

You can find out what is new and exciting with previews, descriptions, and reviews by signing up for Bethany House newsletters at

www.bethanynewsletters.com

We will send you updates for as many authors or categories as you desire so you get only the information you really want.

Sign up today!